I0591227

ISBN:978-1-64456-291-8
Library of Congress Control Number: 2021935524

INDIES UNITED PUBLISHING HOUSE, LLC
P.O. BOX 3071
QUINCY, IL 62305-3071
WWW.IDNIESUNITED.NET

For my grandmother
Hannah Reilly Ray

# WHEN HANNAH PLAYED RAGTIME

## The Fourniers

## VERA JANE COOK

INDIES UNITED PUBLISHING HOUSE, LLC

# HANNAH
## 1892 - 1934

# Chapter One

The morning was grey and damp. Color drained from the earth, washed off by rain that would not cease, might never cease, it seemed so committed. Hannah listened intently to the wind's menacing murmur, stirring up the ground and whatever was on it. There was a clanking sound coming from the side of the house, which she could not place, perhaps the garden tools she had used the day before. They were like cymbals with the drum of thunder, both playful and irritating. The fire in the kitchen was warm, but the chill in her veins remained. She felt her future being written by the patter and the disarray of the storm.

She could smell her father's pipe. It was usually sweet, but the dampness made it pungent, almost sour. It polluted the air like the large Irish setter at her feet, whose wet hair had a bad smell, like soiled clothes. She reached down and touched his head anyway, and the dog's cold nose brushed past her palm.

She would not argue with her father any longer. She would not beg nor plead nor weep. Her father's mind could not be changed; his absurd obsession with things that shouldn't matter was set in stone. She turned her head toward the window, and the dark wind came at her so fiercely. The windows rattled as if phantasmal lunatics were attempting to reach her, as if phantasmal lunatics were about to shatter the glass and take the very life from her.

"Brutal weather," her father said. "Raining pitchforks."

Hannah nodded. "Yes, I hope there won't be much damage."

He went back to his paper and his politics, back to his unreasonable hatred of the Nationalists. None of it mattered a damn to her.

"Ay, there'll be some of it, rest assured."

"What? Damage?" she asked.

"Rest assured," he said.

"Yes, I suppose there will be," she answered and turned her head back toward the window and the angry gusts that took center stage and demanded notice.

Her father mumbled over something he had just read and slammed the paper to the floor. He shook his head, cursed under his breath. "Why the hell would we go backwards?" he yelled out.

Her sister was knitting. The action of the needles seemed to calm her. Contentment nestled around her smile as if the storm weren't taking the roof off over them. Her pretty face was placid and untroubled. She whistled every now and then, adding to the drumrolls of Mother Nature's tantrum.

"What's that you got in your head?" Hannah

asked her. "'On Moonlight Bay'?"

"Will you play it for me later?" Anne asked.

"You think you'll be hearing it over all this thunder?"

Anne laughed good-naturedly. Her laughter had a melody, like violins hitting a high note.

"Well, play loudly then, and I'll sing loudly," she called out, eager to be heard above the storm.

Hannah tried to smile, but she felt the tension in her expression, surprising her by its sudden appearance. *Would there be any singing in the convent?* She wondered. Hymns, of course, but certainly not ragtime. She hoped that God was not her destiny. She didn't want it, nor did she choose it. But that's just the way it was. There was God or there was man ... nothing in between but spinsterhood. Well, she would have gladly chosen spinsterhood, a future dimmed by lack of purpose, over a future dimmed by taciturnity and endless prayer.

"I don't think I will be happy as a nun, Papa," she said slowly, though she'd said it before, a hundred times before. She knew it would make no difference. Her father's mind was made. She hadn't the discretion to choose well, the good sense to choose a man with loyalty to Britain. What unearthly difference it made she could not begin to understand but it certainly proved her inability to make wise decisions, according to her papa.

"What's that?" John Reilly asked.

Hannah turned her head away." Nothing," she said.

Her sister continued to knit, but Hannah knew

3

she was holding her breath. She felt her papa's gaze from across the room, felt the complexity of his thoughts. He had heard what she'd said, she knew it.

Hannah looked at the tip of her shoe, avoiding Papa's irksome stare. Perhaps she should have said it louder. Perhaps she should have shouted it. The gray Dublin sky gave way to a cannonade of thunderous drumrolls. Hannah felt a shiver right through to her bones. She saw her life as one might see a dark cloud descending, swallowing the sun. She shivered again and pulled her shawl closer to her.

John Reilly dismissed what he might have wanted to say, which was rare for him; he always had a response to everything. Hannah knew he wanted to tell her that what she wanted didn't matter, wouldn't ever matter because how could she, a mere child of seventeen, know her own mind better than he? Hannah was used to it by now, her father thought for her, as if her mind wouldn't work without him. She was grateful that this one time he had kept his mouth shut.

"You're too independent, girl," he finally said. "Men don't like that. Not enough good men to go around anyway. Besides, doing God's work is a blessed thing. You should be proud. Happy too, that we've the money for the convent."

"I am not proud," she said. "Or happy."

Hannah knew that if a girl wasn't promised, she became a nun. That's what God wanted if no man had asked for her hand. And of course, God knew best. Her father must have had daily conversations with the good Lord to know his mind so well. But had God forgotten that a man had asked for her hand? Certainly, her father wished to forget. Andy McGregor, with his fine good looks and his golden curls that fell onto his freckled brow, like a perpetual urchin; he had asked for her hand. He'd been teasing her relentlessly since she'd been a girl, too young to realize then that his teasing was boyish flirtation. When it finally dawned on her that he thought she was pretty, she was quick to acknowledge the acceleration of her heart and the flush to her cheeks in his presence. His smile had won her over long ago when he'd stood on the tips of his toes to kiss her. Now it strained her neck to find his smile. But he could never cross the threshold of her father's door again, not with his Labor Party politics. Her father had strong British Unionism roots, and Andy was showing such poor judgment, wanting independence from Britain? How dare he join the Nationalist party and hand pamphlets out around the village that spoke of a return to Gaelic roots and Irish Independence? What absolute rubbish. "You will never marry Andy McGregor," her father had insisted. "He is a dangerous fool, and I will not have a viperous traitor in my family. I will not have us split apart by that man's absurd beliefs."

Hannah shuddered. "Shackled would be more like it," she said softly.

"What's that?" he asked.

"How I feel," she said.

"You'll make me proud, daughter," John Reilly nearly shouted. She knew he was angry with her, frustrated that she didn't bend to his will as easily as he would have liked.

Hannah nodded in his direction. Acceptance now was all she had left. If she married Andy McGregor, he would not be proud? No, he would be ashamed and defensive and probably never speak to her again. And if she went against her father's wishes she would break his heart. Better her own should break.

"You don't like him because he's poor," she said.

She felt her sister's eyes on her. Her father slapped the table with the palm of his hand. "Yes, you want not only to marry a poor man, but a stupid one."

The kitchen shutter hit the window as torrents of rainwater obscured the view of Dublin's hills. They watched as lightning lit up the sky, leaving behind a tenebrous shadow, blurred further by her tears.

"You are entitled to believe what you will, Father," she said.

"I am more than entitled, I am deemed fit by the nature of being your father. I am wiser than you, I've lived longer."

"Is it His will or your will, Papa, that I give my life over to a God who has never asked me directly for anything? I've received no calling except the one in my own heart."

John Reilly did not answer. He picked the paper up and closed his eyes. "I see it as God's will," he said.

*And I have no will?* she thought to say but didn't.

"You girls best be putting on the soup now, it's nearing six."

She would say no more. If she didn't take it into her own hands it was to be her fate. She avoided her sister's glance, knowing sympathy was being offered, but it was not sympathy she needed, it was a bloody miracle.

# Chapter Two

The very next day the sun appeared like a blessing, as if making amends for the storm of the prior night. Hannah was happy to be greeted by the sun and couldn't wait to feel the heat after such dampness. She nearly skipped to the Sweet Shop. Anne was following along as she always did. They'd been going there for years, for crumpets and hot cocoa. Hannah had a job, meager but respectable. She'd recently been hired by Mr. Smiley to teach his daughter to play piano. The back room had an upright, and Mr. Smiley insisted his daughter learn what to do with it.

"Another day looking for miracles," Hannah whispered to Anne as she took her place at the piano bench and Mr. Smiley's daughter sat beside her. Hannah felt somewhat giddy, despite the gloom of the convent hanging over her. Smiley's Sweet Shop always smelled of peppermint and chocolate, and she was sure to get a handful of sweet creams at day's end.

"Today we're going to have some fun, my girl," Hannah said. She was feeling rebellious, though

God knows why; her rebellions were nothing but ripples in a mighty stream, never waves, or hurricanes.

Hannah winked at Anne, and the two smiled at each other, conspirators against the world but never with ill intent. They just had a way of knowing what the other was thinking, and Anne knew instinctively that Hannah was about to alter the agenda.

Hannah played ragtime often. Ragtime was her only real defiance. She loved it, though the older people held their ears. She played a few notes of "*Ragtime Land*," and Mr. Smiley's daughter, Brianna, tapped her foot to the rhythm of it as if she'd been wound up.

"Can I play this, Hannah? I love it." Brianna moved her shoulders to the tune and laughed.

Hannah smiled at Anne and motioned for her to close the door. "Well, your father is terribly busy today. I don't think he'll hear us, and if he does happen to hear us, we'll return to Chopin quick as a wink."

"Rather not quickly enough, I'd say," Anne said as she turned the lock.

"Listen to this and watch what I do. You can do it, too. It's not that hard."

She played Anne's favorite, "*Moonlight Bay*." Then she played all the songs that came to mind while poor Brianna tried to follow all the while saying, *oh, I love this.*

Andy tapped gently on the door, as he did each Tuesday and Thursday. Anne got up to let him in. He could never pick Hannah up at home anymore, not since he and Mr. Reilly had that horrible argument about Britain and the iron hand it had around Ireland."

"Mr. Smiley thinks he's hearing things. Doesn't know what to make of it," Andy said as he entered the room.

Hannah felt the blush to her cheeks, a blush he always seemed to elicit from her. "I'll tell him I'm playing Bach; his music is a bit crazy," she said.

"Ay, I doubt he'll know the difference." Andy smiled at Briana. "No offense, girl."

"None taken, Mr. McGregor."

Hannah caught Andy's gaze as he stood there smiling. Then he started whistling.

"If you don't mind ladies," he said and he began to dance, extending his hand to Briana, who twirled around with him. No one danced to ragtime, it was near impossible, but Andy would attempt it. His brown boots hit the floor like paddles against the sea. Hannah was playing the "*Bacchanal Rag*," a tune she'd learned from a player piano, and he was acting like he'd had too much to drink, comical in his effort to coordinate his steps. Briana gave up and fell to the bench, laughing hysterically. Andy finally slid to his knees before Hannah, breathing rapidly, with his hands outstretched. She swung around and tussled his hair.

"Don't be trying out for any dance choruses, not any time soon." She bent to kiss his cheek. "Well, look at that, the hour has come and gone."

"Come walking with me, darlin'," Andy said, breathless from his rollick. "I've never seen a finer day." He turned to Anne. "Would you mind?"

Anne glanced his way and smiled coyly. "No, I

don't mind, and I'm prepared to tell Papa that Hannah and I knitted after Brianna's lesson, knitted for hours. Hands still stiff from it." She held her hands up. "That's what I'll tell him if you'll buy me a palmier with Irish cream."

Andy reached in his pocket and put a sixpence in her hand. "I'll buy you two if you can convince him he's a damn fool."

Anne and Hannah laughed together. "Ay, it's no use going to the goat's house to look for wool," Anne said.

The sky had burst forth with a brilliant sun, growing hotter by the minute. It had settled the earth, made peace with it. It was like the bad weather of the prior day was suddenly vanishing and, in its wake, revealed the intoxication of pale blue skies. The heat had dried the dampness and had brought the scent of lavender to the surrounding countryside.

Hannah took Andy's hand, and they walked out toward the farms and the winding lanes of Boyne Valley. They were careful not to be seen. If word got back to John Reilly that his daughter was keeping company with a damn Irish Republican she'd be held under lock and key until the nuns took her.

"If it were up to me, we'd run off tomorrow," he said. "But we need just a bit more money to get to America. Can you stall your Papa a wee bit more?"

"He's got my bags packed for the convent; says I'll be leaving next week. He can't wait for God to take me."

"A week is not time enough for me to get the money together," he said.

"And how will I get out of it?" she asked. "He's so proud of me becoming a nun."

Determination settled in his expression like night falling. "I don't know, Hannah, but we'll find a way. I won't have you disappear from my life like that."

"I'll be coming back and forth; I won't be there all the time. At least not yet."

"I could be caught kissing a nun."

She giggled. "Oh, Andy McGregor, nuns only kiss the foot of Jesus."

He smiled. "We could elope."

She pushed him back. "You'll make me a widow in a week if we do that. Papa will surely come gunning for you."

"I say we go to America now then," he said. "If we wait, you'll be locked away for all time. There's nothing your father could do if we eloped to America." He kicked some dirt under his foot and frowned. "I hear they never let you go once you're promised to God. We've got to do whatever we can to prevent that. Not that I don't believe in those that want to worship our Lord but not you, Hannah. Pray, not you."

"I don't want to be promised to God," she said. "I want to be promised to you."

He looked at her sadly. "Can't you talk reason to your father?" he asked. "He's acting like the most pig-headed man I've ever known. If it will make him happy, I'll never talk politics again, well, at least not in his company."

"And will you be in support of British rule?"

"You know I cannot do that."

"We know how you feel. Our friends know how you feel as well, but can you not lie to my Father?"

"I suppose I could."

"He won't let me marry you because you believe in Irish Independence and he doesn't. Is that reasonable? He's the one who told me that I had the calling from God, is that reasonable? Now I ask you, why would God speak to him and not directly to me?"

"I should approach him and pretend to have changed my mind. After we're married, I won't care what I say."

"He'll speak with his fists if he doesn't believe you."

"We've got to try, Hannah. You're right. We've got to do something. I'll come tomorrow night. He won't throw me out, not if you tell him I've had a change of heart."

"I won't let him throw you out," she said. "But do you think it will make any difference?"

Andy shook his head. "I don't know. I'll tell him whatever he wants to hear. If he believes me then it will be worth it."

He pulled her into his arms. They had walked back to adjoining farms. For miles they had seen nothing but foxtail grass, blue-eyed and green. The land was covered in miles of thistle and butterwort. Only cows grazed peacefully across the hills, indifferent to everything but their own enjoyment of their effluvious field of flowers.

Andy smiled. "Before I saw that farmer there waving to us, I thought we were alone on earth."

"I wish we were," she said.

"Run away with me." He spun her around. "Let's just be done with it."

"My father will only hunt us down. I fear he'll put a bullet in you, or make sure you're spending time behind bars. We must get to America as soon as we can. It is the only place we'll be safe from my father and everybody else's wagging tongues. Besides, America is the best place to be, isn't it?"

"I'll get the money," he whispered as he kissed her mouth and she reached for him. "I'll get it or my name isn't Andy McGregor," he said. "Even if I have to steal it."

"You mustn't," she said, a bit startled.

"I won't," he said, "but I will get it."

"You do want to go to America, don't you, Andy?" she asked.

"Sure, I do, if it will bring us peace, sure I do."

"I think it's the only way we can find peace."

"Let's give it one more chance; let's be smart about it. Maybe we can put an end to all this talk of the convent. Tomorrow night I'll come by and I'll apologize to him, tell him I've changed my mind about the British. I'll lie like crazy. I'll do anything to keep you from the nuns. Then once we're married, I'll call him a backwards, cantankerous old fool."

Together they laughed as the warm winds came up behind them, and she tripped backwards. He fell beside her. They were on a hilltop that rolled softly to the grass below, and they slipped down the hill together. She landed on his belly. Their laughter was loud, as if they'd never stop. But soon, their laughter faded, and he put his hands up under her blouse. She felt her skin warm to his touch. She held him tightly and looked around.

"Do we have an audience anywhere near us?"

"Just the birds," he said. "They are singing loudly, rejoicing in our love."

"Pretend they're marrying us, giving us vows, making us man and wife."

Hannah spread her legs and lifted her skirt. She would have her lover the way she wanted him. She would have him completely. She would not be a virgin bride if God put a ring on her finger; that was for sure.

# Chapter Three

Hannah knew she would feel differently after giving up the one thing that made her pure, and she did feel differently. She felt like a woman, no longer a virgin girl, but a woman who had given her body to the man she loved. It was an insatiable delirium, having him inside her, his sweet lips against her ear. He was like music entering her. She didn't think she would ever feel so alive again, not until the next time and the next and the next.

She wanted to tell Anne that it was like a great concerto, to have a man enter you, an answered prayer, two souls in sync. But she would not tell Anne, not yet. It was so sacred that it needed to be kept hidden. Besides, Anne was too young, just a girl. But perhaps she would know just because it must show. She feared her father would take one look at her, and he'd know she'd sinned. She would be a wanton woman in his eyes. But her father did not know anything, nor did her sister. When her Papa looked at her he saw only his virgin child, sweet, virgin child who would make him proud by marrying Christ, and not the man she loved, the flesh and blood man she loved.

Andy rapped upon the window. "Is it safe?" he whispered as she raised the window up, and he stood there glowing in the moonlight. "Have you told him?"

"Yes, yes, I have."

"What did he say?"

She bit her lip a bit. "He huffed."

"Huffed?"

"Well, he didn't really say anything except he'd welcome you if you were like-minded."

Andy nodded his head up and down slowly. "Okay," he said.

"Go to the door and enter like a proper gentleman."

"Look, look at the suit I wear just for you and dear Mr. McGregor."

Hannah laughed. "How smashin' you look," she said as she took him in. His pale grey slacks had black lines going through to his cuffs, and his long coat was made of wool. The black bowtie he wore was perfectly tied around the collar of his pale-pink shirt.

"Thank you, my dear," He stole a peck on her cheek. "May be the last time for that tonight."

"I told him you had changed your ways, and you want to apologize for being such a fool."

"And the words will stick in my throat, I'm sure."

"What we do for love," she said.

Mr. McGregor stood with his back to the fire. Anne sat with Kieran by her side. She stroked the dog's fur as she spoke.

"You look like such a proper gentleman tonight, Andy," she said.

Andy extended his hand to Mr. McGregor as he entered the room. Hannah saw the skepticism in her father's expression.

"Evening to you, Sir," Andy said.

"And to you, young man." He gave Andy's outstretched hand a brief shake.

Hannah watched as the two sat in the living room, and she brought them beers while she and Anne remained in the smaller room. The fire made a lot of noise, and she could not hear the conversation between Andy and her father. She and Anne sat holding hands behind the door her father had closed.

"They seem to be getting on well," Anne said.

Hannah didn't answer her; she was too frightened to speak. She wanted to send hidden signals to her Papa so that he would know what was in her heart and that the only thing on earth that would make her happy would be her wedding to Andy McGregor.

"He must care what it is I want," she said.

"Oh, I'm sure he does," Anne said.

Hannah got up and put her ear to the door, "My God, I think they're laughing," she said and smiled.

A moment later Anne sat upright, "Oh, and what was that?"

Hannah got up and put her ear to the door again. "Perhaps I should enter, I think one of them has spilled his beer on the floor."

"By all means," Anne said.

Hannah returned with a pained expression. "Will you get the dustpan, Anne, one of them has broken a glass."

Anne got up quickly and hurried in. "I'm sure it's fine," she said.

Hannah began to rub her hands together because she didn't know what else to do. Finally, Anne appeared with the broom and dustpan.

"Will you get Father another beer? It was him that spilled it on the floor."

Hannah had an uneasy feeling. As she entered the room with her father's beer, she noticed that both their cheeks were flushed.

"Everything is all right now?" Anne asked as Hannah returned.

But Hannah didn't answer; she sat before the parlor listening as their voices rose. Anne looked at her doubtfully.

"Glory be to God but they seem to be shouting."

Andy's face was flushed with rage as he emerged with his fist clenched. He stared at Hannah with the most pained expression she'd ever seen. He shook his head.

"I'm sorry, but I can't agree with him, or listen to another word out of his mouth."

She watched him leave and looked back at her father. He was standing; his face seemed lit up, it was so bright.

"I'll not have him in my house again," he shouted. "He is a traitor."

# Chapter Four

It was her father who deposited Hannah with Sister Agnes, beaming like a crazy man. She had just a small satchel with her. If it weren't for the plans she and Andy had made together, she would have gone screaming to the hills, offering herself to any wild tribe that would take her. The plan was that she'd spend just a few months at the convent, and then Andy would come for her. He promised her that it would be soon; it would not take long before he could afford passage to America for the two of them.

She looked around the small room they had given her and sighed. It was what it was. There was a bed, a desk, and a window. Poor Christ was hanging all over the walls refusing to meet her impatient gaze. If she sat on the bed and stretched out her legs, they would touch the wall. She picked up the rosary they had placed on the bed. She watched the daylight fade. *How precipitous,* she thought, *to watch dusk swallow the day and leave us with blindness. It's just like entering a church.*

As the days passed, she studied diligently for it

took her mind off worrying if she and Andy would make it out of the country. She wondered what her Papa would do, how obstinate his rejection of her would be. It made her feel awful, but she imagined it would only be a matter of time before they could return, and he would embrace her again. She assumed things would change in Ireland, things always changed. But then she thought of what her Papa used to say, the more things change the more they stay the same.

She picked up the Bible beside her. Why, she would soon be able to quote from the book of Isaiah, Jeremiah, and Samuel, and what good would it do her? There would be endless daily readings of the Bible. It was her least favorite work of fiction. She laughed to herself. Oh, if the nuns could only hear her thoughts, her opinions, they'd banish her. Well, at least she prayed, or pretended to pray, as constantly as the breaths she took. She would kneel on the hard wooden pew, along with the other postulants, and after a while she could feel the cramp in her left leg. She prayed for relief. But prayers aren't answered directly. She knew that much, at least. It would be selfish of her to ask anything for herself what with all the suffering in the world. Sister Agnes had told her that God grants favors to those who pray for others. Still, she needed God's miracles too. If Andy did not come up with the money they needed, she would have to break out and defy her father. There was nothing more desperate than having to remain with lies for the rest of her life, nothing more devastating than being without Andy and in a communion with a

God that she didn't want or need.

But if Andy never came for her, because her father had had him shot, which she often feared, how many hours, she wondered, would she spend on her knees? Let's see, if she lived to be 50 that would be approximately 12,045 days, making that at least 144,544 hours and around 8,000,672 minutes that she'd spend in dire discomfort conversing with a God who ignored her prayers for the freedom to make her own choices.

The other girls disregarded the discomfort of kneeling for so many hours, but she'd see them later rubbing their aching limbs, trying to get the cramps out. But there, in the house of God, they would pretend obedience. Rosaries slipped through their fingers like the finest lace. Their whispered prayers reminded Hannah of scratches on chalkboard, all bundled up in a paper ball, rolling across the floor, sounding like the shaking of a baby's rattle. *Murmur. Murmur. Murmur.* But much more irritating than the murmurs was how a murmur would echo in the magnificence of St. Michael's Church, floating over the quiet pews like the humdrum of distant conversations that were completely unclear, completely.

The eyes of the other postulants were closed as they spoke to their Lord, always closed. Of course, their eyes were closed. Why not? God could not be seen. Well, God is closer to those who aren't looking out at the world but looking within. Sister Agnes had said that too.

Hannah would have none of it. Her eyes traveled the church as she prayed. She would not keep her eyes closed. She couldn't bear the darkness. No, not while the sun teased through the cracks in the door. Stained-glass angels complacently smiled all around her. Perhaps they were blessing the young women before them, all their sweet hopes. Surely all the good deeds of tomorrow sat in their hearts, their promises to the Lord, their worship as deep as the ocean floor, as it should be when God has spoken. But no God had spoken to Hannah, not even once.

The stained-glass angels reminded her of the blessed Lord with his mute tongue. Stained-glass angels are what they would all become, transparent and illusory, hardly living. But she would not become that. Oh, no. Andrew McGregor would take her away. They'd made their plan, and it wouldn't be long before they'd be crossing the ocean to America and she'd be staring at the grey waves and the white foam with her arm in his. She went over the plan every day. She was to wait way back where the nuns never went, back where the peat moss grew, and he'd come for her. He'd have a dress for her to change into and combs for her hair when it grew out and was long and flowing once again. They'd flee to the land of opportunity, him with his purse full of coins and she with her heart full of love and promise. Oh, she couldn't wait. She couldn't wait.

In the meantime, she would adjust, she assumed, for the time being. Andy had said it might take another month or two. She didn't mean to feel so indifferent toward God; she genuinely loved him, but sometimes she felt as if he was standing between the light and the lack of it. She was in limbo, waiting to be carted off to a new beginning by the boy she'd loved all her life. She would never have any regrets. If God held out his hand to her, she would have gone, but she didn't have the calling. God had never spoken to her. She was sorry she wanted more than the blood of Christ on her lips, but she did. She wanted a home and babies. If her father only knew how she really felt he would most likely crumble and die where he stood.

Her hair was gone, cut short as a boy's. It embarrassed her. She was no longer feminine. She'd wept for hours afterwards while fleeting memories remained of auburn trusses that fell to her lap, disappearing like dust. She could still recall how full and thick her hair had been as it lay across his chest, but how long until the memory faded? She told him she wanted green and gold combs to wear in her hair, to look pretty for him. She thought of the colors green and gold. They only existed in the stained-glass saints. But there was no color in the convent. She missed color. When she wanted color, she had to go to the church and stare at the saints, but it was not the same. Colors were more vibrant in Andy's arms, not like inside the convent where everything was sepia-toned, like all color had been drained away. No, the ebullient green of grass and the vivacious blue of sky had been clearer than glass in his arms, as if she'd taken some medicine where everything became more intense. In the convent, there were just shades of shadow, that's all.

# Chapter Five

It was another storm that raged against the walls and the windows of the Harold's Cross Convent. It was a week before he was to come for her, a week before they'd planned to run away to America. She had been at the convent so long she could barely remember what dirt felt like as she ran barefoot through it. But Andy had relayed quietly to Anne that he had the money together for their trip. He had earned it as a clerk in a shipping factory. She was so proud of him. Hannah had planned her escape carefully. Day in and day out she thought of it. Each time she imagined her freedom she would get giddy and stares would come her way, as if she had a screw loose. But she'd go over the plan again and again; she was to take the back stairs at two in the morning when not even the mice could be seen roaming the halls. She would carry her shoes, which were hard and made a tapping sound when she walked; they would certainly make noise on the wood floor.

She could hear the whistle of the wind as she bent in prayer. It was an angry wind that whipped over the land, cursing humankind. It felt like God declaring that the sins of man filled him with rage and despair. God had a right to his vengeance, Hannah thought, certainly he did. She wasn't altogether godless. There were times she felt close to God, and she knew how he loved her, but he was her God in those moments, a God who understood her. He did not belong to anyone else, and no interpretation of anyone else's God would fit hers.

She hurried through her Hail Mary. Anne was waiting for her in their secret place where the peat moss grew and the sun had abandoned, where they could speak without being seen or heard. All the nuns complained it was too damp back there, spooky even, and they would not go there for fear of seeing ghosts. Anne had written that she had urgent news and they must meet as soon as possible. Hannah knew that Anne would not have put in writing whatever the news was. Their father often confiscated their letters, going over them with a fine-toothed comb to assure himself that his daughters had no secret thoughts he would not be privy to. According to her Papa, the thoughts of girls were dangerous.

As Hannah approached, she could see that her sister was pacing, as if disturbed by what she knew. She was pacing with a great deal of anticipation and with short steps. Hannah felt her heartbeat accelerate, an omen perhaps of bad news.

"What is it?" Hannah asked, taking in the look on her sister's face, like something sour was in her mouth. "Get it out quickly because I fear the worst. You appear too distraught."

Anne reached out her hand. "He's going to enlist," she said.

"Enlist?" Hannah asked. "Enlist what?"

"He's going to enlist in the war," Anne said. "Patrick, too. They have this fool idea that is what will unite Ireland, they'll be fighting in a war together with a shared enemy."

"Oh, my God, he can't, he was to come for me in a week."

Anne dropped her eyes. "You know how men are," she said. "Country is everything."

"They could be killed, both of them." If Hannah could have only one prayer answered it would be that she was dreaming this news.

Anne put her arms around Hannah. "What can we do?"

Hannah noticed that Anne was crying, the tears running down her face with the rain that fell from the sky. The rain and her tears mingled, like an embrace.

"Don't worry." Hannah rubbed the tears from her sister's cheek. "It will be all right."

"You mean the war won't last long? Do you believe that?"

"Tell Andy to come to me, to meet me here tomorrow at noon. It is very important; I must see him before he does something so foolish."

"He's serious about the war, Hannah. He feels it's his duty."

"It's his duty to meet me here tomorrow at noon. See that he comes."

She was lucky to have gotten away. Sister Mary Megan had pulled her aside to ask her if she could play the organ for Sunday's mass. Hannah had given her a simple "yes," but then Sister Mary Megan had gone on and on about poor Sister Sally's gout. Hannah had not slept the night before, and she was in no good mood for Sister Mary Megan.

"If you'll excuse me, Sister. Nature calls." Hannah pretended to run to the bathroom, but then, as soon as the Sister walked off, she hurried out the door and back behind the convent, back where the trees hid her from view. Her heart was pounding like a boomerang in her chest. She was out of breath as she approached. Andy was there, looking so serious, so troubled. She noticed he was trying to smile, but his lips wouldn't part. She noticed something in his hands, which looked to her like a small gift with a red bow.

"I don't like that uniform on you," she said.

He met her gaze with a great deal of intensity. "It's going to unite us, Hannah. I must fight. This is exactly what we as Irishmen need."

"Losing men in battle is what we as Irishmen need?"

"This is going to mean everything to Ireland," he said. "We'll be side by side fighting a bigger enemy than each other. We'll be Irishmen fighting on the same side." He pulled her down on the concrete bench where they could sit together. "Your father will embrace me now, Hannah. I don't want to leave Ireland. I love this land. What if... what if we won't have to leave at all?"

"You could be killed, Andy. Have you not

considered that?"

"No, I won't be killed. I'll be back. I swear it. And when I come back, Hannah, your father will be giving us his blessing. I'll be a hero."

She sighed deeply and took his hand. "If something happens to you... I swear I'll...

"Nothing will happen to me." He grabbed her and pulled her close. "I give you my word, we'll grow old together."

"Can I talk you out of it? Is there any way I can talk you out of this?"

Andy looked off. His teeth were clenched, and he would not meet her eyes.

"Is this the right thing you're doing? Why didn't you discuss it with me first?"

"I'm sorry for that. My brothers and I made up our minds so quickly."

"Do you really think this is our war?"

"Britain seems to think so."

"I don't like war," she said.

He held out the carefully wrapped gift in his hand. "A necessary evil, Hannah."

She turned away.

"Here," he reached for her, "this is for you, for all those times you might be afraid, or you might get sad without me."

She took the package and gently removed the colorful wrapping paper. When she saw what was inside, it did make her smile. It was a music box. She lifted it up and held it in the light. It was beautiful.

"This box signifies every precious moment we've shared, back to when we were children."

"It's magnificent."

The box was made of wood, a shiny wood. A piano was carved on the front of the box. She ran her fingers over it.

"Go on, lift the top of it."

As she did another smile broke out on her face so broad it looked hard to contain. "It's playing ragtime." She laughed and put her ear to it.

"Surely it is. '*Precious Moments*' by Scott Joplin."

"Oh, it does make me so happy," she said through her tears.

"It's got your initials on the top."

"And yours too. Oh, Andy, where did you get this? It's expensive, I just know it."

She watched the small gold mechanisms move like the keys on a piano as he spoke.

"I found it in Glencullen for a song. There was this little shop, and I said I was looking for a wedding gift for my bride."

She looked up at him, and then she kissed him. "I will be your bride for sure, Andy McGregor, be it here or in America."

"I promise you, Hannah. I'll be back, and we will be married; we'll be married here in Ireland with your papa at your side. Know that. Please know that."

She kissed him for a long, long time.

# Chapter Six

The days turned into weeks and the weeks into months. Hannah prayed for Andy constantly, lived for his letters. Alone at night, she thought about him and the life they were going to have, the sons that would have his hair and the daughters that would know his smile.

Hannah was oddly happy. Why not? She lived in her head; she lived in her dreams. She seemed to float through her days with an indifference to her chores, to her prayers, and even her conversations. They spoke about the war constantly at the convent, and she blocked out their words. In her world there was no war, there was just Andy, who was absent for a while and would soon be returning.

And soon, there was talk that the war might be ending; it had certainly gone on too long. She hadn't seen Andy in nearly a year, or perhaps it just seemed like a year. They were writing to each other every day, or at least, she was. Just recently, his letters had stopped abruptly, but she assumed they would resume as they had in the past. She wouldn't hear for several weeks and then she would. She kept her faith intact that Andy would be home soon. She prayed that it would be today's news, an end to the damn war. Finally, there would be no prayers, just a victory dinner.

Each week the dead were mentioned at Sunday's mass, and they prayed for hours afterwards. They prayed for all the Irish boys who had given their lives for a larger cause. "There's no greater gift than that," Sister Agnes said.

Hannah had to hold her breath each Sunday and pray that Andy would not be among the unfortunate. She hated Sundays; she hated that list.

On a most dreary day, there had been six of them. There'd been three from Dublin, one from Dundalk, and two from Castlebar. The premature murder of six young men in a war Hannah didn't think they should be in to begin with. When the nuns spoke of duty, she wanted to choke them. Duty had a horrible ring to it, like sacrifice. It was a horrible chore to get up on Sunday mornings knowing the news she would hear, boys losing their lives, coming home in a casket to grieving mothers.

It was always a priest who came to the pulpit and read the list, asked them to pray for the dead. She felt her heart stop as it did each week until the priest got to the last name on the list. Andy McGregor was from Dublin. There had been three dead from Dublin. She closed her eyes tight and put her hand around the gold cross she wore at her neck. It would not be him on that list; he had made a promise, he would be back.

But his name reverberated against the walls. She hadn't heard it, only imagined she had, hadn't she?

Andrew McGregor? The name rang out again like a hammer had slammed against her head. She sat upright with a start. "Did he say … did he say Andrew McGregor?" she asked someone beside her. It was a nod that came back to her, a nod.

Hannah fell out of the pew and on to the floor. She screamed repeatedly and wept aloud. "What name did you call? Oh, please, I heard you wrong?"

"Andrew McGregor," the priest said softly.

They did not understand her grief or the howl from her throat that nearly shattered the glass angels from their tranquil home.

"Thy will be done?" she shouted. "Thy will be done?" It was a question she was asking them. She was angry. She was furious. "How can you believe in this God?" she cried.

All was gone now, every hope and every dream of happiness. His golden curls would lie in the damp earth beneath a foreign field not much different from the one where she had held him in her arms.

They sent her home, of course. She needed to collect herself, they said. Even her father would not deny her tears. As Andy had predicted, they were on the same side now, and Andy was suddenly a hero in her father's eyes. But for Hannah, he was merely dead.

She had heard there was not even a complete body to lay in the ground. When they put Andy on display in the church the coffin was closed. She could not even touch his brow or bend to kiss his lips. She fell to her knees and wept so loudly that Sister Agnes said aloud: how fine is that? Hannah Reilly has surely got the calling for she grieves so deeply. Her soul is full of God's love and compassion. What a good nun she'll make, what a good nun.

Hannah had rocked back and forth on the cold wooden floor for hours. The coffin had held only pieces of him. Pieces? Perhaps with no face to put in the goddamn coffin he was not actually dead. He would suddenly appear and laugh at her lack of faith. "I said I would be home," he'd say, and he'd reprimand her.

The others wondered why she wept so much, but she wouldn't tell them. In her arms she clutched the box, her wedding gift. It did make her smile, despite her misery, but the memory of Andy was so painful, and she felt the ache so deeply, that she rarely opened the lid to hear the tune, the happy tune: "Precious Memories."

Now there would be no wedding. Her life of celibacy was a looming shadow; the absence of frivolity taunted her. Only once in a lifetime a woman finds a man's love, only once. A woman can't love so completely and think she could find it again. She knew that.

"What is your message to me, my Lord, am I meant to serve you?" she asked.

But God was always silent. He spoke in symbols and signs. He spoke in miracles or in disasters.

# Chapter Seven

They were praying when they got the news. Hannah had been at the convent one year, seven months since Andy's death. She was doing her best to adjust, to not carry rage in her heart. But when she prayed it was always for Andy. She prayed his soul was at rest. She prayed that the anguish she carried in her entire being would one day lift. She spoke to him in her prayers; it was the only time she felt happy, the only time she was not alone.

Hannah's head rose slowly when she heard the footsteps; her gaze landed on the altar. She knew who it was, of course. She felt the other postulants stiffen as she approached, her black gown trailing the floor, her coif and guimpe as white as the soap that cleansed her skin. It was Mother Superior, usually the bearer of bad news.

"The five of you will be going off to America. We'll be opening schools. We have spoken to your parents, and they have all agreed. It will be a wonderful opportunity. You'll be trained to teach and to administrate." Mother Superior looked at them each in turn. "Better off in America, I'd say."

Hannah bolted upright. So, it was not bad news she was bringing. Her mouth fell open as the prayer book came to her breast. *I will be free of this place,* she thought, feeling Bridget Regan's elbow hit her waist. Hannah turned to find Bridget's smile and let her expression crinkle up before quickly returning her gaze to the blessed Mother and the solemn acceptance of God's will. Of course, without Andy, it would be a sad journey, but it was far enough away to give her a sense of freedom and a disconnection from Ireland.

"Quite an opportunity," Sister Agnes uttered beside her.

Hannah's expectations had been bleak after Andy's death. A consistent cluster of women and endless hours of prayer were what she had expected the rest of her life to look like. No more barefoot romps through the emerald valleys or bashful glimpses of her sweet Andy McGregor and his unruly curls.

"It's a blessed miracle," she whispered. Though it was not how she wanted to get to America. But maybe it was Andy giving her the sign, hinting of new life and new beginnings.

"You'll be having a fine future," her father said. "A blessed future. You'll be teaching the poor, raising their sights and their spirits. I'll be proud of you Hannah Reilly; I surely will be."

He had never comforted her following her grief over Andy. He had been too uncomfortable to admit to the compromise he felt. He hinted at it, but what good would it do now that Andy was dead? She felt that the oceans between them were as vast as the one she'd be crossing.

"I will do my best," she said, "to follow God's calling."

"And when you return as a novitiate Ireland will be a better place." He laughed as he sat in his chair and lit his pipe. The sun made a path on the wooden floor. "You'll serve God in Dublin or the villages?"

"I don't know, Father," she said. She wasn't thinking about her return, only her journey.

"I'll let you have Patrick Sullivan if I can go in your place. I want to go to America," her sister Anne said.

Hannah grinned. "That's generous of you, but if Jesus had wanted *you*, he would have come knocking."

Hannah looked off. Patrick had returned safe from the war, all in one piece. He and Anne would be married the following year. The beautiful red dog lay at her feet. She watched the rise and fall of his chest.

"I'll be leaving Kieran in your care, Anne. Will you love him as I do?"

"More," she said. "I've always loved Kieran more." She laughed. "God, how I'll miss you, Hannah."

Anne ran to her sister and threw her arms around her. Hannah had experienced joy here in this house. Once upon a time her father was a more reasonable man. Once upon a time her mother had sat in the garden and gently told her to think for herself or the weight of a man would crush her. Why must a woman grow up and face so few choices, Hannah wondered. Could not joy be found elsewhere as well? Wasn't there a world full of choices? But could it ever be found behind the black robes of God's chosen? Yes, the weight of a man, God is a man, and the weight is heavy.

"And I you," she said and kissed her sister on the mouth and on the top of her head.

"I want to play ragtime all night before you leave. I want to rattle the windowpanes with ragtime." Anne began to giggle as Hannah held her hand.

"It won't be forever," Hannah said.

"God does not approve of ragtime," John Reilly called out, and his voice was like a brick falling through lace.

Hannah exchanged one of her conspiratorial glances with Anne. Each sister bit her lip to prevent themselves from looking as if they were mocking their father.

"Then God has a tin ear," Anne said in a pout. "Music brings gladness to a person's soul, and God should not deny gladness."

"Ay, music does bring gladness," he said. "But not the noise of the American brothels."

"Papa," Hannah shouted. "I shall play ragtime for the children in Boston, introduce them to the finest musicians."

"Ay, and the nuns will take a ruler to your hand, daughter. And let's not forget, the Americans are savages. It does not surprise me that their music should reflect them so well."

"Be that as it may, I will do it. I will not be a stodgy nun without a sense of fun. Ragtime music is joyful, Papa, and Americans are not savages."

Her papa had no comment. She felt a sense of power. Now that she was on her way to God's calling, she had the right to her opinions, and even her father would listen, though he might not agree. There was room enough in this world for ragtime music.

"I'll send that damn piano down the road if you tarnish my ears with that sinful sound. I'll have none of it." He stood to his feet.

Anne and Hannah watched as he picked up his paper and settled in the kitchen, after taking a bottle of brandy from the cupboard.

"He'll come round; don't you think?" Anne said.

"Ay, and it won't matter," Hannah said. "I'll be miles and miles away."

"I'm going to be a nun, too." Anne grinned at her, obviously not too committed to that.

Hannah raised her eyebrows. "So, you're giving up the kisses of Patrick Sullivan for the hours you'll spend on your knees talking to someone who never answers you?"

Anne laughed. "Well, maybe to get to America."

"It wouldn't be worth it, little sister," Hannah said.

Hannah had a dream the night she found out she was leaving Ireland. Jesus had appeared to her, his eyes so black it was startling. Then he winked. He looked right at her and *winked. For the first*

*time in her life, she felt a kinship with Jesus.*

"Do you know Jesus winks, Anne? A sure sign he approves of my journey."

Anne put her hands up over her face and giggled like a crazed hyena.

"Oh, yes, a sure sign. Oh, yes, of that I am certain." She threw her knitting at Hannah and made a face that turned her eyes into slits. "Jesus winks? Oh, really, Hannah."

"Well, it's true." Hannah wore a look of determination. "He's given me the sign with that wink. Jesus did look a bit like Andy, though."

"Do you think he'll wink at me?" Anne asked.

"Keep looking. Maybe," she said.

# Chapter Eight

They never strayed far from the dock in Liverpool; they stood anxiously in a line, staring out over the sea; breathless and eager they watched until the *Campania* approached— the ship that would be taking them all the way to their new home. Hannah clutched Bridget's hand so tightly she cried out. Their hearts pounded in unison as the dot in the distance grew bigger.

"Blessed Jesus," Bridget Regan screamed as the mighty *Campania's* anchors splashed into the harbor waves. "That ship is the size of a small country."

Euphoria took hold of Hannah. Fate was unfolding before her very eyes. She thought of Andy and how she longed to see it all with him. She wondered of the fate before her now, how Jesus had given her the sign. Perhaps all of it was meant to be – Andy's death, her voyage. It was as if within that wink Jesus was saying: "Trust me."

She grabbed Bridget's hand again and squeezed it even tighter than she had before. "Blessed be to God," she whispered. "It's His will. I need to believe in it, to trust it."

"I hope I don't throw up," Bridget said. "My brother told me that sometimes a ship can feel like a crazed cradle, rocking back and forth."

"What do you think America will look like?" Hannah asked, as Liverpool faded from sight. They were in steerage, watching as the shore grew dim from a back deck.

"The ground between the rectory and the chapel is about all we'll see of America," Bridget answered.

"But we'll be traveling to schools and distant towns to help the poor." Hannah's eyes were wide with hope. "America will be spread out before us like a great map."

Bridget put her hands on her hips. "You best not be fooling yourself, Hannah Reilly, a map the size of my thumbnail is all you'll see of it."

"Have you no faith, Bridget?" Hannah asked, for she did not want to be disillusioned, not yet.

"Too much faith," Bridget said. "It got me here, didn't it?"

"Well then, maybe, we'll run away, escape from the convent; we'll hop an American train. We'll be vagabonds." Hannah suddenly laughed so hard she fell to the ship's floor. "Oh, God, forgive me."

Bridget Regan made the sign of the cross.

"I think you stole the wine from the ship's chapel," Molly Flynn said, pointing a finger in Hannah's face.

"Ah, but I'd like to do that," Hannah said.

"Where do you think the ship's chapel is?"

Molly Flynn gasped and stared at Hannah. "I think the devil is taking hold of you, Hannah."

Hannah was tired upon arrival at the port and could barely keep her eyes open as they were sent on to the barges that would take them to Ellis Island. She felt like she had been at sea for months. Her legs barely moved, but she followed behind Bridget and Molly as they entered a large building with American flags hanging from the walls, beautiful and flowing they swept over her.

"Stars and stripes," she whispered. "Just like they said, red, white, and blue stars and stripes. Oh, look Molly."

She walked under the flags and could not stop looking up, despite the stiffness in her neck. She was told she was at the main building and would soon be taken to a sleeping room. She would never remember how long she slept in the sleeping room before she was moved to an examination room, but it was dark when she closed her eyes and dark when she opened them again.

"Is this America?" Bridget asked her.

Hannah didn't really have that answer as she looked out over the sea. They told her she would be subjected to questioning, but she had no idea how long she'd wait, how laborious it would be when they finally did question her. Eventually, she was led somewhere else, and she hadn't a clue as to where, but she expected more tedium.

"Where are we now?" she asked Sister Agnes.

"Discharging quarters," Sister Agnes replied. "We will soon be on a ferry to the great city of New York, child."

"Glory be to God," Hannah whispered.

The War had slowed down the immigration to Ellis Island, but there were still many young postulants arriving in 1916. Most were sent off to convents throughout New York and New England. Hannah, Bridget and Molly were promised to the Convent of Saint Anthony in Concord, Massachusetts and were taken to the rail station along with Sister Agnes. The other girls were put into a separate carriage and sent to a small parish in Queens, New York.

As much as she'd wanted to remain awake the motion of the train put her to sleep. When Hannah felt a poke on her shoulder, she anxiously opened her eyes.

"Good Lord," she cried, "we're here, aren't we? We're in Concord?"

They were rushed into a waiting carriage as the sky transitioned into dusk. Hannah squinted as she peered before her, hoping to capture what she could of Concord before the transitioning sky, now the color of ash, completely descended.

"I think I'm going to like Concord," Hannah said, as the carriage finally approached St. Anthony's. "I thought we'd never get here."

Bridget laughed. "You're so exhausted, Hannah Reilly, that you don't know what your eyes are resting on, or even what you're saying. We could be back in Ireland for all you know."

That was the truth. Hannah had come through Ellis Island bleary and bone weary after the crossing, and then there had been the tedious process of going through immigration; it had left her body drained, so many questions, so much waiting. Finally, on the train from New York to Concord, she'd simply passed out. She'd slept so deeply then that she didn't see a thing of this great country. Unfortunately, she woke up just as tired as she'd been before she'd dozed off.

And now there was nothing to see but the dimly lit church. The minute they arrived at Saint Anthony, Mother Superior sent them right off to their rooms, after brief introductions and a tour of the rectory, that is.

"I'm not tired anymore," Hannah whispered. "I want to see the city. It's got me wide awake. I want to see America."

"Shush," Bridget whispered back. "We're not supposed to have any interest at all in the city or in America."

"Mother Superior is nice," Molly Flynn said softly, "though she reminds me of a Jersey cow."

"Best be watching your mouth, Molly Flynn," Bridget whispered again from behind her hand. "I hear they punish nuns for their sins in America; they make them drink salted water."

"Better that than American tea," said Hannah, as the others laughed.

As the days passed, they became dissatisfied with

their surroundings. The church of Saint Anthony looked just like St. Michael's Parish in Dublin. "We might as well be looking out on the Wicklow Mountains," they told each other with a disappointed sigh. Even Jesus looked the same, thin and long on the cross, benevolently silent. The Virgin was blonde, and the apostles all bearded and dark. It was the same everywhere.

"I feel like running away," Hannah said.

"Hush your mouth, Hannah," Molly told her. "We are not supposed to want to run away. We are going to be nuns, wanting for nothing but the good Lord."

The mornings brought no light, and breakfast was meager. Was starving and tedium prerequisites for becoming a nun? Hannah wondered.

"Is there no butter for the toast?" Hannah tried to be inconspicuous as she spoke into Bridget's ear. "Does God not want us to have butter?"

"Be grateful." Bridget smiled. "For the toast, at least."

They would never have expected it. Surely a miracle was about to occur. After three months of studying and praying, Father John appeared in the dining hall one day. Hannah knew something was brewing. Father John was gloating over something or other for sure. *What could it be?* They wondered. Whatever it was, he was pleased to tell them. He walked to the front of the small dining hall and waited for silence.

"I am sure you are going to be very surprised," he said, his smile like taut string.

"I don't think he has any teeth." Molly giggled softly, nudging Hannah in the ribs.

"Shush," Bridget whispered from behind.

Father John held up an envelope. "The oldest Catholic Church in America is in Boston," he said, grinning through a slight gap between his lips. "You've been offered a tour, my good women."

Hannah let out a yelp she couldn't quite hold back as Molly reached for her hand.

"We're going to Boston?" Bridget cried out.

The priest nodded. "Courtesy of the Boston Archdiocese."

Hannah wanted to fall to her knees. She'd be seeing a bit of America after all, before settling behind her vows for the rest of her blessed days.

Father John read from a piece of grey paper so thin it looked transparent. "You must spend some time at our beautiful church," he read loudly, spending at least three seconds on every word. "We — await — your — visit — with — much — anticipation."

Hannah could barely keep her feet from leaving the ground. She was as excited about traveling to the big city of Boston as she had been about boarding the boat in Liverpool. This was the best news she could have ever gotten, just to be able to move in daylight, to see something of the world.

"Are you with me, Andy?" she whispered as she knelt before the window in her room, and one star winked back like the wink that Christ had given her.

"See it through my eyes the way it would have been if the Lord hadn't seen fit to take you."

She clutched the music box in her hand and opened the lid. Of course, she had brought it with her. She couldn't imagine going anywhere without it. It was like having Andy with her, his thoughts when he'd bought it, his smile when he watched her open the top. The ragtime waltz made her feel closer to heaven than any prayer she'd uttered.

"Oh, Andy, I'm taking you with me to the great city of Boston," she whispered.

# Chapter Nine

It could not have been a bluer day the morning the young women set out for Boston. The sky was a whimsical promise of sunshine, dappled with soft, nonchalant clouds that lounged over the long gray train like puffs of cotton. Molly and Bridget ran ahead to the first car like schoolgirls at the last bell. Poor Kathryn got sick and couldn't go at all, and the others promised to remember every moment and relay every detail, so they could tell her one by one when they returned.

Hannah felt blessed to get a window seat in the crowded last car. She was secretly relieved to find herself disentangled from the others. But just as she was settling into the pleasure of her own company, she was startled by a friendly interruption. She found herself staring up at an attractive young man in a fine white linen suit.

"Excuse me," he said and paused for just a moment before lifting his bag and holding it near the small compartment over her. "May I take this seat beside you?" he asked politely.

The train started up its engines as the young

man waited for her reply. Soon the wheels gathered speed. Hannah wanted to slow the train down as it rumbled forward. She looked quickly toward the window. If only she could stop the wheels from moving so fast so she might capture the images and store them away in her purse for future viewing. After all, this was America about to roll out before her.

The man sighed and brought the suitcase down. "May I?" he asked again.

Somewhat apprehensively, Hannah looked up and caught the young man's expression. She noticed the earnestness of his smile and quickly removed her bag from the seat.

"By all means," she answered softly.

Settling back, he stared ahead of him.

*How sharply defined his profile is,* Hannah thought. *And the cuffs of his shirt are as white as milk. He looks like a man on a mission.*

As if he knew she held him in her thoughts, he turned to her. Together they watched as the fleeting images beyond the glass teased their eyes and vanished.

"It does not appear to be so very different from Dublin," she said aloud, "except for the weather, that is. It's raining back in Dublin, I'm quite sure of it."

The smile that fell from his lips was eager, revealing his desire for conversation. "Where I'm going, coconuts fall from the trees and the sun never goes behind the clouds."

Hannah laughed and said she didn't believe him. "Sounds like a fairy-tale place," she said.

The young man's blue eyes found hers. "Your laughter is like a song," he said. "Seriously, you remind me of music. It's your brogue, perhaps. It's full of notes."

She blushed as she turned her face back to the window. *How outspoken*, she thought.

"Wade Hampton Fournier," she heard him say as he extended his hand.

"From?" she asked, shaking the hand in hers, feeling the warmth of it.

"My father was a Royal Canadian horse soldier. He was from a small village near the St. Lawrence River. He died last year. My mother is still alive, though. She's from South Carolina; that's why my English has a bit of a drawl." He paused, taking in her features, studying her face. "I'm named after a Civil War general."

"Really?" she said. "The American Civil war?"

"Sure enough. I was raised in New Brunswick, but I've lived in Quebec since 1907." He shuddered dramatically as he mentioned that he had spent his life dreaming of the sun and hating the Canadian winters that whipped through him with a chill so merciless, it had made his young bones ache.

"You wouldn't do well in Dublin." She noticed the ease in which she laughed again.

"Your home, I presume?"

She took in his smile and nodded. "Hannah Reilly from Dalkey, a small village right outside Dublin. I'm here to join the convent of St. Anthony in Concord," she said proudly.

"Is that so?" he said. Wade leaned his head back. "I'm headed to Jacksonville." He smiled broadly.

"I've got a good job waiting for me."

"Really?" she asked. "What will you do there?"

"I'm going to be selling fine men's clothes on Florida Boulevard, a small department store, but very fancy."

She looked back out the window. "How nice for you," she said with a tinge of guilt, for she envied his freedom.

"My sister, Rena, runs a hotel in Clearwater with her husband. He's an American." He turned his head in Hannah's direction. "They've carved out a nice little life for themselves. Rena's written to me many times about the Florida sun and the ocean air." Wade chuckled. "I told her I was ready to leave the Canadian winters behind me, for sure."

"How did you get the job?" Hannah asked, mildly curious, feeling that the company was pleasing.

"Well," Wade leaned over, his shoulder barely a breath from hers. "One fine day, Rena wrote and told me that one of the hotel regulars from Jacksonville needed a man to work in his store selling suits. Rena went and bragged about me, said I'd look good in all his fancy clothes because I'm handsome, and the man made the offer right then and there. Everyone likes my sister."

"And I'm sure they'll like you as well," Hannah said encouragingly, but feeling he was confident enough for the two of them.

"I could not have been more satisfied with my new arrangements, even though Rena apologized repeatedly about not being able to find me anything in Clearwater, closer to them. 'No, no,' I insisted,

'Jacksonville is a big city and much better suited to a man's future than a little tourist town like Clearwater. It all worked out in my favor, Rena.'"

"That it did," Hannah replied, turning her attention back to the window, but the images were moving so quickly it made her dizzy, so she turned again to Wade, taking in his comely features and wondering if it was a sin to notice.

Wade watched the blush on her skin deepen. He liked that her nose was fine and straight and that her cheekbones were high. Her lips were so soft and full that he had an impulse to run the tip of his finger over them. He leaned in close to her.

"I wasn't lying about the coconut trees," he whispered and folded his arms around his chest.

Yes, life was certainly looking good for Wade. He was headed where the days promised sunshine and he had just met the most beautiful girl he had ever seen. She was certainly far too beautiful to marry God, in his opinion.

"When do you become a nun?" he asked.

"Oh, that's going to take me some time. I'm still a year away from becoming a novice member."

"If you don't mind my asking, you got a calling?"

She stared at him for just a moment before she answered. "I did," she said softly.

He nodded his head and began to pull on some threads that had extended near the cuff of his shirt. He knew she was lying, or at least he hoped she was.

"I wish the ride from Concord to Boston were

longer," he said seriously and a bit forlornly.

"Do you like riding trains?" she asked him.

He shrugged his shoulders. "Not necessarily."

"What were you doing in Boston?" she asked. "If you came in from Canada?"

"Sightseeing," he said. "I wanted to see a bit more of the States before heading south. I'll probably never get up to this part of the world again."

Hannah sighed deeply before answering him. "I won't be seeing much of America either," she said. "Not after this trip."

Wade sat in silence for a moment before he spoke. He had sensed her displeasure.

"You're very young, aren't you?"

She shook her head. "No, not very."

"Do you believe in love at first sight?" he asked. He knew he was being bold, but he felt as if she'd given him an invitation, even if she wasn't aware of it, to be flirtatious.

Truth was, he felt the urge to become respectable; he was no longer a portrait painter on a city street. *A man needs a wife,* he thought, *especially when he's about to turn thirty.*

Hannah stiffened. "Love at first sight? Lord, no," she said quickly.

"Don't lie to yourself, Miss Reilly," he said in earnest. "I think you do believe in love at first sight."

She blushed deeply. "I most certainly do not."

"Don't ignore the subtle changes of the heart." He held her gaze with his. "Do you not feel something between us?"

Hannah studied his chiseled features. "You don't mean...?" She blushed more deeply as his hand brushed lightly against hers. "You and I...?"

Wade noticed they were nearing the city. She hadn't said a word more since he'd completely unhinged her, even made her question her calling. He was quite sure of that.

"You are a beautiful young woman, Miss Hannah Reilly. I could marry you. That is, I'd sure like to marry you."

Hannah turned away. "Don't be absurd, sir, I am promised to the good Lord, and you hardly know me."

"A man knows things when he's as introspective as I am."

"Please don't offend me further, sir," she said, keeping her eyes averted.

Wade wanted to reach for her hand but didn't, not yet. "Don't hide your lovely self away for the rest of your life, Miss Reilly. I'll bet God doesn't need you like I do."

"What about what I need, Mr. Fournier?" she asked him defiantly as she turned to meet the seriousness of his frown.

Wade replied by falling to his knees in the aisle with great flair and drama. "Forgive my theatrics, Miss Reilly, but I'm quite serious. Come with me to Florida and let me make you happy. Why, I'll make you the happiest woman on earth if you'll let me. You'll never feel a chill in the wind again, not with my loving arms around you."

He'd heard about all those women forced to become nuns. He was sure she was one of them.

She'd be a fool to reject him, and he knew instinctively that Hannah Reilly was no fool.

Hannah sat upright and clenched her jaw, though she wanted to smile. The elation she felt was sinful. Instinctively, she reached for her prayer book, ignoring the curious expressions of the people around her.

She did not turn her face toward him again, not until she felt his leg brush up against her own, ever so accidentally, as he sat back in his seat. The very nearness of him had caused a melting in her heart, and the heat of his body had caused her to tingle, even in places hidden by the white long skirt of God's chosen.

*Is this a test you be giving me, Lord?* She crossed herself and bit her lip. Her heart was pounding in her chest so loudly it was a wonder Wade wasn't humming to the rhythm of it.

"Forgive my boldness, Miss Reilly. It's just … well, I believe I'm in love with you … and I've got to act fast or I'll never see you again. I feel I've known you all my life, and we're meant to be together. I don't think we should let this moment pass."

His eyes were so wide; she noticed the blue of them for the first time, such a deep, dark color, like a moody, ominous sky.

He took her hand. "Will you marry me?"

"I don't make frivolous promises, Mr. Fournier." She tried to make light of it and took her hand away.

"Miss Reilly, I believe that fate has brought us to

this moment, and I believe in opportunity. Let's not be haunted forever by an *adieu* that neither of us means or wants. My heart has never felt so light or been so deeply sincere."

"That's an ambiguous statement." She looked past him. It was then he placed his hand over hers once again. She trembled ever so slightly under his touch, as if stirred by the truth she was trying to avoid.

"Please," he said as the train pulled into Boston, "don't leave before telling me where you're staying."

"Cathedral of the Holy Cross. That's where I'm staying."

She searched his face, taking in his expression, one of eager hope.

"Will you just think about seeing me again?" he asked.

"I will think of it," she said impulsively, knowing that if she let him go, she'd be hating herself forever.

"I won't be far from you," he said. "I won't let you out of my sight, not until your mind is made. I'm going to wait for your answer."

"I'm to be a nun," she said. "Can you not see that?"

Wade nodded. "Ask God what to do then," he said. "I don't believe God will lead you astray. There's choice, Miss Reilly, there's always choice."

He grinned at her, and before she could stop herself, she grinned back.

"I will ask God," she said. "I'm willing to question where my path is, but my Good Lord, I've just met you."

"I might be a miracle before you." He let out a long breath. "Yes, I just might be, Miss Reilly."

# Chapter Ten

Hannah embraced the Sisters of Cathedral of the Holy Cross with a guilty heart. They reminded her of the happy penguins she'd seen in geography books, flapping their arms in excitement, their innocent faces adorned by a lack of complexity.

"Follow us," they chatted. "We'll take a brief tour now and then let you get settled."

Hannah felt Molly take her hand.

"Why are there tears in your eyes, Hannah Reilly?" Molly asked, the moment they were out of hearing.

Hannah thought about the young man who was waiting for her just outside the doors of the beautiful old cathedral. She knew he had followed her there. It was as if she could feel his presence. He was bold, but his boldness filled her with excitement.

"I could be out of my mind," she said.

Molly was clearly confused. "What do you mean?"

"I've met a man," Hannah said in a raspy whisper.

Molly stopped in her tracks. They had been walking behind the sisters of the Holy Cross, listening to their talk of the gardens, the stained glass, the haunting up top of the altar.

Molly fell to her knees. "My shoe," she called as the others stopped to wait. "Oh, go on ahead; I won't be but a moment."

She grabbed Hannah's arm and pulled her to the floor.

"Blessed be to God," Molly gasped. "What man?"

Hannah stood back up and craned her neck out the small oval window. "You can't see him from here," she said, "but he's out there waiting for me; he's handsome and kind."

"Where did you meet him?"

"On the train," Hannah said into Molly's wide eyes.

"Hannah, you can't tell if a man is kind by meeting him on a train. Handsome, yes, but not kind, Hannah."

"I am attracted to him," she felt herself blush, remembering the feeling she'd had when he'd brushed her leg. "I've got to trust my instincts. I don't want to be a nun. There, I've said it. I don't have the calling, Molly. If Andy McGregor hadn't died in the war, I would be married to him right now as we speak."

Molly arched her eyebrows. "I don't want to be a nun either."

"Find yourself a man then; you're a pretty girl."

"A pretty Sister, you mean."

"Run away."

"What? I can't do that."

"Well, I can."

"You can't."

"He's waiting for me, Molly. I want babies. I want to live as someone's wife."

"Blessed be to God." Molly made the sign of the cross.

Hannah held Molly by the shoulders. "Go quickly and catch up."

"What will you do?"

"The only thing I can do, turn to the Lord and ask him to forgive me."

Hannah knelt before Jesus in the chapel. She listened to the pounding of her heart. She wondered if she were making a mistake, but it was a risk she would take. She had a choice. For the first time in her life, she had a choice and her father was not there to make it for her.

"Forgive me, God," she said as she stared at the statue's despondent expression. "The truth is staring me in the face. I can't spend my days in a convent, not when there's a man outside the door holding the promise of everything I want. I'm not yet nineteen, how many years will I sit behind bars? Oh, I really do want to have a family, I know it in my heart."

Hannah looked at the quiet figure of the Virgin in her soft blue gown and golden hair. "I can't justify it, Holy Mother. I can't give my life to Jesus when I cherish another, could cherish him. I know that I could. Forgive me," she whispered, "but I feel that Wade is my calling now. It was the good Lord that brought us together, and there's an excitement inside me because of it. If it were not meant to be, then Jesus would not have placed his smile before mine. It's atonement for losing Andy. I know it is."

Hannah left the dark safe walls of the church, convinced the Lord had spoken. She recognized that Wade was a sign from Heaven. He was an escape from everything she didn't want.

As she entered the sanctuary, the nuns looked up as if they knew of her dilemma and were shocked by her decision.

"I can't stay," she said.

*It must be God's will,* she thought, *the way Wade showed up in that seat next to me, making me turn so crimson. It's a wonder I didn't faint in his arms.*

"It's destiny," she said slowly, taking in their confusion.

"Dear?" said one of them.

"Forgive me, Sisters," she said and crossed herself. Speaking so low they had to bend to hear her, she confessed.

"You'll need your father's consent to marry," they told her.

"I have it," she lied, and left.

Hannah ran to him as he stood on the street with his suitcase. He looked amazed, as if he didn't quite believe what he was seeing.

"I was hoping you'd come," he said. "I was afraid you wouldn't, but I would have waited until you sent me away. I would have waited for a thousand years."

She saw the smile that broke out across his face. "I must be crazy." She already felt free, scared but free. "You've got a flair for the dramatic, haven't you? A thousand years?"

He laughed. "Yes, a thousand years. Oh, Hannah, you've made me so happy." He held her in his arms and kissed her on the mouth.

"I hope the nuns aren't looking out the window." She giggled and glanced behind her.

"I like a woman who knows her own mind," he said.

"I feel so elated," she whispered, "and so liberated."

Wade reached out for her hand. "Come," he hollered, "we can just make the next train to Jacksonville if we hurry."

"Will you be loving me, Wade?" she asked, stopping him, turning him to her. "Will you be loving me like you promised? I'm not being some stupid, frivolous young woman, am I?"

Slowly, he bent to kiss her again, and the warmth of his lips made her feel as if she were floating over a cloud.

"I'll love you forever," he whispered when his lips finally left hers. "I'll love you forever and ever, Hannah Reilly. You won't ever be sorry."

They could hear the whistle of the train as they ran to catch it. Wade lifted her right off her feet and carried her all the way to their seats.

"You're light as air, Hannah, like this bag that you're carrying."

"Nothing in it but pen and paper, Wade … and my prayer book, of course, and my music box."

"Music box?" Wade laughed.

Hannah blushed. He didn't need to know she had loved another. It would not be right to tell him.

"I always take it with me. It makes me feel good, brings me luck."

"I'll say."

"I'm not sure I know what I'm doing." She laughed. "I'm being so impulsive."

"We'll get married right away. I need to make a proper woman of you." He was so excited he seemed unable to sit still. "The minute we get settled we'll have our wedding. I'll be working on Florida Boulevard as a married man."

Hannah quickly reached inside her bag for her writing pad.

"I have to tell my papa," she said as she glanced at Wade's exuberant grin. "It wouldn't be right not to."

"Tell him about me?"

"Yes … and about our wedding. You're not an Irish Republican, are you?"

Wade kissed her cheek. "Tell him I'll cherish you, Hannah."

"I hope that will be enough, but he still may disown me."

"Here, here's a post office box; he can write to you there." Wade tore off a piece of paper and put it in Hannah's hand.

She wrote one page after another while Wade talked a blue streak in her ear. *Forgive me, Papa, I have fallen in love. I hope you won't be disappointed in me.* She told her father all about Wade's fine new job and how blessed she felt when Wade Hampton Fournier took her hand in his and told her she was adored. She hoped the guilt her father felt over Andy's death would make him feel more tolerant of what she wanted, what was right for her.

*Please give me your blessing, Father. I so need that from you. We're going to settle in Jacksonville, Florida, where the sun never goes behind the clouds and coconuts fall from the trees.*

Hannah apologized over and over and prayed he would not be angry with her for turning her back on Jesus, but she wanted to spend the rest of her life with Wade Hampton Fournier and have his babies. *Please understand, Papa*," she wrote.

Finally, only weeks after their arrival in Jacksonville, Hannah's father wrote back with his consent. *I am disappointed, child, but you know your heart. I may never forgive you, but I will support your impulsiveness and love you always,* he wrote in his long, beautiful scroll with loops in his letters that circled upward and left trails behind them of black ink dots, letters that bent like dancers leaping and twisting forward, showing off their generosity of spirit like birds in flight. *I will pray for your happiness, daughter. Yes, you know your heart, girl. You always have.*

# Chapter Eleven

Their hotel room had one window, small and covered by glass slats. Hannah rolled the slats up to let in sound and light. She could smell the salt and almost see the grey of the listless ocean from the bed they rarely left. Florida was hot and humid, but the beach was as seductive as a snake charmer's dance. She loved the way the waves teased her toes and then ran playfully away. She liked the way she sank into the sand, and the deep imprint her feet made left a temporary impression, soon to be swallowed by the soft, warm Atlantic.

"There hasn't been another?" he asked her, as he pushed the hair away from her eyes and stroked her cheek.

She wondered if he knew that she'd given herself to Andy that day at the bottom of the meadow, the day she'd always called the best day of her life, until now, that is. She would soon become Wade's wife. Surely her wedding to Wade would be the best day of her life.

"There is only you. I've never had another," she lied.

He kissed the tip of her nose and sat up. He ran his fingers through his hair. She noticed that his hair was wet and looked so dark, and his blue eyes appeared so brilliantly vivid. She was touched by his presence, elated that she belonged to him and he to her. The room was hot, and the sweat ran down his arms. She was pleased that his skin was smooth, and the hair on his body was barely visible. He was smooth, everything about him was smooth.

"I'll have to tear myself away from your lovely arms, Hannah. I'll be meeting with Mr. Lewis tomorrow."

"And he'll make a proper man of you, just as I will."

She was relieved that he'd be starting work right away. She might never have left the allure of their bed if the need for a paycheck wasn't looming over them. She knew he had gone through most of his money, and Lord knows, she had little.

"'Bout time we saw the light of day," she said.

"You should see the suits I'll be wearing, Hannah. I've never seen such fine clothes."

"Well, maybe Mr. Lewis will let you be married in one."

Wade rolled over and smiled at her. "I'm sure he will, chérie. How about next Saturday? Will you become my bride next Saturday?"

"You mean it, Wade?" She sat up quickly. "Have you spoken to the priest? Is there time?"

"There is time. Every night this week we have to meet with the priest, but if we meet all the requirements, he'll give us his blessing."

"But you haven't been out of my sight, when did

you find the time to set this up?"

"Well, your naps are rather long, and rather deeply experienced, I must say. I guess I really knock you out. You never heard me leave or return; you seemed to be enjoying yourself too much."

Hannah leaped from the bed and seemed to skip to the end of it. "I'm eagerly awaiting the Lord's blessing on us." She reached for her robe and tied it around her. "Oh, my God, what will I wear? Mr. Lewis doesn't sell any ladies' clothes, does he?"

Wade went to a closet and brought a box over to the bed.

"You're much thinner, but I think it will do," he said.

Hannah looked wide- eyed and confused. "What's in there, Wade?"

"Compliments of my sister."

She reached for the box and stared at him.

"When I told my sister we were getting married she insisted on sending it. I picked it up yesterday at the post office. I wanted to surprise you. Go on, chérie, open it."

Hannah quickly flipped the lid on the box. She stared at the white wedding dress. She lifted it out and ran her hands over the ivory silk and embodied silk gauze, trimmed with pendent rose buds. At the bottom of the suitcase was a strand of pearls. She felt her heart sink. This dress would not have been her choice. She would have chosen something less gaudy.

"Oh, Wade," she whispered. "It's so beautiful. And the pearls…oh, my goodness."

"Do you think the dress will fit you? My sister weighs a bit more than you."

Hannah held it up before her. "We'll make it fit." She grinned, thinking about how she would alter it, refine the dress, making it more elegant and simpler. She would keep the lace, of course but the flowers would not be missed, they looked so dowdy, and they cheapened what could turn out to be the most divine wedding dress she'd ever seen.

"It's a bit large for me so I'm going to alter it, Wade. You won't recognize it."

"I'm sure my sister won't need it again."

Hannah worked on the alterations every day, up to the moment they were to be married. The dress had to be significantly altered, but as luck would have it, there was enough lace to make a beautiful pair of long gloves. There was also enough excess material that had to be removed so that she was able to make a silk shawl from it, to put around her shoulders. She used the rose buds as trim on the shawl. Her lace veil was made from leftover material that she cut from the hem. She assumed that Wade's sister would appreciate how she had made the dress her own. In Hannah's opinion, she had done the dress a favor.

There were just a handful of people at the church. Wade's sister, of course, and her husband, Charles, a jolly man that Hannah found pleasant enough, but her first encounter with Rena was not as she might have expected. It was like oil and water trying to mix, an instant aversion to each other.

Hannah noticed right off that she looked nothing like Wade. She was clearly older, a rather stout woman with a voice that was so irritatingly shrill, like some high-pitched bird, a turkey perhaps, one who was being chased by a man with an ax. If she had feathers, Hannah was sure they'd be in a flutter.

Rena stared at Hannah without any regard for manners, for it was rude to stare. Hannah noticed that Rena's eyes were round and wide, as if she'd been unexpectedly pinched from behind.

"Is that mine?" she asked as she walked closer to Hannah and took the silk shawl in her hands. "Or should I say, *was* that mine?"

Hannah nodded. "It didn't fit, I had to…"

"I'll say," Rena interjected. She shot a look to her brother. Hannah did not know how to interpret the look, but it seemed to resemble the shock of one who has eaten a rather hot pepper.

"What a disaster," Rena whispered to Wade. "You should have told me she was so, so… aggressive."

Hannah did not know if she was meant to hear the comment or not, but she felt her face turn several different shades of pink. All of a sudden, she felt embarrassed, but her discomfort quickly turned to anger.

"My sister loves you," Wade said later.

"That's nice," Hannah said, feeling a bit unhinged by the nastiness in Rena's demeanor toward her. The dress was a gift, and Hannah merely altered it to fit. It was clear she couldn't wear it as it was.

"I don't want it back, of course," Rena said to Hannah as they were leaving. "Give it to your daughter, if you have one."

Hannah gave her new sister-in-law the perfunctory kiss on the cheek and felt the stiffness in Rena's body, as if she'd been startled by a snake in her garden. Suddenly Rena turned to whisper in her ear. *He's a lady's man,* she said, *keep him on a short leash.*

Hannah was startled by Rena's words. *What a jealous old tart*, she thought to herself. She felt relieved watching Rena and Charles walk away, back to their life in Clearwater, relief that she might never have to see the woman again, not if she could help it.

"I miss my papa," Hannah whispered close to Wade's ear that evening. "I've no one here from my own family."

Wade took her hand. "What a beautiful bride you were," he said.

"He has broad hungry hugs, my papa. Oh, it saddens me, Wade, not having him here to give me away at my wedding and too my sister, Anne, and all my cousins. They need to meet you. They need to know you as I do."

"Shush." Wade kissed her. "I'll marry you again in Ireland; would you like that?"

She looked at her handsome groom, and her sadness faded. Standing at the altar under the arms of Christ, his eyes had been glowing.

"They were glowing for the love of you,

Hannah," he told her.

The newlyweds found a two-story white house on Cherry Street in the prettiest part of Jacksonville.

"I like this house," Wade said often. "Gives me plenty of room for painting."

Wade had made an adequate living as a portrait painter in Quebec, but certainly nowhere near as good as the money he was getting from old George Lewis selling fine men's suits.

"Never could get painting out of my blood, Hannah," he'd say. "Maybe I could sell them."

Wade would stand out on his back porch for hours and paint the way the streets all crossed each other like perfect Ts and Hs. He sketched in the tops of palm trees as they swayed over the rooftops, their long limbs rising to the sky. He'd started working on landscapes right after moving to Florida, which was something he'd always wanted to do, but portraits had been easier to sell on the tourist-lined streets of Quebec.

"That oil on your fingers, Wade?" Hannah asked, grinning broadly.

"Uh-huh," he said as he kept his eyes on his subject.

"No sitting down to dinner 'till you've rubbed your hands good, Mr. Wade Fournier." She handed him fresh lemon. "I'll not have my baby covered with oil paint, looking like a damn rainbow."

Wade laughed. "When we have a baby, chérie, I'm going to paint him from every angle."

"*When* you ask? Well, according to the doctor I'd say in about seven months."

Wade turned to her slowly. "You mean—?"

"That I do," she said.

He grabbed her and twirled her around.

"I'm going to be a father?" he screamed. Then he started to sing, *For Me and My Gal*, and danced her from one end of the backyard to the other, carefully, as if handling glass.

"I hope our baby can carry a tune better than you," she said, laughing and trying to follow his uneven steps.

Finally, when they stopped laughing, he realized she had the blue of the sky on her nose and yellow oil paint under her chin. He took the lemon and rubbed it softly over her face.

"Sweet Hannah," he whispered. "Sweet, sweet Hannah."

Their first child, Wade Jr., was born right before Christmas, 1918. Wade painted and sketched him from every angle just as he said he would, his tiny fingers and toes captured in motion, his smile immortalized on a small square canvas that Hannah framed and nailed up on the parlor wall.

"Isn't he beautiful," they whispered. "The most beautiful baby in the whole wide world."

"We're a complete family now, with Wade Jr.," Hannah said, grinning as she held her son, tickling his belly with her lips.

Wade was at his easel; oil saturated the cloth over his shoulder.

"True enough," Wade said, raising his eyes. "Stay still now, Hannah. You're breaking the pose."

"We best go to church every Sunday, Wade, and thank God for the life he's blessed us with," Hannah said proudly. "To think I might have had none of this."

"I do agree, Hannah. I do agree. Now sit there still, you hear. I'm just about done."

"Photography would be a fine hobby, too, don't you think, Wade?" she teased. "And a lot easier on me, I might add." Hannah arched her eyebrows as Wade approached, his fingers the colors of a thriving garden.

"Just be thankful I sell men's suits, or you'd be my model, Hannah, nude as a newborn all day long." He laughed and touched her nose, leaving behind a big blue smudge. Hannah and the baby had more paint on their bodies than Wade had on his canvas.

"And if I find any nude models in this house, I'll be breaking your fingers, Mr. Wade Fournier, and you'll have to paint with your toes."

Wade laughed loudly. "I couldn't ever do better than you, sweet Hannah. Not a model on earth could be better than you."

Wade worked hard at Lewis & Sons. Men admired his advice and sought out his help. Old George Lewis thought he folded trousers better than anyone, even his own son, Ty. And Ty didn't wear suits like Wade. Nobody's tall, slender body held a pant crease like Wade's did, and his cuffs hit his shoes just at the wingtip.

"He looks so damn good standing there in his pressed suits and his perfect cuffs," George Lewis would say. "And the boy always smells so good, nearly as good as a woman."

Hearing those things said about himself made Wade smile. He cared about the way he looked, always made sure to carefully place his jacket behind his chair when he played cards. He'd roll up the shirtsleeves of his starched white shirt and smile around the table. Much crustier-looking men would smile back at him. Confident bastard, they might have been thinking. Well, he was a good poker player. Wade could bluff better than anyone. Sometimes he even played poker in his sleep, and he'd wake up from a dream in which he had a royal flush. It was easy to like a man who lied so well, but being lucky was like a fugacious friendship: if you were fool enough to trust it, you deserved to go down with it.

Wade thought life was perfect as he walked toward Cherry Street. He loved the Florida sky and the warm quiet air off the ocean. By God, he lived in Paradise. He thought about how well he'd done, he had a wonderful family, a wife who adored him, and a son who was the light in his life.

"Hey, Lola," he whispered as he slipped in through the back door. She had been expecting him as she loosened the tie to her red silk robe.

He walked into her living room and poured himself a drink. Her husband worked nights and had been gone for hours, wouldn't be back for hours either.

She sat on the couch next to him and let her robe fall over her shoulder. She reached out to touch him, and he bent to kiss the cleavage that appeared like two white, soft mounds of snow.

She ran her hands through his hair. He'd gotten stiff on the way over, just thinking about her lips on him.

"Don't mess me up too much, chérie," he said as she dropped to her knees before him.

She smelled lusty, almost like cigar smoke. They rarely fornicated. She said her husband might be able to tell by the smell. *I can't get rid of it,* she said. *But I can swallow it.* She liked the taste of him, and that made Wade happy; he had a certain weakness for playing the skin flute, as the boys he grew up with often called it.

It wasn't long before she was giving him the satisfaction he needed, the way he liked it, feeling her tongue all over him, her tongue, her teeth, her mouth.

"Want me to stop, Wade?" he heard her say. "Push me away now if you can."

He laughed and held her head. She loved to tease him, make him beg for it. He doubted he could stop though, not even if her husband were at the door with a pistol pointed at his head.

There was just something about a woman who liked oral sex the way she did. Not only whores were into it. Plenty of good women had gotten him off that way. And Lola was no whore. She taught first grade at the Catholic academy over in Ponte Vedra Beach. She wasn't the only woman's bed he'd lied in, but hers was the most convenient bed; Lola was a neighbor, didn't live far. He could even stand at the window of her house and see his own at the end of Cherry Street. He found the fear of having Hannah catch him quite exciting, so much so that he often fantasized getting caught. Hannah would be so startled, so riveted that she wouldn't be able to turn away, so she'd have to watch him take his pleasure with Lola all the way to the end.

He lied still after his orgasm just to make sure his breathing was back to normal. Sometimes it was hard for him to catch his breath. Then he stood up and zipped up his pants. Lola was sitting on the floor lighting a cigarette. He was too afraid to return the favor; vaginas were so damn strong he'd never get the smell of hers off his chin.

"You got any money, honey?" he asked her as he put a comb through his hair.

"All you do is take, Wade."

"C'mon on, you got any money?"

"How much are you in for?"

"Three hundred."

"You can't come up with three hundred?"

"Every damn dime I bring home goes to my son. I'll pay it back, I promise. I got a wife and a kid, Lola. That doesn't come cheap."

He wondered who he could borrow the money from to pay his debt. He'd asked George Lewis for an advance on his pay, and Lewis had given it to him. Problem was that his gambling debts kept piling up, and he couldn't go to Lewis every week. He was on a losing streak for sure, didn't happen much, but he was knee deep in it now.

"I don't have it."

"Can you get it?"

"What you going to give me if I do?"

"Whatever you want, honey."

Wade grinned and grabbed her around the waist. While he was sticking his fingers up inside her he asked sweetly if she could make it four hundred.

Wade knew Lola wasn't going to get the money, but maybe she'd surprise him. It certainly didn't hurt to ask. But where the hell would it come from? Her husband certainly wasn't going to give it to her. Stingy Steve everyone called him. Stingy Steve sure wouldn't like to know he was sharing his wife with Wade.

So, where the hell was he going to get the money? He'd run through everybody he knew, even that whore down by the beach who told him he owed her money for not charging him her going rate because he was such a pretty boy.

Wade chuckled to himself, despite his growing anxiety that his luck was running out. Maybe Lola would come up with it. Maybe, by some miracle, it would rain down hundred-dollar bills in his backyard. Either was unlikely.

But the next night, Lola was outside, standing in

her doorway grinning like a Cheshire cat.

"Evening, Wade. Hot night. Want something to drink?" she called, with an offering of lemonade in her hand. She'd waited for him, as she did most nights, watched for him to come up the block. Though he'd just seen her the night before, she couldn't get enough of him, or at least that's what she would tell him. But he had his mind on other things, like where the hell he was going to come up with the money he owed his poker buddies.

Lola must have heard his whistle, and she ran to meet him, her screen door slamming shut behind her.

"What you got for me, honey?" he asked.

She reached in her bra and handed him fifty.

"Fifty?" Wade needed four hundred. He found himself getting angry at her. Her husband worked two jobs; he knew she had it.

That's okay, Wade thought, there was another woman in town that he may be able to get it from. She wasn't as beautiful as Lola, but she was nearly a nymphomaniac, especially around Wade, or at least that's what she'd told him, that he brought that out in her.

"Not tonight, Lola, not tonight." He looked beyond her. He could see his wife out on the front porch from where they were standing.

"I just gave you fifty dollars."

"Yeah, yeah, thanks," he said.

He wasn't going to be visiting Lola that night; if he were, he'd have gone in the back way. Damn woman knew that. He wasn't going inside if he was out in front. No way in hell was he going to let

Hannah see him going in the front way of Lola's house. Lola should know better, but maybe she was just eager to give him that fifty dollars.

He felt disgusted with her. She was an unwanted distraction. He had to figure out what the hell he was going to do, his last poker game had eaten his paycheck, and he owed out much more than four hundred, but that would buy him time. He felt a bit torn in two, he needed to keep Hannah happy, couldn't do that if he were absorbed in his woes. His wife was his responsibility, and he had to make sure his family was comfortable. His family was the reason he needed to better himself. Maybe rise up the ranks in George Lewis's store and manage it. Of course, George's son, Ty, managed it, but Wade felt he did things better than Ty, and George knew it. He would bury his head in Hannah's hair and fantasize his success. Sometimes he was in the mood for Lola but not that night. That night he was in the mood for his wife. He felt so adored when she held him. It was different, there were women and there was Hannah, couldn't be mentioned in the same breath.

He looked at Hannah's fine form from down the block and had the thought that his Hannah looked coy, as if she were hiding a secret.

"Like I said, not tonight, Miss Lola." Wade tipped his hat and moved on.

"Sure now?" Lola purred, pulling him back, wiping the perspiration off her chest as if it were an invitation to something even more enticing on a hot night than the ice cubes she held to her breast. She reached out for his zipper.

"Uh-huh." He jumped back. "I'll let you know, maybe tomorrow."

Brushing back her hair as she leaned over her white picket fence, Lola pushed her arms tight together so her bosoms bounced up and she could show off that nice white perspiration line that peaked up out of her brassiere. He noticed the dollar bills in her bra.

"It's pink lemonade, Wade."

"Dollar bills?" he said, amused.

"Money is money. You want some?"

"Some other time, Lola," Wade said. "Can't do much with dollar bills but wipe my ass."

Dollar bills? Was she kidding? He felt angry again. He thought she liked him more than that. Well, she'd liked him enough to go through her husband's trousers and come up with at least fifty. He was grateful for that, but fifty bucks felt as worthless as dollar bills.

Wade knew he was getting the reputation of a ladies' man. He was on a first-name basis with every woman in Jacksonville. If he could get a dollar from every woman that thought he was handsome he'd be halfway there. He enjoyed the attention woman gave him, but he loved his wife, despite how many beds he happened not to bypass. He hoped Hannah wasn't getting wind of it, but he doubted that. Hannah rarely got out of the house except to volunteer at the Catholic Church when they did their fundraisers. Truth be told, no other woman on earth thrilled him the way his wife did, except maybe sexually. He was a very happily married man though his sex life with Hannah was very predictable and unadventurous. It's not that he didn't like it; he loved being in bed with her. It made him feel complete and whole. Besides, he didn't want his wife expressing desire the way whores did, the way Lola did. Lola wasn't a whore, but she was a very lusty woman. His wife was a very fine woman, a refined woman and had been a good and proper virgin when she married him.

Humor was part of Hannah's charm, what he loved about her, the tease behind her smile; it beguiled him. He loved that smile. She was the perfect wife, exactly what he needed.

Wade walked faster as Hannah leaned against the porch railing and tilted her head. He listened closely for her Irish brogue to start lilting and rising, filling the space around him, giving a singsong motion to the placid Florida air. He wondered what she was hiding from him, standing there grinning like a cat who'd just eaten the pet canary.

His beautiful Hannah looked back at him with a gleam in her eye, like the sun shining down on a stream, her eyes shone.

"Hey, Hannah," he called.

Hannah's laughter hit the night breeze and lingered in the air like an unexpected compliment as he approached the gate.

Wade danced toward her, slowly looking her up and down, holding his jacket over his shoulder with one hand and flipping off his white straw hat with the other.

"Was that Lola Martin I saw you talking to?"

"Hannah Reilly Fournier, you are quite a picture standing there! I'm going to paint you, but don't you know I'll have to go to heaven for the blue in your eyes and, hot damn, all the way to Ireland for the fire."

Hannah laughed out loud and threw her arms around him.

"Oh, but you're full of the blarney, Wade Fournier," she said. "I think that woman was flirting with you."

Wade took her in his arms and lifted her right off her feet, so high she could see clear over his head.

"Put me down, you big fool."

"Happy, chérie?" he asked as he twirled her around in his arms.

"Yes," Hannah said with a wide grin. "Happier than I could have ever been in a convent. Of that I am certain."

Wade stopped just long enough to catch his breath. "*Je t'aime, chérie. Je t'aime,*"

He whispered against the lobe of her ear.

"Give me your hand, Wade," she said softly.

Wade stopped short and stared at her. "What?" he asked, not taking his eyes from hers.

Hannah nodded as she placed his hand on her belly.

"Blessed again," she told him. "Oh, Wade, blessed again."

Wade felt the color drain from his face. "Why Hannah," he whispered. "Another baby?"

# Chapter Twelve

Little Leda was born in 1916. Wade Jr. was almost three. The house on Cherry Street was covered in Irish lace and billowing shades of muted greens and deep hues of yellow. Golden pillows with tassels were tossed on overstuffed chairs, and softly painted paper lined the stairs with a pattern of tiny roses, some opened and some closed. In the nursery of yellow and white daisies, the new baby slept in an ornately-carved mahogany crib — covered by a tiny woolen shawl sent all the way from Ireland and woven stitch by stitch with smiling rocking horses, by her Aunt Anne.

The upright piano was in the parlor, the same one that had stood there since Sister Vincetta had pulled a fast one on Father Timothy right after Wade Jr. was born. Hannah loved that piano. It was like being back in Ireland, playing ragtime. She could almost hear her sister, Anne, singing. She could almost see Andy dancing on the wooden floor.

If the women in Jacksonville didn't like Hannah before she got her hands on old lady Marchand's upright, they certainly didn't like her afterward. It wasn't because she was such a pretty woman that riled them up so much. There were many women who were almost as pretty as Hannah Fournier in Jacksonville, Florida. And it wasn't even because the most handsome man in the city of Jacksonville had married her, or even because she dressed in such fine silks and linens that were imported all the way from Ireland. They hated Hannah because she played the piano as well as she did, and it was so joyous the way that music bounced out into the day and the night. Surely, she was having a very good time. When they heard her play, they felt she knew something they didn't.

But Hannah did have one friend in Jacksonville, Florida, and it was because of that friendship that the piano came to her, as if God had willed it. Sister Vincetta was from St. Stanislaus Roman Catholic Church on Cedar Street, and it had been Sister Vincetta who had made sure that Hannah received Beatrice Marchand's fine old upright. When the old lady died in her sleep in 1913, it was estimated that she was ninety years old. She left everything she owned to St. Stanislaus, including a cocoa-brown French poodle named Tiny.

The two young women had become friends right after Hannah and Wade settled in at the Cherry Street house and Hannah started helping out at fundraisers. Hannah told Sister Vincetta about giving up the sisterhood to marry and have babies.

"I didn't have a choice," Sister Vincetta said, looking uncharacteristically angry. "My family expected it of me. There was no alternative."

"Marriage was not an alternative?" Hannah asked softly, for she did not wish to be overheard by any of the other nuns, who all seemed so stodgy.

"Oh, certainly not." The sister shook her head. "My father frightened away all my suitors."

"Then you had suitors?"

"Well, would-be suitors." She smiled sadly. "I envy you. Your father is so far away. He can't stop you from living your life the way you choose."

"He certainly tried to."

"But look at you now; you have a fine family."

"I hear regret in your voice, Sister."

"Oh, I believe in God with all my heart, but I don't really believe that God has singled me out to follow His call. That didn't matter a damn to my father, though, who most assuredly believed that his daughter was one of the chosen."

"Did I hear you cuss, Sister?" Hannah couldn't help but smile.

"Oh, no, you must have been hearing the leprechauns in your head, Hannah Fournier. Irish leprechauns cuss like hell."

Sister Vincetta had been with the Sisters of St. Stanislaus Roman Catholic Church just under a year when Hannah first started bringing over extra linen and toys for the orphanage and volunteering in any way she could. After a friendship developed between them, Hannah would come often to help in the church gardens, and the good Sister would forget herself with Hannah and gossip and giggle like a schoolgirl.

"So, the lady asks the theater manager, 'Do you know what they're playing tonight, Sir?'"

"'*You Never Can Tell*,' he answers. "'Good lord, don't they even let you know?" she asks.

Sister Stanislaw looked at her, and Hannah knew she hadn't gotten the joke. "George Bernard Shaw's play, *You Never Can Tell?*"

"Oh." Sister Vincetta fell over on her side. She had the roots of several dead flowers in her hand, and she was squishing them all up. "That is so funny, Hannah." She could barely get the words out she was laughing so much. "Do you know what's playing tonight? Oh, *You Never Can Tell* … that's so funny."

"Well, I'm happy to see I can tickle your fancy." Hannah joined in the laughter until the two were tearing dead flowers apart and flinging them at each other.

"I've been asked to do an appraisal of Mrs. Marchand's things," Sister Vincetta said once she finally got hold of herself. "Got to be worth hundreds, she was a rich, old bitty."

"Oh, I'd love to see her house. I'd bet it's like something out of a museum."

"Then come with me. Father Timothy won't mind." Sister Vincetta smiled wickedly. "I'll bet the place is filled with treasures. Perhaps we can pilfer a few?"

Hannah gasped. "I never know what's going to come out of your mouth, Sister," she said.

"How about 'God bless you'? I can always fall back on that."

Hannah took Sister Vincetta's hand as they entered the stately white house, wide-eyed with anticipation.

"Oh, but it looks like a mansion," Hannah cried out.

Mrs. Marchand's fine mahogany tables had legs that seemed to be standing on tiptoe, showing off curved wooden claws. Her vases were painted with colorful intricate patterns that found homes on white doilies, and her paintings were all serious poses of sad young women with light brown hair who smiled ever so slightly from their high-necked collars.

The two women ran through the rooms, and Sister Vincetta tripped on her habit as she flew up the stairs. Hannah stopped to admire the view from the windows as Sister Vincetta tore into one of Mrs. Marchand's bedrooms.

"She faces such a beautiful garden," Hannah called up to the top of the stairs. "She's got a statue of the Holy Mother out there, too. Our Lady of the Lord looks to be sitting inside a shell."

"Look what I have here," Sister Vincetta called from the landing, holding a large velvet box in her hand.

Hannah watched as the sister disappeared behind a door.

"Well, you've got me curious now." Hannah ran up the stairs two at a time, never expecting the good sister to be sitting in the old lady's bedroom, but there she was, comfortable as an old cat in a round chair.

"Have a look," Sister Vincetta said with a wink.

The two women blushed and whispered behind their hands as they rummaged through the old woman's pressed flowers and her faded letters, all of them written with black ink on yellow parchment and signed "with love" from someone named Beauregard Sebastian Rogers.

"Why, who would have guessed it?" The Sister looked bewildered. "I never saw anyone come or go from her house but the poodle."

"Come," Hannah said. "Let's go back downstairs. I think I saw something wonderful in her parlor."

Hannah loved the house and the large stately rooms with their thick green satin drapes and Persian carpets that she could feel beneath her feet when she walked. But it was the piano that had held her in its trance. Deeply rich in walnut wood, it stood near a window and kept watch, as if it had eyes. Hannah couldn't stop staring at the graceful command of the instrument as she entered the room.

"See?" she said. "Something wonderful."

Hannah reached out and felt the wood and then the ivory. She touched the top of the sleek smooth instrument as though it had breath, as though it were a child in need of a gentle stroke.

"Can you play?" asked the sister, still giddy from their discoveries in the velvet box.

Hannah sat on the bench and smiled.

"A wee bit. Do you like ragtime?"

The sister settled in a large plush chair and

placed her hands in her lap.

"The music of the brothels?"

"The music of joy," Hannah said.

She briefly held her hands out before her and stretched out her fingers. The sister smiled politely, as if Hannah were a child about to pretend she could do something she couldn't really do. Then suddenly, Hannah's fingers touched the keys in a motion so brisk that the sister blinked and held her breath. Music filled the room in a sweep and consumed Sister Vincetta's soul as passionately as the tales of the Christ child's birth. She wanted to dance. More than that, she wanted to sing.

"Do you know the words?" Hannah called.

*"We were sailing along on Moonlight Bay. We could hear the voices ringing, they seemed to say, 'You have stolen my heart' Now don't go way! As we sang "Love's Old Sweet Song" On Moonlight Bay,"* the sister sang out loudly.

Hannah joined the singing then swung around on the piano bench. "You never cease to amaze me, Sister," she said.

The sister sat very still. She marveled at her gifted friend. "Can you play classical too?" she asked.

Hannah turned back to the piano and played a Schubert piano concerto.

"Glory be to God," Sister Vincetta said as she crossed herself.

Hannah sighed and sat back. "I had to study the piano in Ireland; my mother insisted on it."

"Your mother was wise." Sister Vincetta nodded and grinned at one and the same time.

"That she was," Hannah said and looked off. "I've missed my piano. Every proper Irish household should have a piano."

"The church only has room for one upright and one organ. They can't use this one," Sister Vincetta said eagerly.

"What do you mean?" Hannah asked, as she turned back to the sister.

"Saint Stanislaus received a brand-new piano just last year from that wealthy parishioner with the last name everyone stutters over."

"I can't afford this piano, Sister."

Sister Vincetta's thoughts seemed to be racing out ahead of themselves.

"Father Timothy has asked me for an account of Mrs. Marchand's belongings, so we have some time before the appraisers arrive."

"What are you thinking, Sister?" Hannah asked, with a perplexed smile.

"We'll just have to sell the piano along with the rest of Mrs. Marchand's furniture anyway." Sister Vincetta sat beside Hannah. "The church has benefited enough from the poor woman's demise."

"Sister?" Hannah smiled more broadly, clearly wondering if a piano would soon be sitting in her parlor.

"You have a gift." Sister Vincetta squeezed her hand. "Surely God wants you to play, to be able to share your gift, don't you think?" Sister Vincetta knew that God had certainly been responsible for bringing the two women together in front of that glorious instrument, and He was surely there smiling at her now and giving her the strength to fib to Father Timothy.

"What a white elephant it is, Father." The sister looked over her papers.

"What's that, Sister Vincetta?"

"Mrs. Marchand's piano, Father." She shook her head from side to side. "A white elephant. Why, it's in horrible condition."

Father Timothy raised a brow. "Really?"

The sister nodded enthusiastically. "Oh, yes, Father."

"Well, I imagine we'll have to junk it then. Would you agree?"

"Oh, I do have a better solution, Father."

"Well? I would care to hear it."

Sister Vincetta told Father Timothy that Hannah Fournier had agreed to take it off their hands. Father Timothy was quite relieved.

"You must thank her for me at services this Sunday. The good woman has spared us quite a backache. The damage it might have done to haul that old piano to the junkyard." He grinned from ear to ear as he gave Sister Vincetta's shoulder a tap.

Wade was just as pleased as he could be to hear his wife play and was eager to hand out cold hard cash to some neighbor boys to cart the Steinway home.

"Easy there, boys. Don't scratch my piano," Wade called.

Hannah couldn't wait to sit herself down before it. "Oh Wade," she cried as it came through the door.

"Set it right there, boys, centered on that yellow wall," Wade said, turning to grin at his wife. "Careful, boys, it's a Steinway. You know how much a Steinway costs?"

"We finally have the right piece on that wall, Wade." Hannah laughed.

"Only rich people have pianos," Wade said as he slapped the boys on the back and put some coins in their hands. "Good work, boys." He grinned so wide it looked like he had an extra set of teeth.

Hannah sat down before the instrument; her eyes welled up with tears.

"What are you going to play for me, chérie?" Wade asked, settling in his easy chair.

"Every song I know, Wade. Every song I know."

Hannah played throughout the night, while Wade thumped his feet on the floor and finished off a pint of bootleg gin.

Hannah played everything from Mozart to ragtime on that piano — yes, she could play Mozart too, but she loved the gaiety of Joplin and Fats Waller and Irving Berlin. Her beautiful head of hair fell back as she stretched and reached her fingers across the ivory keys. She'd shut her eyes and let herself lose touch with the world as each note fell from her hands and landed on Cherry Street like the entrance of the moon, buoyant and playful.

Playing ragtime, for Hannah, was like being

back in Ireland, watching the sun set over the jagged Irish Sea and knowing that right at that moment her spirit felt as full as it was ever going to feel. Her music was her language to something lost but held dear. It hardly mattered that the Irish Sea was so far away she couldn't remember the blue of it. She connected to something precious when she played her piano. The feeling was like nothing she could get from the little Catholic Church on Cedar Street that she attended out of duty. Playing her piano became a hungry obsession, for playing the piano made her feel that she was in a dream, and in that dream, Andy was sitting on the sofa singing along. It was the journey back in her mind to Andy's laughter that gave her peace. It was the comfort of the little house on Dublin Road that made her reverent and grateful for the memory of it. She would never mention it to Wade, but the pastel days of Florida did not please her and she found them bland and uninspiring. Despite herself, she missed Ireland like a limb she might have lost.

Hannah didn't like the coconut trees or the way the sun made her perspire in every decent dress she owned. She was glad, though, that Wade had been wrong about the clouds because what she loved most about the monotony of sunshine was the sudden unexpected rain and the great violence on the ocean of a nasty storm.

"It's raining pitchforks, darlin', like my papa used to say, raining pitchforks."

"All this lightning doesn't scare you, Hannah? Doesn't frighten you to death?" Wade would ask her.

"Lord, no, Wade. This storm is the closest thing to high drama down here."

*Tu es une lunatique. Tu es une lunatique, Hannah.* And he'd laugh as he said it.

# Chapter Thirteen

John Reilly came home to find his daughter, Anne, on the floor and an apparition on his knees beside her holding smelling salts to her nose.

"Good Jesus." John held his heart.

Andy looked up. John could see the confusion on his face.

"She's fainted," Andy said. "She seemed not to recognize me."

"You frightened her." John stared at the young man. He was at a loss for words, he'd never expected in a million years to have Andy McGregor showing up at his door. He thought he'd put an end to that. "She thought she saw a ghost."

"A ghost?"

"That's what she thought."

"I didn't mean to frighten her," Andy said. "Why would she think that?"

"Is she all right?" John ran to his daughter's side just as she opened her eyes. Andy picked her up in his arms and carried her to a chair.

Anne's eyes opened wide as she stared at Andy. "You're not dead?"

John could see the furrow on Andy's brow deepen.

"You should know I'm not," he said. "Care to pinch me?"

John Reilly went back to his chair and sat. "Would you like a whiskey, young man?"

"That would please me, sir."

John went to the cabinet in the kitchen. "I could use one too."

Andy sat and looked around. "Where's Hannah?" he asked.

No one answered him. Andy asked again as John handed him his whiskey.

Anne and her father remained quiet as Andy took a healthy sip.

"Did you know of this, Papa?" Anne addressed her father in a somewhat astonished tone. "Did you know Andy was alive?"

John took a deep breath. "I did."

She had asked him that question as if the decisions he made were not for the best. Good God, his Hannah had moved on, she was married. She had children. He did what he thought was best for his daughter. What did it matter that Andy was alive? What good would it do her now?

"And you kept it to yourself?"

"Yes, I kept it to myself. What did it matter? It was too late." John sat back and rubbed his forehead.

"What are you saying?" Anne said. "You knew that Andy was alive and said nothing, not even to me?"

John put his head down. "I didn't know for a

long time."

"But Hannah got my letters, didn't she?" Andy stood to his feet and stared at Anne. "Would someone care to explain to me what is going on? My letters reached her, didn't they?"

"I didn't know about any letters, Andy." Anne held out her hand to squeeze his. "Patrick and I have married and have moved away. I don't live far, and I come home often but I wouldn't have seen any letters, not if Papa hid them." She turned to stare at her father. "And if I'd seen them, I don't think I would have believed them. It would have been so improbable."

"Why improbable?" Andy was clearly confused. He shook his head back and forth.

"Why, we thought you were dead." Anne stared at him helplessly. "We buried you. We had a funeral for you."

"Dead? You thought I was dead and buried? But I wrote to Hannah."

Anne turned sharply to her father. "Neither Hannah nor I ever knew that. We never saw any letters from you. Why is that, Father?"

"How is Hannah?" Andy asked. "I want to see her."

Anne shot her father another quick look. "Andy," she began, "we buried you, watched them put you in the ground."

"You buried the wrong man. The army corrected their mistake. My parents have known that I'm not dead for over two years." He stood up and paced the room. "You must have known." He stared at John. "What did you do with my letters?"

"I don't speak to your family, you know that. We had no way of knowing you survived." John looked off. "Your family never notified us. They would not have had any reason to."

"I wrote to the convent, to Hannah Reilly." Andy stared at Anne, hoping for some explanation.

"We didn't doubt that you were dead." Anne looked at him. "Hannah and I didn't doubt that you were dead, Andy. As far as we knew, you died in the war, we never heard otherwise. My God, there was a casket in a church with your name on it."

John did not know how to read his daughter's expression, but she most likely wanted to boil him in hot oil.

"I wrote letters to the convent, to Hannah." Andy looked at John. "What did you do with them?"

"I destroyed them," John said. "The convent sent them to me, and I destroyed them."

Andy shook his head, as if trying to make sense of it. "Why would you do that? She's a nun now, is that why? Wait, the convent sent my letters here? Then Hannah has left the convent?"

"If I had known. If Hannah had only known," Anne said.

"She's a nun now, is that what you're telling me?" He looked from Anne to John. "Or isn't she?"

"Hannah needed to go on with her life, you must understand that." Anne began to cry. "She thought she'd lost you."

Andy came and stood before her. He took her hands in his. "I would never cause this family pain, especially not Hannah."

"What happened to you, Andy?" Anne reached out and took his hand.

"I was held in Wittenberg, Germany, where my troop was captured. I was gravely wounded when they brought me in after nearly a year of fighting. After that, typhus nearly killed me. There was a horrible outbreak of it. I was transported to a hospital. The minute I was able I wrote to Hannah, to let her know I'd be returning to battle, to fight alongside Britain, and then I was coming home to her. I was certain it would not be long."

"It was two years." Anne lowered her head.

John lowered his. "I'm proud of you Andy McGregor. God bless you."

"You never gave her my letters?" Andy walked to John and put his hands on John's shoulders. "Why?"

"Yes, why, Papa?" Anne asked.

"She was married by then."

Andy fell back. "Married?"

"Ay, she went to America with the St. Joseph Convent, and she was on a train going to Boston, I think it was. Anyway, she met a man there and she left the convent for him. They married, have two children now."

Andy put his hands on either side of his head. "It is not the will of God that she should be married to anyone else but me."

"You can't question God's will," John said.

"No, not God's will, but the interference of other people, I can certainly question that."

"I'll make no apology to you, Andy. I did what I thought was right." John stood to his feet and scowled at Andy, scowled the way he used to.

"This is insane." Andy's hands had become fists.

Anne reached out, "Andy, if we only knew."

"Will you tell her at least that I'm all right?" His voice had come out shaken and low as he looked into Anne's expression.

Silence fell between them, and then Andy took his leave, looking as wounded as he might ever have looked in the war. The door slammed behind him as he left.

A silence fell between John and his daughter before they spoke. "You are not to tell her, daughter." John Reilly stood in the center of the room and stared at Anne.

"Don't you think she has a right to know?"

"If she were still in the convent, yes. But she's married now. This would confuse her. It would hurt her, unsettle her."

He couldn't read his daughter's thoughts as she looked away from him, but he knew he would not have liked what she was thinking.

"I will tell Patrick that you are not permitted to relay this information to Hannah."

"My husband does not tell me what I can say, or what I cannot say to my sister."

"Go home to your husband, Anne. Hannah does not need to know that Andrew is alive. The news of it may upset her marriage."

"And who are you to make that decision?"

"Do not disobey me," John roared out, but Anne had slammed the door behind her.

# Chapter Fourteen

By 1919, good liquor was hard to come by in the state of Florida. Wade was ambitious and understood opportunity when it held out its hand and offered up a silver dollar. There was an old distillery right outside the city. Jack and Jeremy Sanford owned it and were getting rich selling bootleg whiskey up and down the state. They had been getting rich since 1915. Jeremy Sanford bought himself a new Edison, and Jack Sanford had moved his family into a mansion on Old Grove Manor two years back. Wade watched them get rich while he sold them silk ties and three-piece suits.

"Sure looking good, Mr. Sanford," Wade said as he smoothed down the material on Jack Sanford's shoulders.

"I don't think I ever had a suit look this good on me," Jack said as he smiled at Wade.

"I think the pinstripes make you look very distinguished, sir. Why, you could run for governor. I'd sure as hell vote for you."

Jack laughed. "You don't think the pinstripes make me look more like Big Jim Colisimo?"

"The gangster?"

Jack nodded.

"Well, aren't they one and the same?" Wade asked with a smile. "Gangster? Governor?"

Jack took a moment to digest what Wade had said, and then he laughed loudly and grabbed Wade around the shoulders.

"You're a smart boy," he said, "I don't know if you're living up to your potential."

Jack Sanford had always liked Wade. He liked him as much as old George Lewis liked him. Wade was sure of that. He also recognized his discontent at being a "yes" man for someone else's profit.

Suddenly Jack got serious and leaned in toward Wade. "All over town that you're into Mac Benson for a grand."

Wade sucked in his gut and clenched his mouth, feeling like a fool that his business was the latest gossip. Jack slapped him on the shoulder.

"You want to earn some real money, kid?"

Wade couldn't think fast enough to answer him. He couldn't think of anyone he'd rather work for.

"Why don't you come work for me and my brother, Wade? I like your style, and people sure do take to you." Jack Sanford put his cigar back in his mouth and puffed. "I need someone nice and personable handling the business up there Kentucky.

"Kentucky?"

"Things get tough sometimes. Think you can handle it?"

"Why, I'd like to talk to you about that, Jack. I feel my talents are not being utilized."

Jack Sanford looked at the crease in Wade's trousers and the fine smooth wave to his hair. "You're a smart kid, like I said. You like nice things, don't you?"

Wade ran his tongue over his mouth and nodded. He felt his heart thumping with a mind of its own. "Willing to work for nice things too, Jack," he said.

"Heard you had a new baby?"

"Yes, a daughter."

"Daughters are very expensive." He took Wade aside. "Look Wade, that gambling debt of yours? I'll take care of it, okay, son? Call it an early bonus."

"Oh, no, sir, I can't let you do that. I'll sell you a painting for it."

"A painting? All right. I'll take your painting. Look, son, I want you staying out of debt. Money works better for you if it isn't promised out."

"You're right, sir."

"You go into debt, and I might have people knocking on my back door. You understand?"

He looked at Wade intently. "Yes, sir," Wade said. "Yes, sir."

That night, when Wade came home, elation was settling in his soul the way religion would have if he believed in it. Something had happened between him and Jack Sanford. He felt as if he'd been picked for something, chosen by someone smart.

He sat in his easy chair and listened to Hannah tell him about his son's toothache and how she had to dip some gauze in vanilla extract for him to hold on his aching tooth and it had really helped.

"That so?" he said.

"And baby Leda is getting as saucy as she can be. Stuck her tongue out at me when I told her it was time for her nap."

Wade laughed. "Chérie, he said. "Some good is coming our way. I can feel it. I think I'm going to be a rich man. As a matter of fact, I know I'm going to be a rich man."

Hannah looked over at him. "You're already a rich man; you've got two beautiful children."

Wade went to her and took her in his arms. "No, I mean really rich, the kind of rich that doesn't cut costs in the supermarket or cut back on the things we really want, like a new car. I mean rich like having money in the bank and being able to drive over to Clearwater and spend time with my sister and her husband and my children, frolicking on the beach without a care in the world."

Hannah looked at him and smiled. "I don't need anything more than what I have, Wade."

"But if it came your way you wouldn't turn your back on it, would you?"

"No, I guess I would not," she said.

Wade never thought twice when Jack Sanford told him he needed another man handling his affairs. Wade never even told George Lewis he was leaving Lewis & Son, and Ty Lewis had to knock on his door to get some answers.

"Haven't seen you in days, Wade," Ty said.

"I've got me a new sales job, Ty. I am going to

get so rich I'm going to buy out your store." Wade filled Ty's shocked silence with a hearty laugh and invited him in for some of Hannah's tea.

Ty stood back and looked at him. His face was sad, and his voice broke.

"You are never going to buy my store, Wade Fournier," he said and started back down the walk.

Wade yelled after him, "I didn't mean I was going to put you out of business, Ty. I meant you were going to sell me suits, lots of suits. I'm going to be working with Jack Sanford."

But Ty didn't even look back, and Wade felt a strange foreboding, as if he just might have lost something he never knew he had.

"Strange man that Ty Lewis," Wade said as he walked back in the door and looked at his wife. "Doesn't believe in opportunity. Hell, I told him I was working with Jack Sanford now."

She gave him an odd smile. "Guess he doesn't see that as opportunity, Wade," she said.

He looked at her serious expression. The weight of it made him sit. When he'd first told her he was going to work for Jack Sanford she had a fit. "Bootlegging?" she had screamed.

He was surprised that she knew that Jack Sanford was a bootlegger, but he guessed she'd heard it from that gossipy nun she was friends with. He'd planned to lie to her. He was going to tell her that Jack sold encyclopedias.

Hannah hadn't spoken to him for days after that, and now she was still acting like he'd skinned a cat.

"What is it?" he asked, seeing the sadness in her expression. "I told you that this is going to make us very rich."

"Jack Sanford is a gangster, Wade. Is that it? You want to be a gangster too?"

"It's business. It's opportunity."

"I'm pregnant, Wade."

He felt the room spin. He didn't know what to say, it had been so unexpected. She started talking then. He could hear her going on and on, just talking a blue streak, begging him to keep his job with George Lewis, but not all of her words were registering with him.

"You're working with criminals, Wade. You can't jeopardize this family, especially now with another baby on the way. You've got to think of us. What will become of us if they throw you in jail?"

Wade couldn't find the words fast enough. "You're just like Ty. You don't understand opportunity, Hannah. You're not looking at this in the way it's meant to be looked at."

"And how's that, Wade, you in a jail cell?" Hannah scowled at him. "That is what I am seeing."

"Rich people have small families. It's the poor that overpopulate, chérie."

"That sounds like the dribble of that fat cigar-smoking lush that's made you a criminal, that despicable Jack Sanford." She stared disbelievingly at him. "What does having a small family have to do with your decision to break the law?"

Wade cleared his throat. "Look, listen to me, Hannah." He got up and began to pace the room.

He couldn't deal with another baby. It would take him six months to get out of debt, even with Jack Sanford's generous gift. They'd just start to get on their feet, and she'd cut him off at the knees, wanting this for the new baby and that for the new baby. He thought of what Jack had said about not accumulating any more debt. He had to keep things in perspective. He had to have control.

Wade reached around to the end table and grabbed the cigar he had left there before Lola's mouth had made him forget what planet he was on.

While she was straightening her dress and reapplying lipstick he wondered if she knew any kind of doctors that performed abortions.

"You ever have an abortion?" he asked.

She looked startled. "I don't think it's possible for you to make me pregnant, Wade, you're only going in through my mouth."

"I didn't mean me." Somehow, he felt insulted. "You want to get laid? I can do that," he said.

She laughed. "Maybe. One day."

"Well, have you ever had an abortion?"

"No, I'd rather have the kid than have one of those."

"Any doctors in Jacksonville that do that kind of thing?"

"Why don't you ask Jack Sanford? He knows everything illegal going on here."

"Why I guess he's knocked up plenty of women." Wade winked at her. "Why didn't I think of that."

Of course, Jack Sanford knew of a doctor, a good reasonable doctor. He had shared a conspiratorial grin with Wade. "Tough luck having to pay for a good time, huh?"

"No, no, no, it's for Hannah," he said. "My wife."

Jack looked surprised but he didn't say anything. Wade felt that he was judging him for putting Hannah in that position, couldn't be much fun for a woman to have an embryo sucked out of her womb.

He weighed his words carefully, weighed the way in which he would approach the subject. He knew it was not going to be easy, but in the long run she would not disobey him. He waited until the children were asleep, and then he reached over and took her hand.

"There's a doctor over on Forbes Street I want you to see." Wade brought her close to him. "Let's be smart about this."

"What is wrong with Doctor Lauder? He's a fine doctor, Wade." Hannah stared at him, perplexity written all over her.

Wade inhaled for at least ten seconds. "He's not that kind of a doctor. The doctor I'm talking about is the kind of doctor that gets rid of babies."

Hannah's eyes grew large, and she gasped. Her body went limp.

He went on talking even though he knew he'd devastated her. "Two children are all we can afford, Hannah. I don't want another baby eating up the profits," he said firmly and stood to his feet. He faced her. "This money is for us right now. Maybe, you know, in a year or two. Let's give this time, get on our feet first, then have another baby if you want, but not now. I'm going to be traveling a great deal, won't be here to help you."

"You are not serious?" she said.

He set his jaw. "You will obey me, Hannah. We're paying a visit to that doctor tomorrow. Only poor people have more babies than they can take care of. We aren't poor anymore."

Hannah didn't know what to do. She thought that Wade had made some harsh transition into a monster, a man she didn't know, didn't want to know. She could not love this kind of man. She felt betrayed and confused. He was not cherishing her; he was forcing her to go against the very fiber of her being. She rushed through the gates of St. Stanislaus Catholic Church on Cedar Street in tears.

Sister Vincetta turned abruptly and looked up. She was in the garden tending to Father Timothy's clematis vine.

"Hannah, what is it?" Sister Vincetta stood and wiped the dirt from her habit.

"He wants me to kill my baby," Hannah cried.

"Dear God." The sister took her hand quickly. "What are you talking about? "

"Abortion," Hannah said sadly.

"Dear God, an abortion?" The sister dropped to her knees. "It's illegal."

"You think that matters to Wade?"

"Abortions are not safe. You do know that, don't you?"

Hannah nodded and rubbed her red eyes with the sleeve of her dress.

"What could he possibly be thinking? Why would he want that?"

"He says it's safe; they've improved them. He knows women who've done it."

"Oh, it is not safe, Hannah. *It is not safe.*" The sister vigorously shook her head from side to side. She was furious. She pounded her fist into the palm of her other hand.

"He will never love this baby. He's so much as told me. He says we have enough children. He's threatened to leave me if I have it. Good Jesus, what am I to do?"

Hannah held her arms across her chest, and large choking sobs escaped from her like a sudden storm laying claim to a July sun.

"I'm going to pray for Wade, Hannah. I'm going to ask God to forgive him."

"That isn't going to solve my problem, Sister."

"No, but it clears my head."

Sister Vincetta took Hannah's hand and walked her inside the church. The nun dropped to her knees before Christ on his cross. She turned back to Hannah.

"I'm going to ask Jesus to bless your baby and all the descendants of your baby, damn it. That bastard has no right to ask this of you. Perhaps I should go to the police?"

"I'm his wife, his property. Do you think the police will care, will arrest him?"

Sister Vincetta's small, lithe body leaned over in prayer. Passionately she rocked back and forth as she held her rosary.

"Most likely they'll slap him on the back in sympathy."

Hannah looked up. Jesus glanced down from his wooden cross with sad, beseeching eyes. All the angels in the high effulgent windows caught the light of the sun as they smiled sweetly at Sister Vincetta and glistened in their blue glass gowns. Hannah remembered the glass angels back at St. Michael's Parish in Dublin, *I should have stayed*, she thought.

Hannah wanted to pray but couldn't find the words on her lips, so she held her head to heaven and asked God to talk some sense into Wade. Perhaps that was prayer enough.

# Chapter Fifteen

Wade poured himself another drink as Lola rubbed his shoulders. She brought her lips down to the back of his head and kissed him.

"Abortion isn't altogether safe, Wade," she said.

He stared at her and pulled her close to his face. "Would you do it?"

"For you," she said. "I'd do it for you."

That's what a woman is supposed to say, he thought. But he knew she was lying. The other night she had said she'd rather have the kid than abort. Well, he did not want any more children. He wasn't going to piss every penny he made to dust.

"Don't you mark the calendar?" Lola asked.

He looked at her as if she had asked the most ridiculous question in the world. Hannah had mentioned marking the calendar, and he had ignored her. When a man wants sex, a woman is just supposed to be there giving it to him. He reached out and rubbed the inside of Lola's thigh. "You're a good woman," he said.

Lola smiled and put her finger in her drink. She stirred the ice cubes.

"She used to tell me when it was a dangerous day. Told me I'd be putting a little one in her womb if I wasn't patient."

"Looks like she was right," Lola said.

"Damn it, it's up to God." Wade slammed his fist down on a table. "She should know that—she was going to be a nun."

Lola stared at him with a hint of sympathy. "Then God gave the two of you another baby, Wade. Let her have it, I say. She'll be busy, and you'll be able to visit me more."

She reached out for his belt. If only his wife believed in oral sex, he would have been fine, never would have demanded more than that. Maybe he just should have run over to Lola every time he needed release.

Penny, the teenager next door often watched the children for Hannah. She gave the girl a few dollars and it was such a relief to be able to just have the time for herself.

She let Sister Vincetta in through the back door. Hannah was wearing a pair of Wade's trousers and one of his shirts. Her hair was pinned up under his best straw hat.

"Why you're looking mighty handsome," Sister Vincetta said as she closed the door behind her.

"I've laid out his grey trousers for you. Take any shirt from the closet and here's a hat." Hannah tossed another straw hat the sister's way. "You see how short hair comes in handy?"

"And the children are where?" Sister Vincetta

asked.

"Penny has got them next door."

"Perfect. I wouldn't want to confuse the little tykes."

The two women walked down Cherry Street all the way to the beach, looking like two college boys going for a walk. When they got to the ocean, they haphazardly dragged their feet by the water and laughed as the sand stuck to their skin. Hannah was happy to be feeling giddy, as if there wasn't any weight pulling her down.

"You can call me Vinny," the Sister said.

Hannah laughed loudly. "Henry will do for me."

"Good name for you, Henry."

"You know, Sister, his job has turned out to be a blessing, not a wretched curse," Hannah said.

"What do you mean, Hannah?" Sister Vincetta asked. "What he's doing is wicked; he's a bootlegger."

"I don't care about that. It's a godsend not having him around so much anymore, that's what I mean. It's an opportunity not to be near him, the unpleasant stench of him."

"Is he becoming an alcoholic? Is that what you're saying?"

"He stinks like an alcoholic."

Wade had been traveling the state with his bootleg gin for so many days out of the month that she rarely saw him.

"So, it thrills you then, to be alone?"

"Yes, alone without his suffocating mindless chatter. He talks so much and never says a damn thing."

Hannah had absolutely refused to have an abortion and even though Wade raised his fist to her, he seemed to accept it, and did not hit her or demand that she not refuse him. She thought they had put at least that much behind them, though nothing was the same between them anymore. She sensed it and thought to correct it, as if it were her duty to correct it.

"Do you think he accepts it then?"

"Me having this baby?"

"Yes, does he?"

"Well, I thought he was fine with it, and I prayed that the distance between us would narrow and we'd be happy again."

"Are you happy, Hannah?" Sister Vincetta asked.

"He never brings the new baby up, never wants to pick out a name, or even shop for a rattle. How can I be happy knowing my husband hates the child I'm carrying?"

"Maybe… after it's born, he'll change."

"He won't change," Hannah said.

"People do."

"I could live without his earnings." Hannah turned to her. "Don't you think?"

"What would you do?" the Sister asked.

"I'd give piano lessons or work in a store. Maybe George Lewis would hire me."

"I would help," Sister Vincetta said.

"He sleeps around on me," Hannah suddenly blurted out.

The sister's eyes grew wide and round as pennies. "I have heard that," she said.

"Thank you for not lying to me, Sister. It's common knowledge."

"Have you confronted him with his infidelities?" Sister Vincetta asked.

"Yes, and he told me I had quite an imagination."

Hannah watched as Wade walked up the street. She was so sick of his lies — his lies and the smell of him when he passed out in bed beside her reeking of whiskey on those rare occasions he saw fit to come home. Now that he was a bootlegger he seemed to drink as much as he sold. She was not happy to see him. Oh, she was not happy at all.

"We have to talk," he said as he walked through the door. "There's still time. The doctor told me there's still time."

Hannah followed him into the parlor. She hadn't seen him in weeks, and their unborn child was still obsessing him. She thought he had laid it to rest, but apparently, he hadn't.

The children were playing in the dining room. She could hear their laughter as she faced him.

He stared back at her. "I'm giving you one more chance," he said, raising a finger in her face.

Hannah felt despondent. She knew when she looked at him it wasn't love she was feeling.

"You want that damn baby more than you're willing to honor my wishes," he said.

"Yes," she said. "I do."

"I'm just trying to keep my family comfortable." He walked away and began to pace, taking long walks from one side of the room to the other.

"You don't love me, Wade. You couldn't possibly love me. If you did, you'd never ask me to do this."

"That couldn't be further from the truth. I do love you, but I need to teach you a lesson, Hannah. You can't disobey me."

"I can disobey you. Why shouldn't I be able to think for myself?"

He looked at her for several moments. She couldn't read what she saw in his face, but it made her angry.

"Then you'll pay the consequences." He looked away.

"I already have," she said.

She watched as he climbed the stairs. She heard him retrieve a suitcase from the closet and listened as he threw some clothes into it.

After a few minutes he came down the stairs. Hannah had not moved.

"You won't see a dime from me if you have this baby," he said as he came into the room.

"I'll not be killing an innocent child."

"Then you'll be wiping the bastard's ass without me," he hollered as he slammed his fist into the wall, sending a tiny-framed painting of Wade Jr. crashing to the floor.

"It's not an option," she said. "How many times do I have to say it?"

"Can't you come to your senses, woman?"

"Only *I* say what I'll be doing with this body of mine. Not you and not some murdering doctor."

"You don't have any rights. You can't make those decisions. Remember that, Hannah. You're my wife, and if you don't do what I say, I guess you won't be my wife anymore."

Hannah watched as he put the last of his things into the bag and closed it. For only an instant, she wanted to crawl into his pocket and curl up near the warmth of his thigh. She wanted to dream away the man he had become after he started selling bootleg whiskey. But perhaps he had always been a bastard.

"What's happened to you?" she screamed.

"I'm leaving," he hollered over his shoulder as he approached the front door. "Just like I said I would."

"May the devil take you," she said quietly, as the door opened and closed on his words, like the taking in and letting go of breath.

# Chapter Sixteen

Sheela Anne Fournier was born on April 14, 1920. She was named after Hannah's favorite aunt from Londonderry. When Hannah was a child, her Aunt Sheela would take her out for long walks on the great rocks overlooking the sea and tell her that nature was God's way of revealing his heart.

Hannah had not seen Wade in nearly six months before the baby arrived. So, she was surprised to see him walk through the door like he'd never left. It was the day she'd brought Sheela home from the hospital. He stood over her and stared at the baby.

"What are you looking for, Wade?" Hannah asked. "She's perfect. Were you hoping she wouldn't be?"

"I wanted to see if her eyes were blue," he said. "That's all."

"Yes, they're blue—now leave us be."

"You must need money." He reached in his pocket and counted out some bills. He placed them on the side table.

Hannah put the baby in her bassinette and turned to face him. "What color eyes would you be expecting on our baby, Wade? Both our eyes are blue."

"That may be so, Hannah, but our friendly neighbor, Mister Jonathan Palmer? His eyes are as brown as shit, so I'm just checking."

Hannah reached for a small porcelain vase. "You bastard," she said. "You couldn't possibly be insinuating that I am as common as you are?"

She didn't give Wade any time to answer. The porcelain vase hit the back of the door about one split second past the slam Wade gave it. He hit the dirt running as she followed him out, her dark auburn hair falling over her shoulders and her voice scratching in the back of her throat as she screamed out. "Leave us be, Wade Fournier. Go back to your women and your whiskey and leave us be. I don't ever want to be looking at the likes of you again," she hollered as she ran out to the road — the hot, humid air engulfing her in a sweltering confined assault.

Wade slammed the door of his brand-new Ford. She could hear him yelling back as he started the engine.

"I'll be back, woman. You are raising my children! You can't deny me my children."

"Don't you be knocking at this door again," Hannah called as she caught the tail end of his car's engine and watched in disdain as he disappeared into the giant red glare of the sun.

"We don't need you," she screamed.

No one knew where Wade was living these days.

It could have been with that young whore on the south side; it could have been with anybody. But the whole town suspected he was selling bootleg whiskey by now with the Sanford brothers and traveling with it as far north as Covington, Kentucky.

Hannah had gotten herself a job at Lu-Anne's, a small dress shop not far from Lewis & Sons on Florida Boulevard. It did not pay much, but it was buying food. Hannah left the children at St. Stanislaus Orphanage during the hours she worked and picked them up afterwards.

All the rich women in Jacksonville shopped at Lu-Anne's. Hannah couldn't help but envy them. She envied them their husbands because Hannah believed that most women married well, married good honest men who came home in the evenings with chocolates and fresh flowers for their wives. Hannah would imagine these good, honest men nestling into a favorite chair with the evening paper. She could just see them watching their women with amusement as they walked through well-appointed rooms, chatting endlessly about all the things she used to bend Wade's ear about — weekend picnics, and which one of the children had misbehaved.

"Women without men these days are viewed as missing a limb," she told Sister Vincetta. "We're oddities, pitied and ignored."

"Nuns are viewed like prostitutes," Sister Vincetta said.

Hannah was shocked. "Sister!" she exclaimed.

"True. We're both outcasts of society. We don't

belong in it, yet people can't seem to live without either of us."

Hannah couldn't help but laugh. "You know what they call me behind my back?"

The sister shook her head slowly. Hannah knew that her friend had heard the gossip but did not want to repeat it.

"That uppity Irish girl with her poor children and her philandering husband. They make fun of me."

"And what do you call them?" the sister asked and waited for Hannah's reply, which didn't come, so the sister continued. "Well, here's what you should be calling them: a bunch of bitches with nothing to do all day but feel good about the suffering of others."

"Bitches? Oh, Sister Vincetta, God is surely shaking his finger at you."

"Oh, poo," said Sister Vincetta, you think he hears me?"

Hannah and Sister Vincetta still met once a week for their walks on the beach. Wade had left just enough clothes behind so they could appear innocuous as they ran along the water, looking like young men frolicking. If only Wade knew what good use his clothes had come to.

Only a week after she'd heard from Anne, she watched Sister Vincetta tie the belt on Wade's slacks and slip his hat over her eyes. Hannah wanted to laugh but laughter was not something she was able to do, not on that day.

They walked in silence the two long miles to the beach. The day was overcast and grey. "Looking a bit like Ireland," Hannah finally said.

Hannah sat on the sand looking out over the waves as if some poor pet dog had died. Usually, wearing men's clothes made her lightheaded but on that day she could not smile. No, on that day she felt as if she may never feel lightheaded again.

"What's on your mind, Hannah? You look as if you're listening to sad music."

Hannah reached into her pocket and pulled out a letter. "It's from my sister, Anne," she said.

"Is she ill?" the sister asked.

Hannah shook her head. "No."

"Did someone die?"

Hannah looked at her oddly. "That's just it," she said. "Someone didn't die."

"For God's sake Hannah, what are you talking about?"

Hannah put her face to the sky, wanting to feel the sun, but it was so listless and pale she could barely feel the heat from it.

"There was a boy in Ireland that I knew all my life. We loved each other so very much. We were going to be married. We were going to run away and come to America together." She turned to sister Vincetta. "I thought he died in the war."

"Thought? You mean he didn't?"

"No, he didn't."

The sister put her hand on Hannah's arm. "False information?"

"I suppose." She held up the letter. "My sister has written to tell me that he's very much alive. It was some sort of mistake. He was wounded, too wounded to write to me. He's been captured and was being held in a foreign land, I think."

The sister shook her head in astonishment. "My God, Hannah, what will you do?"

"Nothing I can do."

The sister stood to her feet and looked right into Hannah's eyes. "You certainly can. I will help you raise the money to return to Ireland. You should marry this man, have a proper husband."

Hannah smiled. "You are quite a romantic, Sister."

"I am not a romantic, Hannah, I am a realist."

"We Catholics don't divorce; you know that."

"And I say rubbish to that. There are extenuating circumstances. Wade Fournier would have seen you dead to get his way; you deserve happiness."

"I will never have it," Hannah said sadly.

"That is no way to think."

"My sister wrote to tell me that he's married now, and he lives in Dublin working for some land development company. I think he's expecting his first child. She's sorry she didn't tell me sooner, but Father forbade her to. Now that he's married, I guess it doesn't matter."

Sister Vincetta sat back down. "I'm so sorry, Hannah."

"It would not have mattered if I'd known sooner."

"I guess not. He must have married because you were."

"I thank the God Lord that he lived, that he's alive." Tears fell from her eyes. "I thank the good Lord for that."

*After I thought about it,* Anne had written, *I realized that Father may be right, it would only hurt you to know that Andy had lived, for nothing could be done about it. But then I also thought you had a right to know. Oh, Hannah, he was so distraught to learn of your marriage. I will never forget his face.*

Hannah felt like the brunt of some cruel joke, maybe God's joke for leaving the convent. It was painful to think about Andy now, because she would never see him again, never lie in his arms or play ragtime and watch him dance. Hannah wanted to make the best of her life, such as it was. That's all she could do now, live for her children and find solace in that, even pleasure. Fate was so cruel, and it could not be undone.

*Fear can make a woman mad;* she wrote to Anne the following day. *There are nights when I can't find my way home in the dark. My skin has become sensitive to tree branches, so much so that I can't bear to be touched by them. I've begun to imagine that there are people inside the shadows who follow me, and this confuses my sense of direction. Sometimes I can feel myself separate from my skin and float somewhere outside my body, and there are even times when I cannot tell what side of the street I am really on. If the moon is very bright, I can follow it and find the red flowerpots that I placed on my front stairs and filled with geraniums. I can reach the warm touch of my piano and play ragtime for the children. They're always smiling at me and reaching out their small arms for a hug. Sheela's baby scent and sweet infant sounds are so sweet to snuggle and lay my face beside. It is the children that ground me and restore my senses, the children and my blessed piano. Thank God for that, Anne. But still, it doesn't change; I confront fear nearly every day. I can't put a name to what it is I'm afraid of, maybe it's just another punishment from the good Lord for all the mistakes I've made. I should have stood up to Papa the way I stood up to Wade. But I would not have had these same blessed children, so maybe the Good Lord knows best.*

# Chapter Seventeen

As the years passed, and the children grew, Hannah nearly forgot that she had ever been married. Her sadness eventually lost its daily presence in her life and remained only in the background, mostly, whenever she thought about Wade. There was too much in life to be grateful for — her children, for one, and for another, a soft night of piano sounds drifting through the evening stillness, reminding her that the soul is greater than life's disappointments and the heart, more resilient to sorrow than she might have guessed.

"I loved Wade," she often told Sister Vincetta. "But he muddied my soul — put me at a distance from it."

"I hear marriage can do that to a woman," the Sister answered. "But you can't have your children without a man."

"So, the devil is good for something." Hannah laughed. "Where would I be without my babies?"

Hannah could hear Leda and Wade Jr. arguing

over something or other, their voices rising to levels of torture. But that was fine, welcomed. Sheela was much more contemplative, tied to Hannah's waist, fascinated with stories about Ireland and horse wagons and emerald fields. Sheela especially liked her mama's story about how Jesus had winked and given her the sign to come to America. She loved the idea that Jesus would wink at all when he appeared to be in so much distress.

"It was in my dream, child," Hannah told her often. "He looked right into my eyes and he made me feel that everything was going to be as fine as a long summer day. I had a lot of anxiety coming to America, though I was so excited."

"Will he wink at me, Mama?" Sheela asked.

"Maybe. One day, maybe he will." Hannah stroked the child's hair and pulled her close.Sheela yawned and Hannah laughed softly. "You should all be in bed now," she said. "It's nearly eight."

"And eight is what time, Mama?"

"Ah, yes. Shame on me for forgetting." It had become a ritual. Sheela appeared in the doorway every evening before bedtime.

"Do you want to brush my hair, Sheela?" Hannah held out the brush.

The little girl ran for it. "I thought you'd never ask," she said.

Sheela loved to brush her mama's hair, especially because her mama's hair fell all the way down to her waist and was so soft and silken.

"Oh, but you come from good stock, little lady," Hannah said as she watched the child stroke back and then down with the silver brush.

"You've got the Brannon good looks, Sheela, taking after my mother the way you do, your darling grandmother, Colleen Fitzpatrick Brannon Reilly, hair as black as yours. Died so young, she did." Hannah sighed. "Well, of course you've got your father's eyes, blue and dark as a threatening sky. That's the best of the man, Sheela. Pray that's all you have of him."

"I wish my eyes were green or brown then." The child put her hands on her hips and pouted.

Hannah tried not to laugh. She never wanted to give the impression to her children that Wade was not a good man but sometimes things just fell out of her mouth that she could not control.

"Well, your grandfather is a good man, child, difficult but good. John Reilly. How I miss him. Oh, how I miss my papa."

Sheela watched her mother in the glass.

"You come from good Irish stock," Hannah repeated as she looked back at her daughter. "Don't you ever forget that, little lady."

Sheela giggled as Hannah reached up from behind and grabbed her for a kiss.

"Good stock like Papa's whiskey?"

Hannah wished Wade would abstain from his vulgarity. He often referred to whiskey like that: "good stock."

"Lord no, little lady. Good stock like me," Hannah said.

Wade had shown up intermittently over the years and had taken Leda and Wade Jr. to Mayport

Road for ice cream sodas. He would throw some bills in a box on the side table and shut it loudly right before leaving.

"For incidentals." He'd grin.

He barely looked at Sheela and always assumed she would remain behind with her mama. He noticed that the child never wanted to sit on his lap or hang off his coattails like Wade Jr. and Leda. Didn't matter, his other two children loved him.

Sheela could see her father from where she was hiding. She didn't want him to see her, though, so she made herself as invisible as she could. She hated the way he looked at her, like a fine piece of lace, something admirable but apart; someone worthy of attention but certainly not approachable, or even lovable.

She watched as he sat there staring off into space while he waited for Leda and Wade Jr. to show up and act as if he were someone special. Sheela didn't like the way he was just sitting there in her mama's parlor, following the crease in his pants with his fingers and shaking his two-toned shoes as if there were music playing somewhere.

She looked away. She hadn't meant to, but she heard her brother yelling from upstairs. When she peeked back, her father had gotten up.

"Sheela?" He stood over her like a forest monster. "What are you doing down there?"

"Nothing."

He smiled without parting his lips. "Now, I know little Sheela doesn't want to come out with her papa today. Isn't that so, little Sheela?" he said, standing behind the chair, his voice startling her so much she might have lost her lunch. "You never want to come out with your papa. Damned if I know why. You're missing out on ice cream."

"No, thank you, Papa." She scowled at him. "I can get ice cream here."

"So you can."

She stood up and faced him. She always tried to be polite, but she never wanted to call him anything but "bastard" just like her mama did when she didn't think the children were in hearing range.

Leda and Wade Jr. came tearing down the stairs and circled Wade as if he were Santa Claus himself. Sheela watched as he took their hands in his and bent down low to Leda's eye level.

"Why, here are my fine children now. You ready to go with Daddy in Daddy's new car?"

He glanced over at Sheela. Leda squealed like a baby pig as Sheela found her mama's frown. Hannah had come down the stairs and stood there scowling at Wade. Sheela was sure she thought she was smiling, but she was scowling.

Wade opened the door as if he still lived there. He turned before leaving and nodded as if he were coming back to small talk at the dinner table.

Sheela stood very still and reached for her mama's hand.

Despite his shiny new Ford, Wade still owed people money, so whatever he gave Hannah barely covered her expenses. She continued to work at Lu-

Anne's, but her wages were never enough to both feed and clothe the children. The fear of not having enough food to eat if she lost her job was causing her to awaken in the middle of the night breathing in short, quick breaths and perspiring so badly the bed would be soaked with it.

"If not for my children, I would take my vows. Would the church still have me, Sister Vincetta?" Hannah asked, as she and the sister walked together in the warm sun, past the lilac and yellow gardens behind the church.

The sister noticed the two deep lines above Hannah's nose and the sadness in her eyes as she spoke. "God has a plan, Hannah. He always has a plan." The sister swallowed as if she had sucked on a sour candy. "You must have faith in the path you're on. If you lose your faith, you'll surely fail God."

"I think God is punishing me for marrying and not following the course I set out to follow when I left Ireland." Hannah turned sharply to her young friend. "I made God angry when I married Wade, didn't I?"

"You'll only make God angry if you lose your faith. He gave you a choice. He's not angry at you for choosing." Sister Vincetta stopped abruptly and stared at her. "Have faith, Hannah."

Hannah turned and looked squarely into her friend's expression.

"I am still a good Catholic. No matter what."

"I know that, Hannah."

"In the end, he was not a good man, not a good man at all. God has punished me for not heeding

His call," Hannah said and looked up at the blue sky; looked up as if God were up there sitting in an easy chair, frowning down on her and shaking His head in disapproval.

Sister Vincetta laughed. "No, Hannah. God has no such intention. He has more important things to do than punish you."

Hannah looked at Sister Vincetta as if she were a small child. "You are not Irish, are you, Sister Vincetta? We have the all-knowing gift of prophecy, we Irish. We've only to use it. It comes in the form of a dream, sometimes. Dreams are the language of prophecy. But you've got to figure the dreams out, read the images. I dreamed once that a large wave came out of the darkness and took me under."

The nun raised her eyes to heaven and made some indiscriminate sound from the back of her throat.

"I keep dreaming I'm in sand, buried to my neck. I scream, but the children can't hear me, and the wave that's coming toward me is so high and fierce."

Sister Vincetta adamantly disagreed. "Nonsense, Hannah, dreams mean nothing."

"Are you saying God holds no grudges, Sister? Because he's surely angry at me."

The sister smiled, but she was firm when she answered. "That's exactly what I'm saying, Hannah Reilly Fournier."

"Then you haven't read the Bible," she whispered. "I feel it. I'm doomed to punishment, to an early death."

The young nun took Hannah's hands and

pushed her backward. "Death is a bit too much like poetry to you Irish. That's what I think." She grinned so wide she looked comical.

Hannah finally grinned back. "You may be right, Sister Vincetta, but I'd give up a year of my own life to set foot on the blessed poetry of Irish soil, I would."

"I'll pray for you, Hannah," Sister Vincetta whispered as she opened the doors to the quiet chapel and walked inside. "I'll pray that one day you'll be back on Irish soil."

Hannah followed and closed the tall, stately doors behind them. The bright Florida sun teased through the tall glass windows like inappropriate flirtatious laughter.

# Chapter Eighteen

On most days Wade drank more whiskey than he sold. When he was drunk, his eyes turned cold as steel. On those infrequent visits to his children, he would sneer at them as if fire might come from his nose. He often stumbled into walls, his long hands grabbing at doors and curtains or anything else that might hold him up. The afternoon Henry Fournier was conceived, Wade was in just such a state.

"Wade Junior! You come here now!" he bellowed as he looked for his chair, his face a maze of red blotches.

Wade Jr. stood in a corner fingering the fine edges of Hannah's lace curtains. His long, skinny legs were covered by short blue pants that ended in sailor-boy cuffs, revealing his black strapped shoes. His dark blue eyes were resting on his papa as if he were watching a large dog find its way to the floor.

"Come on over here, boy."

Wade reached for his son with one eye opened. His slender feet were planted on the carpet for balance while his outstretched hands bobbed up and down, as if he were floating over a wave.

"I said, come on over here, boy."

Wade Junior gave the lace a final run up the hem and then let it go. He never moved quickly for his papa anymore, not like he moved for his mama, especially when she came home calling his name and singing up the walk. He didn't know anyone who could sing like his mama, could make him feel like he was listening to the start of one of those concerts they gave on the beach over July 4th holidays that got everyone so excited.

He knew that when his mama sang like that, she was bringing home dark fudge, long sweet bars of dark fudge that made him so giddy he'd dance around her while she held the chocolate high over his head and called him her "silly boy." He would just get sillier then and dance wilder, and Hannah would laugh and lift her skirts and kick her heels to some wild Irish song she'd be singing — while he twirled and skipped into the kitchen.

She'd follow his skipping right on over to the counter so she could cut the fudge into tiny squares and watch while it disappeared and lay under his tongue. And for as long as the captured candy could be held and sucked and slipped from side to side in the soft, sweet prison of his mouth, she'd be smiling.

Wade leaned back against the cushions and let out long, low breaths that made his eyes stare straight through a person as if he had just lost his sight. It was one of those deep wheezing spells that passed over him like those summer lightning bolts that turned the sky all white and then moved on without striking anyone dead.

Wade put his hands to his throat and closed both eyes for about thirty seconds. When he opened them, Wade Junior had only made it midway across the room.

"I said get over here, boy!"

"Yes, Papa," he said and walked directly in front of the chair, staring into his father's blue eyes with his own.

"Where's your mama?"

"She's upstairs with my sisters, Papa," he answered.

"You go tell your mama I'm here and take your sisters out back to play. You hear me?"

Wade leaned into his son; his breath permeated the air between them with an over-powering rancid odor. His son winced and stepped back. His father laughed loudly and grabbed his arm.

"Whiskey, boy. That's what you smell. Whiskey! A man's drink. You and me are going to be drinking buddies one day. Here. Give me your hand."

He took the boy's hand to his lips and turned it over. "Keep it cupped, son," he said.

The boy looked up, confused and curious. "Yes, Papa."

He then spat three times in the palm of his son's hands. "Drink up, boy." His laugh was boisterously unnerving. "Go on, drink up."

Wade Junior stared as the foamy moisture stuck to his skin like a stick of gum that had been chewed all day. "I don't want to drink it," he said.

Wade laughed. "Can't waste it then." He

chuckled and licked it off his son in one large sweep of his tongue over the boy's palms.

"Now go tell your mama I'm on my way upstairs and take your sisters out back," he uttered and pushed the boy aside.

"Yes, Papa." Wade Jr. ran to leave, eager now to take the stairs two at a time and breathe in the hot clean air that waited just beyond the room, beyond the sour odor of his father's breath.

"And son?" His father's voice stopped him just at the arch that separated the parlor from the front hall.

"Yes, Papa?" Wade Jr. turned quickly, wanting to get over the bequest. Whatever it was, he would grant it.

"You keep your sisters outside for half an hour or so, you hear?"

He'd been headed to Lola's when he saw the Ford in front of her house, a stamp of ownership. Wade assumed that Lola's husband either lost his job or took the day off. Maybe a drink would get his mind off his disappointment. He hadn't planned on visiting Hannah that day but sitting there in Dewey's Pub he started feeling angry. Maybe he was angry he couldn't drop in on Lola or maybe he was angry he didn't live at home anymore. He didn't like to admit to missing his wife, missing his wife more than he missed Lola's mouth playing him.

He could always get himself a whiskey or two at Dewey's. Jim Dewey didn't care much for laws. It was like a private club knocking at the gate in the alley three times and waiting for the door to open. Besides, Dewey was a favorite with every corrupt politician in Jacksonville. They left Jim alone and looked the other way on Saturday nights when the street outside Dewey's was lined with automobiles and boisterous men who were about to blow their paychecks on getting themselves soused, and if they were lucky, some woman as well.

Wade always found a buddy or two at Dewey's. Sometimes all a man needs after the noon siren is a stiff drink. He sought out conversation, was eager to encourage it. He liked a good argument against bringing in moonshine whiskey from the Caribbean and letting women into government. Soon enough, the conversation would always swing back to crass jokes and sexual innuendo, and Wade would start feeling big in his britches, too big not to take what was due him.

He rode on back to what was now "Hannah's House" and flopped into his favorite chair. His son stared at him like he was some freak let out of the carnival. When Hannah finally came in the room, he was nearly asleep, but he jolted upright.

"What do you want, Wade?"

He rubbed his hands on his pants. She looked beautiful standing there in the sunlight with the highlights in her hair looking like fire.

"We are still married, Hannah." He grinned and watched with a certain amount of disappointment as she backed up toward the wall.

"Leave now," she whispered. "Before I call the authorities."

"And tell them what, that your husband has

come to take what's his?"

Her eyes darted out the window, toward the children. Their laughter was almost like music, he thought. He put his arms on the chair for balance and got to his feet. He was a bit unsteady, and she jumped back, as if he were going to fall on her.

"Shit, I won't fall on you. I'm in control of myself."

Her smile was snide. He didn't like it.

"You get on upstairs, Hannah. We don't want the children to be afraid now, do we?"

He came toward her, and she slapped his arm. He reached out and brought her close. He felt her warmth, and he wanted to fall into her arms like a small boy, but he didn't. He picked her up and carried her up the stairs and into the bedroom. The whole time he was trying to appear amorous she stared at him like he was the devil, but she wouldn't scream, she wouldn't upset the children, and he knew that. He threw her on the bed and undid his belt. He didn't want to be violent, but he couldn't control the passion he felt for her, the rage that she no longer loved him, and the sorrow that he had succumbed to rape, like some lowlife ape from the ghettos.

Hannah watched the light as it hit the wall. She counted the tiny balls of dust that ran in circles through the light and spun around so quickly, the way she always counted the dust when Wade came and took what he called "his right." The beam of light danced all over the room, and she followed it with her eyes as Wade held her down. She could hear the children playing outside as he fumbled with his zipper and attempted to lift her and force himself through her barricaded legs, all covered in tangles of sateen. She could smell his hunger between breaths of sour whiskey and cigarettes as he slid inside her and pounded her with the force of his body, knocking her head against the bed frame and loosening her hair, causing her eyes to lose track of all the little balls of dust she had been counting.

She knew he was through with her when the pounding ended in a long frozen moment of release and he landed like a large fish on her belly. She watched him leave her then and walk about the room gathering his things, touching his pocket watch and crisp clean shirt with a tenderness he had denied her.

She felt an odd contentment.

"What are you staring at, Hannah?" he asked as he tied his tie and smoothed the wave in his hair.

"I'm staring at my blessings," she answered. "I'm certainly not looking at the likes of you."

"What are you talking about?"

"Don't you see the beam of light, Wade? Don't you see my pathway to heaven?"

She pointed to the shimmering ray of light that had settled between them.

"No, I don't see it," he answered after a loud burp.

"Didn't think you would," she said.

"I don't see what isn't there," he said with an obvious degree of sarcasm.

Hannah ignored him. "It's filled with all my blessings," she said, "and I'm counting each and every one."

He laughed and burped again. "I said I don't see it."

She sat up and kneeled at the edge of the bed and put her hands in the light. When she brought her hands together, the light all but disappeared in her palms.

"Blessing number one," she said. "Wade Jr."

She extended her hands and spread the light in the room. "And little Leda." She laughed. "Blessing number two."

She stood up before him and ran her arms around the circle of light until she was standing directly in it like a sweet, disheveled angel.

"And baby Sheela. See little baby Sheela, Wade? You remember her?"

She danced in the light for several moments before she spoke again.

"Blessing number three."

He looked perplexed. "What the hell you doing, Hannah?" he asked her, almost sobered by her behavior.

"Whack!" she said as she slammed her hands together. "Wade Senior. Whack!"

Her laugh had an odd raspy quality as she pulled down the shade. The room was now shadowed in semi-darkness.

"You're crazy!" he said nervously and reached for the door.

"No light shines on you," she said as he stood there and stared at her. "You're a bastard."

"I'm going to have you committed," he told her. "You're a lunatic."

He turned sharply and left the room. She heard his footsteps trip on the stairs and knew he had fallen into something or other after he'd slammed the door.

"Drunken son of a bitch," she whispered and waited until the house returned to its comforting silence without the wheezing sound of his breath or the creak of his shoes that caused all those creases and squeaks in the floorboards as he walked in a place he was no longer wanted.

# Chapter Nineteen

Nine months to the day, Henry Richard Fournier was born. There was a terrible thunderstorm the evening of his birth. The sky was black as coal and fiercely lit by bolts of lightning. Howling dogs provided a fitting backdrop to the hurricane-force winds that swept the city up in a melodrama of unrelenting passion. The children of Jacksonville huddled in the safety of overstuffed living rooms and screamed out loud after each frightful strike sent them running for cover.

The children at the St. Stanislaus Orphanage, however, did not have the luxury of safe and warm living rooms to enfold them from the storm and had to seek their shelter from the Lord. They sat upright, staring at the little plates of food in front of them and avoided looking up at all the ghostly shadows thunder and lightning left behind when it popped and cracked so loud it sounded like the world was ending.

The children were waiting for Sister Irene, who was often referred to as "that old witch," to hurry up with her *Hail Marys* and ring the dinner bell so they could eat yet one more meal of macaroni and butter.

Sheela sat at the orphanage dining table and watched the other children as they pretended to pray. She felt a tinge of guilt. Her mama had told her that she and her sister, Leda, and their brother Wade Jr., were blessed by God to have a mama, and the other poor kids at the orphanage didn't have any parents at all.

"Promise to be kind," her mama had said. "Don't act any better than anyone else for having a home to go to, because in God's eyes, everyone is worthy of respect."

But that night, Sheela felt special anyway, and it made her a little sad not to be able to brag about it.

"*Blessed is the fruit of thy womb...,*" the nun droned.

The thunder clamored and drowned out the sister's prayer as the children scattered their gazes around the table and took advantage of so much distraction by rolling their eyes back in their heads and making faces. But Sheela's expression never changed. She was too lost in thought. *What if the damn storm blows out the lights over at the Good Samaritan Hospital?* She wondered anxiously, *and there's Mama trying to have a baby.*

She could see Wade Jr. on the other side of the room playing with his spoon. She wondered if he knew something she didn't. It seemed Wade Jr. always knew what was going on before anyone else; maybe because he was the oldest.

Her sister Leda sat opposite her. Leda's eyes were closed, and her head was adamantly bowed in prayer.

*Sissy*, thought Sheela.

As if Leda could read her thoughts, she lifted her head and motioned for Sheela to pray. Sheela wrinkled up her face and stuck out her tongue as quickly as she could before Sister.

Irene's peripheral vision could find her. She looked back at Wade Jr. and caught his smile. Was it just a week ago that she and her brother had found the pictures over at the library of some woman giving birth?

"It looks like it hurts," Sheela had said. "Do you think it hurts?"

"Nah, it don't hurt," he had answered with authority.

"No?" She looked closely at the picture.

"Nah, the babies just slide out real easy. They're all wet and greasy. The doctor wipes them off. See look."

Wade Jr. pointed to the picture and traced the baby's form with his finger.

Sheela stared at the photograph of a smiling doctor as he held up the screaming infant for the camera.

"It hurts the baby more than the mama. See, that's why the baby cries and the mama doesn't."

He turned the book around to give his sister a better look. Sheela saw another picture on the opposite page of the mother reaching out her arms to the infant. She felt an indescribable sense of joy.

"Are you going to have babies?" she asked Wade Jr.

"Boys don't have babies, you dope," he said and

tousled her hair.

Sheela smiled and remembered her mama's face the day she announced that she was going to be bringing home a new little brother or sister.

"Having a baby is knowing God in a very special way." She had reached for Sheela and drawn her near. "God gives us the glory of creation when He gives us children."

She remembered her mama's smile as she held her hands over her stomach.

"Come here and listen for the new baby, little lady," she had said.

Sheela had put her head down on her mama's belly and listened for the tiny stirring of the unborn child.

*I'm going to have a baby someday*, she thought. *And I'm going to know God in a special way, just like my mama does.*

The sister's intrusion startled her back to the loud wet night.

"Didn't you hear the bell, Sheela?"

"Yes, Sister." She nodded.

"Then eat your food or I'll take it away," snapped Sister Irene.

Sheela stirred her spoon around the bowl of mushy macaroni and thought about her mama in the hospital under all those clean, white starchy sheets. The rain raged against the glass and shook the windows. Sheela watched the stiff and stern sister who sat feeding herself as if she enjoyed the mushy macaroni. Sheela reluctantly moved the food around her mouth and watched the sky as it lit up all those black-and-white nuns hovering about the dining hall cloaked in silence and staring at the children as if they were hardened criminals.

Suddenly, Sheela heard the thunder crash and the lightning follow like a whip of stars. The room shook with the charge and glared pure white for an instant; then the dazzling light disappeared back into the black sky. The children screamed, and the nuns scattered and attempted to calm them.

Sheela closed her eyes and imagined her mama reaching up with her new brother or sister in her arms. She could hear her mama's words. "What a miracle it is, little Sheela. It's His will laying here on my breast."

Wade Sr. insisted that the new baby wasn't his even though little Henry could have stolen his face. The other children fussed over the new arrival and fought over helping their mama care for him. Sister Vincetta pitched in and talked the parish into hiring Hannah three days a week to give the children piano lessons and tutor them in reading and writing.

"It won't pay much," the sister said, "but it will cover diapers for little Henry and even an occasional bar of fudge for Wade Jr."

Then Andrew and Ty Lewis bought out Lu-Anne's from Brett Strickland when he moved his family to Tampa, and Ty offered Hannah her old job back. Hannah was happy to get the work, but she missed being with the children. She was holding down two jobs now and getting less than five dollars a month from Wade.

Wade seemed to own more suits than any man in Jacksonville, and he always drove a new car, but he told Hannah he could only afford to give her what he gave her. She saved whatever extra money she could and kept it upstairs in a locked chest; right next to the music box that Andy had given her so long ago.

"This money is for us," she told the children. "We're going back to Ireland someday. I'm going to show you the valleys I loved as a girl. I'm going to walk you past the great drama of the sea. We'll bicycle ride on roads bordered by yellow-green fields, alive with purple and white flowers. We'll dance with the flowers under the prettiest sky you've ever seen, as the great hills of Ireland enfold us."

"How high is a hill, Mama?" the children would ask.

It was difficult to explain to them what Irish hills looked like when they were being raised in a land as flat as the palm of her hand. The children would tease and tell her that the hills of Ireland sounded like the humps of camels.

Hannah missed the morning horse wagons and the early mist as it lay on the emerald earth. Many nights she sat alone and tried to remember the chill in her veins as she followed her father through the winding dirt lanes that curved up through trees with branches that hung in long embraces, making her think of violins crying out a song. How she longed to sit in the open air and watch her father lift his grandchildren up to the moody Irish sky. She ached to hear his laughter. *Oh, I know what you'll be saying when you spin the children around in your arms,* she'd think.

"I'm over the moon, little Hannah Reilly. With the grandchildren you've given me, I'm over the moon!"

Oh, how she yearned to hear him say that.

She found joy with the children; they became her port in the storm, her anchor against the drowning of fear. Henry was growing into a chubby, solid little boy who followed his big brother around as if Wade Jr. wore a silver magnet that held little Henry in constant pursuit of his footsteps. Henry's hair was as black as Sheela's, and his sweetness tickled Hannah's heart. She knew instinctively that he would become a kind and gregarious man.

Wade Jr. had his father's good looks and the silent way he captured attention just by entering a room. But Wade Jr. could play piano like his mama. When Wade Jr. sat down at the piano stool, the music moved through his fingers and hit Hannah's heart like the caress of an angel. He could capture her in his playing the way the hills and valleys of Ireland had made her weep in the early morning hours, with the fog laying low over the land like the breath of God. He played those old Irish tunes as if his own blue eyes had held the vision of pennywort and dog rose over the hills of Killarney.

Leda was as pretty as an Irish rose, which is what

Wade called her, his little Irish rose. He'd bounce her on his knee whenever he appeared for one of his infrequent visits. Hannah dressed her little Leda in pink and yellow dresses with lace around the cuffs of her sleeves. Leda adored her father and would often pout for days after he had come and gone. Hannah found it difficult to discipline the child because Wade had spoiled her with so many compliments and myths. He always brought her peppermint candy and told her a bunch of tall tales that she would hold onto and repeat at the dinner table. Hannah worried for the child, filling so many of her days repeating Wade's chatter and his French cuss words and sleeping in his old shirts.

Sheela was as sweet as maple brittle and as coy and aloof as the spring in March. She had the kind of beauty that made you look twice and wonder how her eyes got so blue or her smile so sweet. Her laughter trailed behind her walk and teased a tip of the hat from every young man she passed. She was her mama's favorite child, though Hannah hated to admit it. But it still brought a tear to Hannah's eyes to think back on those days when Wade was pleading with her to destroy the child in her womb. Her rage still made her tremble when she recalled his ultimatums. *I defied you, Wade Fournier*, she'd think. *I'm proud of the child you would have had me kill.*

So often, at the end of the day, in the quiet moments of sunset, Hannah reflected on the choices she'd made, and she made her peace with God. In the stillness of the day's transition, as she watched the sun burst and fall in the sky, she felt strong in the slowly fading fear and the creation of hope. It was as if the dusk would bring miracles that the dawn would sow.

# Chapter Twenty

It was the Christmas of 1926 when Sister Vincetta and Hannah decided to put on a play about the birth of Jesus.

"What fun we'll have," Sister Vincetta cried. "I'm going to let you do all the work."

"And what work would that be?" Hannah asked.

"I expect you'll write me a script and choose the music."

"Is that all?" Hannah said.

"We'll use all the orphanage children in the play."

"I'll be keeping my own children in the limelight, thank-you. Henry will be the tiniest angel. Leda and Sheela will be two of the wise men."

"My god, why not make one of them the Virgin Mary at least?"

"Well, because the two oldest children at the orphanage should play Joseph and Mary. The others will sing in the chorus."

"Good enough," the nun said.

Hannah made all the costumes, and both she and Sister Vincetta directed the play. The sister insisted that the organ be saved for the Mass and the performance be set to piano. She wanted Hannah to begin the evening with Handel's "And the Glory of the Lord," and she wanted Wade Jr. to end the evening with Handel's "He Shall Feed His Flock." In between, of course, the children would sing "O Little Town of Bethlehem," "Come All Ye Faithful," and there would be a solo performance by one of the children singing "O, Holy Night." Hannah also decided to let one of the orneriest of the orphanage children join Wade Jr. in playing Handel.

"The little devil incarnate?" apprehensively questioned the sister. "Do you think the child is up to it?"

"God speaks through his fingers, Sister. Have no fear." Hannah gave her a confident pat on the back.

There was a great deal of excitement on the evening of the performance. The children were helped into golden wings and false beards. From backstage, they could hear the scurry and mumbled tones of voices that praised the beauty of the warm and glowing altar where the baby Christ lay sleeping in real straw and glittering white shawls.

The church was filled that night with wealthy Catholics who heard that Hannah Fournier and Sister Vincetta had rehearsed the orphanage children in a play, and that Father Timothy would be giving a special Christmas sermon on charity, followed by a Latin mass. Father Timothy had a flair for the dramatic and bore a striking resemblance to John Barrymore. The women loved to watch as he gestured and threw his voice around the church as if he were really standing on a Broadway stage as the Prince of Denmark.

The men closed their eyes and reflected on the philosophical puzzles Father Timothy pondered over, as if they all had a superior male intellect that connected them to Jesus in a way woman would never understand. Most of them believed intellect was a male privilege and that women graced the church to nod and pray but not to question doctrine, and certainly not to disagree with anything that had already been agreed upon as truth. The men felt secure in the luxury of their religion and held the assumption that if there were anything new the little women needed to understand, their husbands would explain it.

The room was hushed to silence when Hannah appeared that evening. Her rich auburn hair twirled above her head in a deep red bonnet of waves. Her dress was a brilliant blue that caught her eyes and sent their color to the farthest pew. She sat at the piano looking like a long, lean Modigliani figure, all elongated lovely lines as she held her fingers over the keys for an instant of complete stillness and then lightly let them fall in a slight caress before the first note was played.

The night was filled with tears that slid down the cheeks of men, laughter that hurt the stomach when the children appeared in their little beards and white robes. The wealthy couples of Jacksonville embraced the children that night and wanted to take them all home and fill their bellies with Christmas turkeys and fill their pockets with futures that protected them from any more nights of canvas cots or motherless days. They could not stop praising Hannah Fournier or talking about the performance of Pierre Lucian, the "bad little French boy" turned angel, who had ended the evening playing Handel's "He Shall Feed His Flock."

"Where did he learn to play like that?" they asked Sister Vincetta.

"Why Pierre has been studying piano with Hannah for three years now. Ever since he's been with us."

The women of the congregation patted his head and hugged him as they continued to praise him.

"The little devil is sure to be adopted tonight," whispered Hannah.

"I have an idea." The sister clapped her hands together and grinned like a Cheshire cat.

"And what would that be?"

"These people can pay you a lot more than St. Stanislaus."

"What are you saying?" Hannah looked at her carefully.

"How would you like to become independently wealthy?" The sister beamed.

"Whatever are you talking about, Sister Vincetta?"

"Do you want to see those green valley's again, my friend?"

"God knows, no wish is greater."

"Then watch this."

Sister Vincetta turned to the congregation and held up her hands for silence. Before she began to speak, she winked at Hannah, who stood at rapt attention.

"My good men and women, I am very pleased to announce that Hannah Fournier has offered piano lessons for your children."

A stirring of whispers filled the church as people turned to each other with gasps and brief exclamations of approval.

"The children can go to her home for an hour after school, and let me add, she has promised to be very reasonable."

The congregation applauded loudly. They turned to Hannah with smiles and outstretched hands. It certainly seemed that Hannah's way with children compensated for the haughty airs she had been accused of.

It wasn't long before word spread all over Jacksonville that Hannah Reilly Fournier could perform musical miracles with incorrigible sons. Not long after that, Hannah had enough students to give up working in the old dress shop that Ty and his father had renamed Lewis's Ladies Wear. She was able to spend more time with her children, and she had even saved up an extra fifteen dollars by the end of the month.

"It's the tail end of a dream, my darlings," she'd write home in the evenings to her father and to her sister Anne.

"I'll be in Ireland with the children before the

wink of an eye. Oh, if I'd only known my music would serve me so well. Certainly, the good Sister Vincetta has created a miracle. We'll soon be talking a blue streak, our laugher picked up in the Irish wind. I'm sure of it. A year or so is all the time it should take. Thank God for that blessed piano. At the end of a whisper, you wait."

# Chapter Twenty-One

There was nothing like a river town. Wade could smell it on his hands, damp and cool. He could see the dirt rise in the air and pile up on his shoes. It was a city made from wood and smoke and honky-tonk music. It had an energy that kept him up until dawn counting stars, while the night breeze lay warm on his body hair like a woman's mouth.

Wade had found himself an apartment in the center of town overlooking an old cathedral. He sat in his second-floor window with his fine, lean leg propped up against the window frame. His white undershirt firmly covered his strong, hairless chest, and his long black socks were held up with garters that were perfectly anchored around his calf.

He watched the city. He could taste the dirt in the air on his tongue, blown in from back roads or else caused by new construction; he could feel his eyes burn from it. He smiled to himself as he thought about women, all those available St. Louis women, blatantly bold with their interest as they clicked their heels on the newly paved sidewalks and swished their dresses under his nose. He was almost drunk on the changing times, new and daring women with their short hairdos, and short dresses, and nothing much else keeping him from their flesh except the whisper of silk.

It was 1927 in St. Louis, Missouri, and Wade had just bought himself an interest in the McGreery Distillery. The bootlegging business in Florida had become too crowded, and he was unable to survive the split back to the Sanford brothers. Besides, it was time for Wade to buy into his own business, own a piece of something. He turned to his closet of dark new suits; suits that made him feel as if all that happy music he heard in the street was playing just for him. Why, he could fly right out his window and dance round the world. He was, after all, 10-percent owner of the finest, purest Missouri whiskey that money could buy.

Wade leaned his handsome head back against the window frame and breathed in deeply. This city was his home now, and he was a profit man in it. No more roads to travel selling whiskey to any punks with money. He was a gentleman caller once again, and his fine French-Canadian manners were purring in his veins as he reached for his silver flask. He popped off the top and ran his fingers around the edge. With the dry dirt lying on his mouth, he rubbed his lips with whiskey and felt it sting and tingle and trickle down his throat like gold dust.

He coughed badly. He felt the wheezing begin deep down in his chest, and he had to stiffen his back and wait for his breath to rise again through his nose. He had to wait to feel the back of his throat open and allow in the air, breath that he could release back into the smoke and dust of the St. Louis street.

Someday, he thought, he would bring his oldest son to this town. He couldn't help but frown thinking about Wade Jr., remembering their last encounter.

"I'm proud of you, Wade Jr.," he had said as he threw his arm around the boy's shoulder. He was nonplussed by the shift away from his touch, the silence that fell between them. *This will pass*, he thought.

Wade Jr. had developed a somber, distant way of never looking his father in the eyes anymore. Father and son shared a strong physical resemblance, but the boy had a lot of his mama's traits. He could play pool with his eyes closed, but he could also play that damn piano. Wade had listened with wonder the very first time he'd heard his son play. Why, the boy had pulled the piano concertos of Franz Liszt from his fingers as easily as Wade shuffled cards.

Impressive, perhaps, but he hoped Hannah hadn't made a sissy of his son. He missed him. It was an emptiness he believed he could fill with a few trips to the speakeasies of St. Louis. He needed to win the boy over. It was a matter of time. That was all. One day he'd bring him around the city and show off the amazing dexterity of his son's fingers around a cue stick. The boy was only fifteen, but he handled that stick like the great master of pool, Ralph Greenleaf himself. Now that was something to be proud of. In three more years, he'd get him away from Hannah and show him what the world was really like. Damn woman coddled him way too much.

"I'm giving you a partnership in the distillery, son, soon as you turn eighteen. I've got to provide you with something more to survive on than piano tunes," Wade said.

He had made a special trip to see his son, had purposely avoided Hannah, insisting the boy meet him at the bus station.

Wade watched as his son looked about to cry. "I like the piano, Papa," he said.

Wade put an arm around his shoulder. "No way to get to the top of the world playing pool or piano, no matter how good you are at either. Now, Wade Jr., there is more money in whiskey than in music. Nothing like that burn slipping through the gums and slapping against the chest like gunfire."

Wade Jr. kicked some dirt with the tip of his shoe and shoved his hands down low in his pockets.

Wade continued, "And then, of course, there is the glow, the one that takes a man closer to God than religion, the goddamn glow of good liquor." He laughed so much he started spitting.

Wade Jr. stared him down with a hateful expression.

"How many times do I have to say it, Papa? I like playing the piano."

Wade quickly got up from the window. The

memory upset him. He looked around his fancy room. The bed was dark and high, and the sheets were so clean he couldn't wait to sleep. He was paying good money for this room, but a man of his caliber had to have the best. His interest had cost him 750 dollars, but he was going to turn that 10 percent of McGreery into 70 percent of McGreery.

"I'm going to own this little honky-tonk town, Wade Jr.," he said aloud. "And one fine day I'm going to turn over a thriving business to you, whether you like it or not."

*Yes, sir.* Wade thought. He was going to tell Wade Jr. that life has priorities, and a man has to take what a man needs.

"I'll replace the damn piano, Wade Jr. Hell, I'm good for it," he said into the air, as if his son stood before him.

Wade walked to the mirror over his dresser and combed back his hair. "How else was I going to own a piece of this town without selling that clunker? I couldn't pull anything out of my own pocket. I'm into Jack Sanford for a thousand," he said to the reflection that bore into his soul.

"You hear me, boy?"

Wade pulled off the silver top of McGreery's flask once again and followed the fire all the way down to the pit of his belly. The street sounds of St. Louis stirred under his window, and the dusty red dirt came in with the wind.

# Chapter Twenty-Two

Sheela sat in the middle of the floor and stared at the dust balls that kissed the wood and flew in spirals toward the open door. As if a phantom had left behind its shadow, the emptiness stared back at her. The piano was gone, and all that remained on the wall was a gray smudge. Some men had just come out of nowhere and moved it out.

"Sold," they told her brother. "Sold to a Mrs. Penelope Granger over on Owls Nest."

"Sold by who?"

Wade Jr. grabbed one of the men by the shirt as he started bringing a dolly through the front gate of the house.

"Hey, don't get so hot under the collar, kid. Here, look." The man stopped and reached into his pocket. "Your father sold this piano to Penelope Granger, and I'm here to deliver it to her."

He handed over a small piece of paper to Wade Jr.

Sheela watched as her brother rolled it up and threw it on the ground.

"Look, kid, I'm just doing my job," he said and

reached down to pick up the crumbled piece of paper and put it back in the pocket of his shirt.

The men came back in, hoisted the piano up on the dolly and rolled it out the door. It couldn't have taken more than ten minutes. Her brother, Wade, didn't say another word. He just ran past her up the stairs to his room.

Henry held his fuzzy old white bear and stood by the dark thick arch that hovered over him like a cave. Leda wept softly and sat with her back to the wall, her tiny shoulders rising and falling into pillows that muffled her cries.

They could hear their brother upstairs as he paced above them. Every few seconds something would hit the wall and slide across the floor; they could hear him yelling out words they didn't understand. But when they heard their mama coming up the walk, the house took on a silence. Wade Jr. flew down the steps two at a time. The baby ran to Leda's lap and held his bear across his eyes. Sheela looked up at the barren wall and felt her heart flutter like the wings of a captured bird. Hannah met her son's winded rush with a laugh as she pushed through the open door.

"You'll be knocking us both off our feet, Wade Jr."

He stood very still. Sheela could hear his breathing, knew that sadness had settled in his expression like the onslaught of bad weather.

"Why, what's wrong with you, darlin'?" Hannah asked as she followed his eyes toward the parlor.

Sheela put her head in her hands as Hannah turned from Wade Jr. and slowly entered the room.

She could hear Leda's muffled sniffling and the floorboards creaking under her mama's step.

Hannah stood behind Sheela and stared at the gray smudge on the yellow wall. Sheela could smell the scent of fresh flowers and feel the sun as it streamed through the open window and landed on her arm. A soft wind picked up the lace and lifted back the curtains like playful ripples running in a stream. She stared at the emptiness and tried to imagine that it still held music, but all it held was her mama's sigh.

Hannah turned around. Her eyes darted over the golden room.

"My piano," she whispered.

She turned around again, and Henry began to cry.

"My piano?" she repeated as she stood back.

Leda held on to Henry as Wade Jr. ran from the house.

"My piano!" she said to the children as she turned around again, as if she were about to dance to one of her Irish folk tunes.

Sheela stood very still. Hannah's auburn hair was falling to her shoulders now as she continued to turn. Sheela watched her mama take in the absence.

Hannah fell to her knees. She reached out to touch the yellow wall as if the ivory keys still moved beneath her hands. She stretched her fingers before her and ran them over the emptiness.

"My piano!" she screamed.

The dust gathered, as if frightened, and then scattered in the air, as if pushed by music.

# Chapter Twenty-Three

Lucy had blonde silken hair, sort of like the texture of one of those long, delicate flowers children like to blow on. Her family came from Clayton, a wealthy suburb of St. Louis. Her Father, Aaron Lloyd, owned the town bank and made it his business to know everyone else's. He was the kind of man who called everyone by his first name except for women, who were always "dear." He'd slap his clients on the back and shake their hand at the same time, while he thanked them kindly for entrusting him with their financial futures.

Lucy's laughter followed every sentence she spoke, and she always gave men her undivided attention. She wore white dresses with lavender or yellow accents, and when she walked you could hear the skin on her thighs touch. Her cheeks were a dash of peach, and her lips were a hint of pink. She wore bonnets with narrow brims and ribbons that fell to the side. Her hair bounced in the latest bob, and her breasts rose with a gentle swell from the bodice of her crisply ironed dress.

It was Aaron who brought Wade home for

dinner one night. He was impressed with the gradual accumulation of funds that were neatly tied with a rubber band and deposited into his account on a weekly basis. No one much cared how Wade earned his money because his fingernails were clean, and his smile was infectious. His shirts were always starched, and the pleats in his slacks were always pressed. His eyes were so blue, you looked twice, and he threw his French around like he was visiting royalty. Lucy had just about run out of men when she met Wade. Too many men in St. Louis were soured on toil or just too damn married to be exciting.

But Wade made her feel as giddy as a schoolgirl stopped at the top of the Ferris wheel. After he had dined with the Claytons, he mentioned that he'd like to paint Lucy's portrait and would she mind sitting for him.

"Would you mind, sir?" He stared at Aaron Lloyd.

"Why, that would be splendid. We'll pay you handsomely for it, too." Aaron beamed proudly at his daughter.

"I wouldn't take a dime for it, sir. Your daughter is so perfect a subject that it is I that should be paying you for the privilege of putting her on canvas."

Aaron laughed and shook his hand. "Thank you, son," he said. "I accept your offer."

Wade had picked up painting again after about a year in St. Louis. He started sitting in his window and sketching the street below. Then he began driving out to the riverbanks and painting distant barns and sunsets. It was around this time that he started sketching his children from memory, especially his oldest son. He aged Wade Jr. ten years and gave him a dashing mustache, thin and narrow and turned down toward his shoes, the way he imagined his son would look one day, and he sketched a challenge in the boy's eyes that would never be there.

Lucy sat perfectly still. They were in Wade's fancy room above the street. As he mixed the yellow for her hair, he watched her breasts swell under her breath and the faint red blush that lay on her skin. He found the perfect blush color under the soft nylon brush and, too, a color for the tiny drops of sweat that lingered as the heat of day permeated the high-ceilinged room with its lush, tall windows. His hair was wet, and his shirt stuck to his back, but he held her there in his gaze until he had filled in her face and given a soft, young pout to her lips, lips that he brushed in with delicate strokes of reds and browns. The air was rich with oil, and they both seemed drunk on the attention they held as they spoke between brushstrokes in brief sentences and nervous laughs.

He didn't have to rape her, though he had the impulse, the fantasy ran through his mind as he watched her.

"Why Wade, what are you thinking, you look so serious?"

"Your breasts are quite beautiful, like white hills."

Lucy giggled. "White hills? You saying they're large?"

"I'm saying I like the way they sit up straight. I imagine they curve so nicely."

He could feel the energy as he walked to her and adjusted her low-cut blouse. He let his hands linger on her flesh as he caressed her right breast with his fingers.

"I have the impulse to kiss you," he said. "To run my tongue down your white hills."

"Oh, Wade." She gave in with total surrender and surprised him with aggressive tugs at his crotch as he tore open her dress and fumbled with her undergarments as quickly as he could before exploding from all the poetic foreplay of having brushed in her bosom.

"You are so sexy," she said afterwards.

He fell back against the pillows. "Think a poor boy like me could court you?"

"Why you are not poor, Wade. Daddy says you're always depositing lots of money each week."

"Next to your daddy, I'm poor, darlin'."

"You're rich in lovemaking, should I tell Daddy that?"

Wade laughed. "No, I don't think you should tell Daddy that. Tell him I'm rich in manners instead."

Their courtship lasted only a month before Lucy insisted on an engagement. Wade couldn't think of a more lucrative arrangement. Aaron welcomed Wade as a potential son-in-law and promised to hold a mortgage on a large white house in Clayton that he would help finance.

"Why, thank you. I've had a few deals fall flat lately. Nothing is moving this week, but you know how valuable Missouri property is. Next week I could be sitting on a gold mine."

Wade had told Aaron that he had made his money in real estate, but neither Aaron nor Lucy would have cared if they knew Wade's money came from selling bootleg whiskey. They certainly didn't seem to care that while he was courting Lucy, he was married to some other woman down south.

"Go on and plan the wedding, Lucy. I'll be divorcing Hannah just as soon as I can," Wade told her. "It's only a matter of time."

So, Lucy went to her mother, who had shown an understandable amount of skepticism at the morals of a man still married and courting another.

"I do not altogether trust Wade's intentions," Mrs. Lloyd had proclaimed.

"His divorce is just a matter of time, Mother, a minor inconvenience," Lucy insisted.

Mrs. Lloyd sighed. "Well, if your father says he's good enough for you, well then, he's good enough for me. But I will plan no wedding before that man is free of any disturbing attachments."

Wade had his eye on a white house in Clayton. It was probably thirty years old and appeared to be looking back at him when he stood on the front lawn gazing at it. The windows were paned and as tall as doors, and the rooms seemed as large as tennis courts. Wood was everywhere he looked and so dark and richly carved into complex patterns that swirled and dipped, he grew dizzy following the maze from room to room. He noticed that the banister was smooth as butter and the floors were bordered in walnut. He touched every inch of wall and peered out of every window. His eyes finally rested on a parade of evergreens that hid the road and lingered in the breeze with a sway so lovely, it just about made him weep.

"Yes, this will do darlin'." He smiled at Lucy Lloyd and took her hand. "Yes, this will do."

Wade knew she loved him. She loved him so much he could barely keep her hands from tearing at his fly and reaching in to grab at him. He really didn't have to do anything but let Lucy bounce all over him and make those funny little groans women make when they just can't get enough of a man.

"I can't keep my hands off you, honey," she said.

Wade burped. He knew he'd had too much to drink and wondered if he would be able to keep her smiling.

Lucy fit herself over his hips and began losing her eyes somewhere in the top of her head.

Wade felt himself getting hard. Sometimes he enjoyed this kind of sensual pleasure even more than good whiskey. "Oh darlin', oh darlin'," he whispered.

She moved with him slowly for a long while, and then, more frantically. "Baby, baby, baby," she uttered breathlessly.

She pumped away until her moan became a scream, and he exploded up inside her, feeling his semen and her feminine discharge dribble back on his stomach like paste being poured on his skin.

It was over for him, but not for Lucy. She lay beside him and cried, as if she were still having some experience he didn't quite understand. All he wanted to do was wash her lusty womanly scent off his body and send her home, but the gentlemanly thing to do, he supposed, was to just let her cry.

Wade reached over her for his silver flask and wondered what the hell there was to cry about after such a damn good exhausting time. As the whiskey ran down his chin, Lucy licked his face. He could feel the tears on her cheek.

Wade closed his eyes and tried to find sleep, but Lucy reached down for his tired, pasty organ as it lay wilted and still against his inner thigh.

"Oh, Wade," she said.

She began to breathe funny all over again as she pulled and yanked and refused to let him shrink back to size. All Wade ever wanted to do after she satisfied his momentary lust was disappear — find a good dream and disappear.

"I just can't keep up with you, honey," he said.

Lucy ignored him; she always ignored him and played with his body like some kind of food she was hungry for.

Eventually, he drifted off to sleep. When he awoke, hours later, he was gratefully relieved to find that she had finally stopped her pulling but her head was on his chest, as if he were a prisoner in her arms, and he could feel her fingers on his legs like too many flies on flesh.

He thought about being married to her. He'd be a real respectable Missouri gentleman with a fine house and in-laws that knew everyone who was anyone. Wade felt proud of himself. He knew he didn't love Lucy, though he told her he did. She was frivolous and foolish, though he imagined she was the type to look the other way when he didn't come home some nights. If old man Lloyd got wind of his affairs though, he'd be driven out of town. He'd have to be careful. Maybe other women weren't all that important, but then he thought of having to please Lucy for the rest of his life and he felt like some poor fool in quicksand. He gulped hard and fast for air. Then he reached for his silver flask, and it went down easy. He smiled and closed his eyes.

# Chapter Twenty-Four

Wade returned to Jacksonville in 1928 and checked himself and Lucy into the St. Charles Hotel on Beach Boulevard. Lucy had never seen the ocean and couldn't stop squealing and pulling on his arm, just begging for a long walk by that raging wonderful swell of waves.

"I love the loud slap the ocean makes when it hits the sand. It sounds just like your sweet, excited breath in my ear." She giggled.

He held out a large white hat and told her to cover her head with it every time she went outside. "And rub yourself with this to keep from burning," he told her and tossed her some white cream.

"Oh, no, I want to be tan and dark just like a chocolate baby," she said as she slipped out of her traveling dress and held a long-ruffled bathing suit out in front of her.

He watched her lay across the bed and lift her naked legs high in the air as she struggled to pull herself into her suit. He tried to ignore his erection as her short fleshy legs dangled in midair, and she panted like a little happy puppy after a tug-of-war.

He turned away from her and reached for his flask. He thought about seeing Hannah and wondered how quickly he could get it all over with. He didn't like being back in Florida smelling salt air and feeling as if the sun were going to bake him to death. He didn't want his skin turning red anymore, and he hated the sweat pouring all over him until dusk. He thought back nostalgically on the days he never used to sweat and assumed that middle age was leaving its mark on him. Well, he'd be out of the state of Florida soon enough, and he'd never have to look back, not after he talked Hannah into giving him that damn divorce. Then he'd finally be able to move on with his life. St. Louis was the most comfortable place he had ever been, and he longed to return to that little river town, where a good blue suit stayed pressed in January.

"Come here and help me, sweet cakes," Lucy suddenly called out.

His eyes traveled up the mirror, and he caught her reflection behind him. Her face was a red huff between her legs. He didn't like the idea of her yanking at him now. He felt that Hannah's eyes were everywhere, and she was laughing at Lucy's grotesque position.

Wade tried to conceal his erection by taking his shirt out and letting it fall in front of him as he walked over to the bed, but he couldn't hide anything like that from Lucy. Her eyes grew wide, and she smiled softly as she stared between his legs.

"Oh, my sweetie pie," she purred.

He wanted to leave the room and relieve himself in private, but she reached out and clung to his legs.

"Lucy's going to get you, sweet man," she whispered as her excited hands tore at his fly and out it flipped, like an accusation.

She had never taken him in her mouth before. He was surprised and almost pulled himself away. But he was glad he stayed there, letting Lucy suck at him. He didn't think nice, young girls did that kind of thing. But he was ecstatic. He felt his thighs stiffen as she pulled him more deeply into her mouth. The hot Florida sun poured in through the window, and for the first time since he had arrived, the heat felt good. He closed his eyes but not for long. He knew he had to exercise control; he couldn't let himself go all over his good cotton trousers. He didn't know for sure if she'd swallow it. Some women didn't, and that would certainly be a mess.

Despite the distraction, he kept thinking about Hannah and wondered if he could ever have gotten her to do what Lucy was doing.

Wade pushed Hannah's teasing Irish smile out of his thoughts. Best to just enjoy Lucy's lips around him, but Hannah's vision stayed there like some goddamn haunting. No matter how hard he tried, he couldn't help but hear that wild laugher of hers.

"Gotcha like a lollipop, don't she, darlin'?"

Wade shook her image off and stepped back, feeling his penis slide out of Lucy's mouth.

"That was good. That was good," he whispered.

He then excused himself and went into the bathroom alone to finish what she'd started.

He left Lucy sleeping and drove the few miles over to the house on Cherry Street. He hadn't seen Hannah in two years. Since he met Lucy, he'd been sending her more money than usual. His luck in St. Louis had been good, but there was talk of repealing Prohibition, which would destroy his income. He counted on buying a legitimate business when that happened, but for now, McGreery was serving three states and Wade's share was adequate. By 1927, right after he'd bought into the McGreery Distillery, things changed, and bootlegging was pretty much owned and operated by organized crime. Wade was no more than an errand boy for gangsters. His 10 percent was eventually reduced to whatever the boys in Chicago allowed him to take, so Wade started setting his sights on buying up land.

The town assumed that Wade Fournier had a real estate business that he ran from his room on Taylor Street, overlooking the old cathedral. So, buying up land seemed like the most natural thing for him to do with his money if Prohibition were repealed. People liked Wade. Women still flirted with him, and men thought he was an interesting sort because he always wore little bow ties and perfectly creased trousers with two-toned shoes. He frequented speakeasies and made it a habit to be generous and gregarious with younger men, especially if they reminded him of his son. They could always count on Wade to buy a round or two and offer a bit of advice about business and the ways of women. Wade figured he wouldn't have any trouble at all getting his new father-in-law to agree to his business loan. Repealing Prohibition was all people seemed to be talking about these days, and he wanted to be ready for the next opportunity. Hell, there wasn't a man in St. Louis who wouldn't do business with Wade Hampton Fournier.

The first thing Wade noticed as he turned up the old familiar corner was that the white fence was broken in several places. It looked as if a large dog had gnawed it. The paint was almost gone, and the wood looked gray. But the trees were still lovely and held the house in a sweet protective shadow. As he approached the door, he felt his heart leap to his throat, and he thought he would change his mind and run all the way back to St. Louis. But he didn't. He stepped inside with a key that still turned the lock.

The first thing he saw was the yellow wall. He couldn't see the emptiness on the other side of the wall unless he stepped inside the parlor, but he knew what it would look like and didn't really want to be reminded that he had never replaced that damn piano. So, he went the other way into the kitchen. A girl of about twelve stood at the stove and turned a large wooden spoon around a silver pot.

"Sheela?" he asked.

She stepped back quickly. He had startled her.

"What do you want?" she said and returned to her pot as soon as she recognized him.

"I'm here to see your mama." He leaned against the door.

"My mama doesn't want to see you." She put the

lid on the pot and placed the spoon on a small wooden board. She then stood there and stared at him.

"Where's your brother?" he asked.

"Upstairs playing with his trains," she answered, still trying to stare him out the door.

"I mean your brother, Wade," he said with amusement.

"He's playing pool in Pensacola this week," she said quickly and then added through steely eyes, "You better go."

He noticed how lovely she was and how warm the little house seemed to him. He had an urge to sit at the table and have Hannah come in and scratch his back and pull on his ears the way she used to.

"He's playing pool these days? For money? He's only seventeen," he said.

"What do you do for money?" she asked and pursed her lips.

"I'm a bootlegger, honey. Now when's your mama coming back?"

He put his hands across his chest and stared back at her. He noticed the tiny bumps behind her white undershirt.

His cold blue stare seemed to unsettle her, and she went back to the pot.

"You can wait in the parlor," she said and pointed him out the door. "She's only in the yard," she added when she noticed he wasn't moving.

He didn't want to sit in that damn parlor. He would have preferred tasting what was in the pot and attempting to charm his daughter into giving a good goddamn that she hadn't seen him in two years. But she'd be a hard heart to capture. That was for sure. He could feel an unexpected sadness stirring in his chest as he watched her; it caused his eyes to water, and for one split second he wanted to hold her in his arms and ask for her forgiveness.

"You're a beautiful girl," he whispered. He came toward her and stood a foot or two behind her. "I'm glad your mother never—"

She turned sharply and cut him off. "Yeah, thanks," she said.

She flipped back her hair. He might have slapped her for her sassiness if he didn't think she'd overturn that pot on him; the little girl was always too damn saucy. He walked closer to her and put his hands on her arms. He felt her shrug him off. He returned his arms around her and pressed his thumbs hard over her chest and stood closer. He felt her body stiffen. This child might have been the most beautiful girl he'd ever seen. He rubbed his hands over her tiny breasts and moved behind her, as if he were slow dancing. He had grown hard in an instant. He began, to pump her from behind. He wouldn't fuck her, he only wanted to. She struggled to free herself and he held his body closer and moved more forcefully. He wanted to slide off her shorts, but damned if Hannah wouldn't kill him for that, and she could come flying through the door any minute. He reached his hand under the girl's shorts and pressed again, going inside her with his finger. The child was clearly frightened and began to cry. It took all his strength, but he moved away.

"You're quite a little girl," he said. "Going to be a

heartbreaker."

Her expression was hateful, but he also saw the confusion.

"Sorry honey," he said. "Really, I am. Never could resist a pretty face. No man will ever be able to control himself around you."

He stood for a moment and lingered by the door before retreating into the parlor. He tried to shake off the little girl's expression. He felt like some unwanted spirit returning to haunt the material earth. But, damn, he felt an ownership, however devoid of responsibility it might be, for everything Hannah claimed as hers, including that little girl. He could take her, why the hell not? He squared his jaw and drew in his breath. Could he really be nothing more than a looming shadow in this house, with all the indifferent significance of a ghost? This was his goddamn family after all. Despite himself, it hurt so deep inside that he felt a physical ache from it. Could it be that Hannah might no longer love him, that his children might not even care for him?

He found his old chair and slid into the cushions. He returned his thoughts to his original purpose and counted his justifications for securing a decree of invalidity. That is what he would need in order to marry Lucy in the Catholic Church. Old Aaron Lloyd wouldn't have it any other way. So, he counted those justifications the same way he had once justified abortion.

"We're just starting to get ahead," he remembered telling her.

But Hannah didn't care about cold, hard realities, no, not Hannah. She had looked at him with so much disappointment lining her eyes that he almost felt pity for her. But then she spat at him. "No. I will not," she had screamed. "No! I will not kill my baby."

He lit a cigarette and inhaled as deeply as he could before he felt a sharp jab just above his rib cage. He stared at the shadow on the yellow wall, the gray smudge that once held the piano. He wondered why the hell she had never cleaned it. He blew the smoke in front of his face and looked at the empty wall through swirling clouds. He could smell the nicotine on his fingers, but they were only slightly yellow, and he knew that the scent of tobacco was like a rich man's cologne, one that he wore on his hands with pride. He brought his fingers to his nose and smiled.

Hannah must have seen his car when she came around the front of the house because she came in like fire. She stood there looking at him with eyes that bubbled out of her head and lips that curled up under her teeth like a smoking dragon.

He stood up quickly and almost fell.

"I'm here to talk to you," he managed to get out before she began to push him toward the door.

"Get out!" she yelled.

"I need a divorce."

"Then get one."

"We need a decree of Invalidity. She's Catholic."

"Our wedding vows were said before God in my church, and I will not dishonor my church."

Wade knew Lucy would not be happy if he could not take the sacraments. If he married Lucy without that decree, he would no longer really be a Catholic.

"I would not be able to receive Holy Communion. My marriage to Lucy would not even be recognized by the Catholic Church."

Hannah laughed. "You think I give a damn?"

"Let me go on with my life," he pleaded.

"As bad as it is, our marriage is recognized by the Church as a sacrament, a partnership for life."

Wade laughed. "Nothing lasts that long. You need to be reasonable."

"I am being reasonable. My church sees our marriage as a sacrament that I will not take lightly. So, you'll have to kill me because that's the only way you're going to get me to agree to that decree," she said as she poked him.

"Please, Hannah. Her parents are even more Catholic than you."

He retreated backwards as she continued to jab her finger into his flesh.

"Didn't you hear what I said? I will not dishonor Jesus."

"I want a divorce," he repeated.

"Do you now?" she asked. "Are you really a Catholic, Wade?"

"You know what the hell I am," he sneered at her and held his fists tight.

"Then you know damn well you'll never get a divorce from me," she said, confronting him at eye level.

"I *want* a divorce," he repeated. "I need that decree."

Hannah laughed. "So you can marry some little tart you got up in St. Louis? If you honor nothing in your life, honor your church."

"I'll have you committed. You're a lunatic. Always been a lunatic. I hear your little friend over at the convent has to come find you at night because you can't even get yourself home."

He retreated more as she moved closer and closer to him.

"You stink, Wade, and you're going to die of it. You think you're going to live high on the hill with some little woman for the rest of your days? You're going to die married to Hannah Reilly Fournier. I will not offend my God anymore for the likes of you."

"Then that money I send you every month will stop, and you'll be out on the street with your bastards," he hollered.

Hannah stopped in her tracks. She stood very still.

"Is that your car out front?" she asked him as she peered through the lace curtains.

"Yes," he answered with a perplexed tilt of his head.

"Are your keys in your car, Wade?" she asked as if she were inviting him to dinner.

"Why, yes, I believe they are," he answered, convinced she was going to tell him to get moving and never look back. But instead, she ran out of the house and slammed the door behind her. He could hear her dragging something out on the porch. He wondered what the hell she was up to.

It took a second before he realized that she had left him standing there and wasn't coming back through the door. He shook his head and went to the window. He cursed as he saw her getting into his car. He had to struggle a bit to push the front door past the red flowerpots she had used as a barricade, but by the time he was able to reach the street, she had already started his car and driven off.

He chased her down Cherry Street, running as fast as his feet could fly, but she left him in the dust. He followed the dust, and when he couldn't see the dust anymore, he followed the road. He just kept running. He ran as fast as he could until he finally saw her way off in the distance. He pushed his legs hard to get to that car. Finally, he could see her sitting there behind the wheel, as calm as a sea breeze. His car, on the other hand, was kissing the trunk of a large tree and the front hood had popped up, and from underneath the dented gray hood came wisps of black smoke.

He could hear her laughter as she tossed his keys on the road. He went to reach for them, but he was breathing rapidly. He seemed unable to catch his breath, and his face felt on fire.

"Hannah, you crazy bitch!" he managed to scream before he finally fell to his knees.

Hannah turned to watch him as he put a hand to his throat and tore open his shirt. As he leaned on the ground with his other hand, she could hear some horrible wheezing sound coming from him.

"Wade?" she began and started toward him. For just an instant, she wanted to run and hold him in her arms and cradle his head in her lap. She wanted to ease his discomfort, stroke his brow, and feel the warmth of his body against hers.

*Oh, if the bad times and the harsh words had been nothing more than a dream,* she thought.

Hannah went back to the car and stared ahead of her, silently waiting for help. Finally, two old buggies pulled off to the side of the road to offer assistance.

# Chapter Twenty-Five

They took Wade to Cypress Hills Hospital and admitted him overnight for observation. Lucy paced around his bed like a cooped-up cat. Every now and then she would pull his blanket up to his chin and kiss his forehead.

"That dreadful woman," she kept repeating. "What on earth ever possessed her to act in such an undignified manner?"

"I asked her for a divorce, Lucy," Wade muttered.

"Precisely." She put her hands on her hips and stared at him from the foot of the bed. "Precisely," she said again. "That's what we came here for, wasn't it?"

He lowered his eyes.

"I presume she will agree to a decree of Invalidity?"

Wade said nothing and avoided looking at her.

"I assume by your silence that she will not?"

"She will not," Wade said.

"How dare that woman deny us our happiness."

"No cause for divorce in the Catholic Church.

Must be some way though."

Lucy sat herself on the side of the bed and let out a barrage of choking and wailing sobs. Soon the ward was filled with concerned nurses who cradled her and led her off into a corridor to collect herself.

They gave Wade a small tablet to swallow. He gulped it down and lay back on the white pillows to reflect on his dilemma. He had been told he had chronic asthma. They showed him some odd apparatus and told him to stick it in his mouth when his breathing became short. They also insisted he not smoke his cigarettes anymore or pet Lucy's longhaired Angora kitten.

He wasn't quite sure if "chronic" was serious. He surveyed the hospital ward. Everywhere he looked, there were white metal beds. He counted himself as the fifth bed from the door. His eyes traveled the room, and his stomach turned over in tight anxious knots. He felt a cold darkness lying on his chest as he closed his eyes.

A nun sat at his bedside. "God loves you," she said, placing rosary beads in his hand.

The beads felt cold against his palm. He held them up and stared at the silver cross.

"He is too consumed by his own pain to care a damn about me," Wade said.

But the nun was gone.

He realized then that he must be dreaming. Of course, he was dreaming — he was standing at the wedding altar with his beautiful Hannah. He tried to change the dream and think of other things — like the way Lucy's breasts were always warm and moist in the crease, or how whiskey stung his tongue and sat in his belly like fire, but all the images vanished — all but the blue of Hannah's eyes and his own lips vowing to love and cherish her until the end of his days, the way it was supposed to be.

Might as well go with it, he thought. So, he leaned in to lift her veil. Her face flashed before his eyes and quickly disappeared.

"Come back!" he screamed. It was his dream, and if she'd shown up in it; well, then so be it. He struggled to find her again, but she kept eluding him. "I'll get you," he said. But his illusive bride was nowhere to be found.

"Ha! I'll sketch you." He laughed out loud. He could control his own dream for God's sake. So, he sketched her back into his mind, and when he had her image in front of him again, he pointed his finger at her and laughed. He watched her drive his automobile into that tree, and he laughed so hard his sides hurt. He lifted her up and spun her around, and she laughed with him, laughed so hard that her beautiful hair fell all around her face the way it used to.

From so far away he heard someone say he was laughing in his sleep. "Don't wake me," he whispered. "Don't wake me."

But a hand touched his forehead and took him away from the dream.

"No, come back!" he kept repeating until Hannah must have taken pity on him. She reappeared before him, and he couldn't feel the hand on his forehead anymore.

"My chest is cold," he told her. "And Jesus is

angry at me, as angry as you are."

Hannah smiled and took him in her arms. He felt as if he glowed from the love of her. That was when he noticed that the Jesus on his rosary looked at him. His eyes were a deep brown, almost black, with tiny flecks of gold.

"I want blue eyes," Jesus said. "Blue as heaven, blue as Hannah's."

"Hannah," Wade called. "I need your eyes to give to Jesus."

But she'd left him again. Now he'd have to disappoint the Lord.

When he awoke, Lucy was blowing her nose.

"You were just a chatterbox in your sleep," she said. "Who were you talking to?"

"Why, I've been thinking," he said.

"Daddy is not going to like this," she told him. "Mother is going to have a fit. We have to be married in the eyes of the Church. We have to be accepted."

"But I have an idea, darlin'," he whispered. "Now dry your eyes and go pretty up. I need a little more sleep so I can think clearly about this."

He lay on his back and pressed the rosary against his palm. He tried to remember his dream, but he couldn't. Oh well, he had other more important issues to attend to. He lay there with his eyes open and stared at the ceiling. The cross in his hand felt cold against his palm.

"How perfect," he said as he stared around the white, steel room. "There is a way. Always a way out of anything." He remembered back to when he was working for Jack Stanton, how Stanton had laughed about it.

"You can commit your wife," he'd said. "With just one other family signature."

Wade remembered how they'd poured the whiskey in their glass. "Ain't that a bitch? Fellow over in Seminole County had his wife committed. Poor fool woman can't get out."

Jack had slapped him on the back. "Tell your wife she'd better toe the line." And with that they'd clinked their glasses and downed what was left of their bootleg liquor.

# Chapter Twenty-Six

Rena Soldar owned and operated a hotel on Bay Street in Clearwater. Her husband, Charles, was a second-generation proprietor of the grand and glorious Sea Spray Inn. The original Inn had been built in 1860. Back then, it had a great dining hall and five rooms upstairs for guests. The Inn was renovated in 1900 by Charles's father to accommodate more rooms, but a great deal of the early Spanish architecture remained intact.

Impressive palm trees, allowing glimpses of the grand white pillars to peek through, hid a visitor's first view of the Sea Spray. The hotel's windows were blue-shuttered, and fine old wicker rocking chairs sat on the porch, slightly stirred by the sea breeze. A friendly "Welcome" sign hung above the door. Lace curtains faintly revealed a front parlor with straight-backed French chairs that swooped up in richly carved swirls of wood. The fabric on the chairs was a light green with delicate pink feathers that swept around the back and seat. In front of a window stood a small wicker desk that looked out on beautiful tall multi-colored flowers. A painted lamp sat on a wooden table that shone with a luster so rich it captured the reflection of the old white cat that perched upon it. The hotel faced a small park that was graced by a choir of banana trees. Just on the other side of the park a bus station made the Sea Spray one of the easiest hotels in town to reach. The popularity of the hotel, however, would not have been compromised even if the Sea Spray were clear across town because Charles and Rena had a reputation for serving a hearty breakfast and a reasonable dinner. All eight rooms in the front were tidy and had private baths. Charles had added four smaller rooms in the back that could be reserved for half the price. All the rooms had mosquito nets over four-poster beds, and the morning breeze always brought the scent of mimosa with it. The rooms and the hospitality made people feel that they were staying in a private house and sitting down to dinner with the most gracious proprietors in all of Florida.

Rena Soldar was a plump, bouncy, dark-haired woman with round eyes and lips that turned down at the corners. Her features were sharp, and her mannerisms were demonstrative and expressive. She spoke with her hands. She talked loudly and constantly cursed in French. She dominated her husband with winks and flirtatious demands that he fulfilled with the eagerness of a schoolboy.

Rena had been insisting that Charles build a trellis in front of the back garden when she received a surprise visit from her brother.

"Why, Wade, you look as thin as a scarecrow," she said as she kissed his cheek.

"I have asthma." He laughed. "Don't even know how to spell it, but I have it."

"It can't kill you, can it?" she asked as she led him to a chair in the parlor and yelled out to Charles to start the measurements for the trellis.

"I suppose it could if it got bad. It can cut off my breathing."

*"Mon dieu.* What did they give you for it?"

Wade pulled the odd apparatus out of his pocket and showed it to her.

"Strange-looking thing," she said.

"Yeah." He put it back in his pocket and sat quietly.

"I'll get you some tea," she said.

"No, no, not quite yet. We have to talk."

She sat opposite him. "You have my complete attention."

"I'm doing quite well in St. Louis."

"Yes, you wrote me. Got yourself a business, no?"

"I'm engaged to be married, Rena."

Rena sat back; the surprise showed in her face. "Married? You are married."

"Hasn't been a marriage for years."

"Well, that's true."

Wade got up and looked out the window. "She's not right in the head, you know. Hannah? She's not right in the head."

Rena laughed. "You're just beginning to notice? I told you that years ago."

"She cracked up my car last week, drove it into a tree! She doesn't know how to drive, never did. She's not right in the head at all," he said again and waited for his sister's response.

"But don't you remember? You taught Hannah and Wade Jr. to drive that summer you bought the new Ford. She did well; you told me."

Wade swallowed hard as the memory of Hannah's laughter brought up images of his son sitting on his lap and his wife at the wheel of his car. She "drove like a man" he had told her. She had one hand on the wheel as she took to the road at thirty miles an hour, and he kept yelling at her to slow down. Wade pushed aside the memory. She had been a good driver.

"She's crazy," he whispered. "Crazy people do some things well one day and not the next."

"I told you that when you married her, Wade. Let's not forget what she did to my beautiful wedding dress. I didn't have to lend her that dress. I didn't want it back, the way she ruined it. Without my permission, mind you. Just took a scissor and started cutting."

Wade nodded his head. "Ruined it, didn't she?"

"Yes, she did. And remember that night she took off walking on the beach and we couldn't find her for two hours? We didn't know she had decided to take a walk, to just disappear. We were all afraid she had gotten lost and was lying out on the road somewhere, maybe hit by an automobile like some dumb dog. Remember? It was right after you married her." Rena cackled like a witch in a children's play. "The woman was always getting lost." She cackled again.

Wade closed his eyes. He could still see how salty and full of fire Hannah had returned from that walk. He was furious at her when he realized her disappearance had been based on some frivolous impulse, and he had reprimanded her severely for causing such worry.

Charles and Rena had wrapped her in blankets that night while she kept going on and on about the ocean.

"She put on a pair of your slacks and rolled them up at the cuffs and just took off. She came back looking like some lunatic. She kept saying the ocean is God's blood. Remember, Wade? God's blood? Ha! Crazy woman. Dressed up like a man? Crazy woman."

Wade remembered how she had talked about the ocean. She said if she closed her eyes, she could imagine she were back in Ireland walking by the sea. She said it frightened her and calmed her at one and the same time, and she wanted to walk by the ocean every evening because it felt like walking with God and with a silent part of her soul.

"But I've got to wear your slacks, Wade," she'd said. "Slacks give me freedom and allow me to tease the waves and run along the shoreline without having to worry about dragging some silly skirts in the sand."

"They'll lock you up if you're found on the beach in my clothes, Hannah," was his response. But when an old pair of his white trousers turned up missing, he always wondered if she took them and put her hair up under one of his hats and walked the beach at dusk.

"I've got to do something." Wade brought the purpose of his visit into focus. "Lucy is from a wealthy family. I'll be set up for the rest of my life after we're married, but her parents will break it off if I can't get a proper divorce. Hannah's refusal to give me that decree of Invalidity makes me look bad."

"Well, get an improper divorce then."

"Then our marriage is not going to be recognized by the Catholic Church, and Lucy's family won't allow us to marry."

"You've got yourself another woman, that's grounds for divorce."

"Hannah won't divorce me. She won't go through the process. Lucy is Catholic. I won't be able to take the sacraments." Wade's hands came down hard on his knees. "There is a way though. It came to me, like an omen, like something necessary."

"What are you talking about?" Rena asked. "You going to push her off a cliff?"

Wade chuckled. "No, but if she's mentally incompetent I've got grounds for an annulment and the Catholic Church can't get involved."

"That sounds like it would be hard to prove."

Wade shook his head. "No, it won't be. The laws are all on my side. Can you come to Tallahassee with me?" he asked. "I'm going to need you there. I'm going to need your signature."

"Tallahassee?" she asked slowly. "Why Tallahassee?"

"That where the Florida State Institution is."

Rena stared at him. He could tell it was starting to make sense to her, though she might think of it as being cruel.

"Leda, she can't get herself home at night. She talks to herself. She wears my old clothes and goes to the beach and just runs up and down by the water, getting herself all wet. I'm not being frivolous about this."

"*Ah, une lunatique, une lunatique.*"

"I've got children. I've got children, Rena," he rattled on. "She isn't fit to raise my children. Her mental state is too precarious."

"I never liked that woman, Wade. Never did trust her. Now I told you that, Wade. Remember all that stuff about God? People that talk so much about God are crazy. *Mon dieu*, remember what she did to my wedding dress? Let's not forget that."

"If I try and talk to her, she just looks at me and screams. She just stands there and screams! I can't trust her with those kids. Henry is only a little boy, and my Leda is so impressionable."

"What can we do about this in Tallahassee?"

"I looked into this. It only takes two family signatures to admit her. That's the law. If I, as her husband, say she's unstable then the hospital will take her in for observation with one other signature. Your signature." He stared at her.

Rena took in a long breath. "You want me to sign something that will put her away, is that it?"

"If I can prove mental illness, prove that she might have been incompetent at the time of our marriage the church will grant an annulment."

Leda stood to her feet. She smiled at him. "Charles can handle things while I'm gone. The sooner you are rid of that lunatic the better. We'll leave in the morning. Now, tell me about this new woman of yours."

Wade went out alone that evening. He felt like his life was about to alter and change for the best. He felt settled and secure. He let himself inhale for as long as he could stand it. His chest began to burn, and his insides shrank around his throat; it seemed to paralyze his body for a moment, before finally releasing him back to a normal breath.

He made it to an old speakeasy and settled into the noise with a grateful abandonment. He drank his whiskey quickly and sang along to the old roll-top piano that cranked out a song by Cole Porter ... something about having an ace in the hole. He stood up and put his arm around a pretty brunette with a red headband. He sang loud, as loud as he could. Before he knew it, the whole room was singing with him. Their voices were like a shield; their exuberance was like a hug. He'd done the right thing, the smart thing, the only thing he could do under the circumstances.

# Chapter Twenty-Seven

Wade signed the hospital papers quickly. They were in a small office, and he and his sister had just given an account of Hannah's behavior. They also managed to get signed reports from some of Wade's old drinking buddies. The men had been somehow coerced into swearing that Hannah kept getting lost right out in front of her own house, an eccentricity Wade liked to joke about, but it was clearly a serious issue, they said.

Wade turned his head and stared out the window as one of the doctors looked over the sworn testimony concerning Hannah's poor sense of direction.

He and Rena were sitting before a board of three people. Rena kept wringing her hands and following Wade's lead as he turned back to her with an encouraging nod; he did this several times. Finally, he dropped his head in his hands and rubbed his eyebrows. Rena dabbed at her eyes with a white handkerchief as Wade slid the papers over to her for her signature.

"*Mon dieu. Mon dieu,*" she whispered and

looked at Wade. His face was a deep pink, and his eyes were in an unyielding slant. He looked around the room and nodded again at Rena.

"She's too high-strung to raise my children. She goes off by herself and can't find her way back home. She wrecked my car. She injured me. Here look."

Wade stood up and bent down to show the doctors a tiny scar on his forehead that he'd had since childhood.

"She threw a vase at me. It broke into a hundred pieces. Cut me good."

"And how long ago was that?" one of the doctors asked him.

"Oh, some years ago. She's been acting crazy for years. Scar never healed."

He noticed that Rena had begun her signature, but he didn't sit back down. He walked over to the window and stared out over the grounds.

"This isn't easy for my sister. It isn't easy for me. I love my wife. But we have to protect the children."

He put his hands in his pockets and let out his breath. When he turned back to the room, the doctors were standing to leave, and Rena was biting her lip.

"Your wife will be given the best treatment," the elder doctor said as he reached out for Wade's handshake.

"Thank you, Doctor."

Wade grasped the doctor's hand in both of his.

"We'll hold her here for observation," the doctor said and reached out his other hand to cover both of Wade's. "Dr. Russell will be assigned to your wife's case. I'm sure she'll be released in three months. Perhaps it is not serious."

Wade dropped the elder doctor's hands and reached out for Dr. Russell, who returned his handshake vigorously.

"Doctor," he said, as he looked him squarely in the eyes.

"We ask that you not visit your wife for thirty days. It's routine."

Dr. Russell gave Rena a reassuring smile as he filed out.

"I'll take good care of her, ma'am."

"Don't worry," said the last doctor to leave as he gathered up the paperwork. "Sometimes all people need is a rest."

Wade looked back at his sister. They were finally alone in the small room.

"Well, it's done." Wade said. "That's that."

"*Oui*," Rena said firmly.

"I'll have to stop in on that nun over at St. Stanislaus, Hannah's friend. Let the nuns take the children for now. I can't be moving them up to St Louis. Not yet. But I'll come get them soon, real soon."

Rena looked at him. "They could always help me at the motel," she said. "The girls at least."

"Sure, let's wait the three months though. I'm sure that's all I'll need. Let the nuns take them for now, then once I know I can prove her incompetence, I'll have the girls go with you."

# Chapter Twenty-Eight

Sister Vincetta was surprised to see him. He could see that clearly she appeared to be looking at a ghost. Well, why wouldn't she be surprised, when was the last time he'd visited a convent?

"Wade?" She looked at him as if she expected him to be somebody else.

He suddenly felt like an adolescent about to be reprimanded for a prank. He felt his heartbeat race and hoped he wouldn't have to pull out his breathing apparatus.

"They told me you wanted to see me?"

"Yes. I need to speak to you, privately, if that's all right."

She led him into a small office off the hall. There were portraits of priests on the dark-paneled walls. The heavy drape was partially closed so the light was dramatically obscure. He observed her features in semi-darkness. It seemed to him that she knew he was there with bad news.

"I'd like for you to take my children in, just until I can send for them. I have to settle some things in Missouri first. It shouldn't take me long."

The nun looked shocked. "Take your children in? Has something happened to Hannah?"

He wet his lips and cleared his throat. "Hannah is going to be away. She needs to be observed."

"Observed? Observed for what?"

"For… for her mental state."

"Her mental state?" The poor nun looked about to faint. He watched as she slid into a chair.

"As you know or may not know. My wife is unbalanced."

"Your wife is no such thing."

"Yes, yes, she is. You wouldn't be aware, of course. She recently wrecked my car, hit me with a vase. She screams constantly. It's not good for the children. They think of their mother as a lunatic, you know."

"They do not think of their mother that way at all."

Wade watched as the nun's face reddened. She said nothing more. She sat in silence looking as if she were damning him to hell.

"Where are you sending your wife, Wade?" she finally asked.

"The Florida State Hospital in Tallahassee."

The nun stood to her feet. "The mental institution?"

Wade nodded.

"Do you really think that is necessary?"

"Of course, or I wouldn't be doing it."

"You are an evil man."

She had shocked him. He stared at her a good minute before he was able to continue. "Will you take the children?"

"I will do anything for Hannah," she said. "I will take them for Hannah."

"Thank you. This is the best thing for my wife." He stood and extended his hand. The nun did not take it.

"What is your purpose for doing this? Surely you have one," she asked him.

"I love my wife," he said. "She needs this."

"Have you ever known what she needs?"

He stared at her, and she stared back.

"You don't know what goes on between a man and a woman," he said.

"I know what goes on in the mind of a devious man. I know evil when it's standing in front of me."

Wade reached into his pocket and handed the nun a roll of bills. "For the care of my children."

The nun pushed his hand away. "There are those of us who can't be bought. I will care for your children because I love them."

"I'm glad that you do love them."

"Far better than you, Wade."

He could feel her eyes on him as he walked out. The bright sun felt good, the clean air hit him like a caress, but his breathing was shallow, and he could not take his breath. He fished in his pocket for his breathing apparatus and collapsed to his knees in the church gardens. From the window he could see the nun watching him, damning him.

"You cannot allow this to happen," Sister Vincetta whispered as she knelt before the feet of Jesus. *In the name of the Father, the Son, and the*

*Holy Ghost.*

She made the sign of the cross and bent her head.

"Blessed Jesus," she began. The candles flickered under the watchful eye of the Virgin Mary. "Blessed Jesus," she began again.

The quiet church could not comfort her. Jesus looked down from his martyrdom, but even he could not console her.

"Jesus," she whispered. "I am consumed, I am consumed with rage."

But Jesus had nothing to say. She waited. The silence lingered.

Father Timothy appeared suddenly from out of nowhere. She had not seen him enter. He glowed in the dim church light like an apparition and watched as she stood up and threw her rosary on the ground.

"Child?" A startled Father Timothy gasped.

"You cannot allow this to happen," she said defiantly and fell to her knees. "We cannot allow this to happen."

"Do not make demands in the house of God," said the father as he stepped from the altar.

"God has forsaken her," she said loudly. "We cannot."

"Child!" he reprimanded as he came to her and raised her up. Her eyes were filled with tears. "Whatever is the matter, child?"

"The children?" she whispered.

"What children?"

"What will become of her children?" she screamed out. "He won't be back for them. I know it."

"You're distraught." Father Timothy stepped back into the shadows. He had never seen her so upset.

"Yes," whispered the sister, "I am."

She bent her head and prayed. She asked the good Lord to forgive her anger.

Father Timothy knelt beside her and put his hand on her shoulder.

"Jesus will protect her," he said.

"She isn't insane," she told him.

"Jesus will protect her," he repeated.

"Do you think?"

"We'll pray," he said softly.

So together they knelt and stared at the dim sweet light of the candles. Father Timothy began to pray. Sister Vincetta bowed her head again.

"Bastard," she said in the stillness. "Bastard," she whispered under her breath.

She felt Father Timothy's hand on her own. Sadness filled her.

"Child," he whispered, "life has a way of working out."

"Father," she said aloud, "why do we live with so much suffering?"

And she heard Father Timothy answer. "Polarity, child. Contrariety."

"Father?"

"Grief will be followed by joy and joy again by grief."

"So it is."

"Yes. Pray with me now, girl. Pray with me."

They sent only one doctor's assistant to remove Hannah Reilly Fournier to the Florida State Institution in Tallahassee. Two more assistants had to be summoned. A small crowd gathered around the house on Cherry Street, and they watched as Hannah appeared and then disappeared back behind the window.

"Leave my property!" she screamed.

But the crowd remained, and the doctor's assistant remained and periodically checked his watch. He was waiting for the woman's sister-in-law to arrive so he could gain access. Soon, the two other assistants drove up to the house on Cherry Street and all three of them approached the door, but Hannah kept it locked and would not answer.

Hannah was expecting Sister Vincetta, and she would not budge until the good sister arrived and told these fools that she was not insane. She had learned from Sister Vincetta that Wade had asked St. Stanislaus to keep the children while she was being held under observation at the hospital in Tallahassee. The children had surreptitiously been gathered up and taken to the orphanage while Hannah was working at Ty Lewis's Lady's Wear Store.

Ty Lewis had given Hannah back her job after he'd heard that Wade went and sold her piano, and she lost all that income she was getting giving lessons. For the last two years, Ty Lewis had been showing up at Hannah's kitchen on Friday evenings with his sleeves rolled up. Together they chopped the onions and simmered the broth for fish stew. It wasn't long before those "fish-stew Fridays" became a habit. He'd started off bringing her mussels for the stew, and when he learned she loved shrimp, he never showed up without a quarter pound of it.

"It's potluck you be bringing me, Ty Lewis. Shrimp in me kettle."

He loved to tease her about her brogue. "I can't understand a word you're saying, Hannah."

Then after about a year he started to sound like her himself. She told him he reminded her of Paddy Ryan, the baker's boy, who taught her how to bake soda bread.

Ty asked her to marry him. It was the evening her little boy, Henry, had fallen and hurt his knee. She sent Ty up the road to Miller's Pharmacy for iodine. The child was screaming so loudly that all the neighbors on Cherry Street opened their doors and peeked over, only to see Ty Lewis holding Hannah's arms and telling her he'd be quick.

"Uh, oh," said Ty. "We'd better make it legal now. God knows how the neighbors will interpret that."

His eyes turned serious, and he took her hands in front of all the neighbors and in front of all the neighbors, he got on his knees.

She looked down at him so sadly the color drained from his face.

"I'm already married. You know I'm already married," she told him. "And I'm Catholic, Ty. I can't do anything about that."

"Please let's just do it and get it done. He's a bastard, Hannah."

"Be that as it may, he's my husband."

And so, they never spoke of it again.

Hannah had felt sad a good part of the time, especially during those late years of the 1920s, but she had not been altogether unhappy. The children had given her enormous pleasure, and she held fast to the dream, the one that assured her that she would return to Ireland one day and recapture the comforting familiarity of her own people and her own land. She missed her home, and her sister Anne, and the dirt fights they had had as children. She didn't want the memories to ever get so far away, but there were times when she felt so removed that she couldn't altogether capture them.

*What I wouldn't give to be tossing Irish dirt in the air*, she thought as she paced around her parlor and glanced behind the curtain.

Suddenly, she heard another knock on the door.

"Go away!" she screamed.

But she knew they remained on the porch, and she could see one of them peering through the lace.

She finally sat down in the old chair that used to be Wade's and thought about the carefree days of her childhood, following her father home with bread and cheese from the village store. She thought of Andy, how different life could have been if she'd only waited. She should have defied her father and never gone off to the convent. She should have trusted he'd be back.

She put her head in her hands and wept. If only she had never met Wade. She cursed the very first time she laid eyes on his face. What a foolish young girl she had been to succumb to his fine good looks and his happy chatter. She shouldn't have been talked into marrying him and going off to Jacksonville, as if she weren't supposed to be somewhere else. It hurt to remember it, how Wade had given her the window seat on the train and kept leaning over her shoulder, pointing so quickly at things that he made her giddy.

"Yes, it's a whimsical place," she had told him, glancing around at the short square houses on a Florida street. "Life must be easy here. You've taken me to Paradise, Wade Fournier. Surely you have." And with a blush, she'd kissed his cheek.

Ha! Paradise. She had loved Concord also, the little she saw of it. And she had wanted to teach children and spend her days praying. That would have been a fine life. God was completely in her heart before she ever set eyes on Wade.

*I wanted more than the Church in my life, didn't I? And now I'm going to pay for it*, she thought.

Hannah got up and walked back to the window. She looked at the crowd of people that remained to stare at the house. She looked out at the faces that shielded their eyes from the sun and struggled to get a glimpse of her.

"If only you'd made me a smarter woman, Jesus. I'd be sitting in the cozy lap of the church counting my rosaries," she whispered.

She went back to Wade's chair again and sat. She

held her hands around her legs and put her head down.

"Will you not help me now, almighty God? I know you are with me, but I don't know what you want of me. Will you not show me the way out of this?"

She thought of her children and felt a deep well of longing envelope her. How she loved her babies, how frightened she was of losing hold of them. Soon she was shaking uncontrollably. *That bastard, that bastard, that bastard*, she thought.

That is how Sister Vincetta found her, holding herself and shivering as if she were very cold. The sister had promised the men from the institution that she would deliver Hannah right into their arms if they would allow her entrance inside the house.

"Just give us a few moments alone," she'd begged.

They'd eyed each other suspiciously.

"I've a key to the house. I can let myself in, but I'll take no man with me until I'm given some time alone with her."

"As you wish, Sister … but don't be long." The men reluctantly promised to keep their distance.

Sister Vincetta went quickly to Hannah and held on to her tightly. "Jesus will protect you," she whispered.

Hannah laughed. "Not anymore." She sat back and stared into the sister's sad expression. "I need a miracle now, Sister."

"It's only for observation."

"We read, don't we, Sister? We know what happens in those places. Some people never get out. He wants to declare me incompetent. He'll get his divorce then."

Sister Vincetta looked away uncomfortably. "Perhaps you should give him what he wants?"

Hannah stared at her. "You are full of surprises. You know I can't do that and call myself a Catholic."

The sister sighed. "I wish you'd consider it."

"Did you tell them I'm as sane as you?"

The nun nodded. "Of course, I did."

"And?"

"It's your husband's word they're taking over mine or anyone else's."

Hannah closed her eyes. "I'll never see my children again," she said quietly.

"Hannah! That's ridiculous."

"You are not Irish, are you, Sister Vincetta? We've the gift of prophecy, we Irish."

"You've stopped trembling. Good." The sister sat back on the floor and stared at her. "I don't believe in your Irish prophecies."

"Pray for my children."

"Of course," the sister said, trying not to show her fear. She could hear the knocks on the front door. She went to the window and opened it. "Please, give us more time. Leave us be," she shouted out to one of the men as he stood stoically in front of the door. She then turned back to Hannah.

"Everything will be all right. You'll see."

"Sister Vincetta," Hannah began, and her words came out like pebbles being dropped to the floor, landing hard in Sister Vincetta's heart. "I cannot fight this. I don't know what to do. I haven't the money for a lawyer."

"Nonsense. Of course, you can fight this. Now let's pray that you get this ordeal over with as quickly as possible. After they speak with you, they'll know there's nothing wrong with you and they'll release you."

The sister knelt beside Hannah and reached for her rosary. She quietly prayed while Hannah stared silently ahead of her. The men shouted at them from the street to get on with it.

It was right after Sister Vincetta finished her third *Hail Mary* that they heard another car drive up. Hannah got to her feet quickly and went over to the window.

"It's Wade's bitch of a sister."

"Damn!"

"She'll let them in now," Hannah grabbed Sister Vincetta's hand. "Watch over my children for as long as you can. Wade will never take them. He wouldn't know what to do with them."

They heard Rena open the front door, and they knew the men were now inside the house.

"Promise me, Sister," Hannah pleaded.

"I promise," Sister Vincetta said, close to tears.

"Oh, before I forget." Hannah reached under her shawl and brought the music box to Sister Vincetta.

"That's lovely," the Sister said.

"I'm afraid of what will happen to it if I leave it

here. I want to leave it with you. Will you hold it for me?"

Sister Vincetta nodded her head as she opened the lid.

"Ragtime?"

"I want Sheela to have it. If anything happens to me, please give it to her." Hannah came and put her hands over Sister Vincetta's.

"Nothing is going to happen to you, Hannah," the Sister said.

"I want to be known. I want to be known to my children and my children's children. Known for loving them. I cannot go to my grave thinking they might be sad, thinking they might be hurt. It's their pain that bothers me most, Sister. And being helpless to prevent it no matter where I am, be it here, there — or in God's almighty heaven."

The nun looked at her, her eyes lined in red.

"You are not going to your grave, Hannah."

They watched as the men from the institution stood under the arch and stared at them.

"Promise me?" Hannah whispered. "Watch over my children."

The nun nodded quickly and pushed Hannah to her knees.

"Pray," she told her.

The men paused.

"Excuse me," said one of them.

Sister Vincetta looked up. "You promised to let me take her."

"Sister, you promised to bring her out sooner, and you didn't."

Hannah slowly got up and walked to the side

table as the men observed her movements. Stoically, she reached for her bag.

"Do not touch me. I will go with you."

She turned to Sister Vincetta. "Tell Sheela to be my little lady. Will you tell her that, Sister?"

"I promise." Sister Vincetta glared at the men as they walked toward Hannah. "Bastards," she whispered under her breath.

"You say something, Sister?" One of the men turned to her.

"Bless her," she answered. "What else would a nun say at this moment?"

# Chapter Twenty-Nine

Anne was expecting another baby that summer. She was so happy about the child, but there was a cloud over that happiness. She could never be completely happy again. How could she ever be happy when Hannah was so unhappy? It disturbed her deeply that Hannah could not be there for the birth of her second child. What joy they could have shared together. Hannah had not even been there to hold Sean in her arms when he was born. She had not been there for Hannah's children either. It was through no fault of her own, that was for sure. That man her sister had married was a monster and gave her nothing, certainly not his love or his protection. Hannah had written that she could barely afford bread so much of the time, much less jam or butter. It seems her husband drank every penny away or spent his money on other women.

Now, it seems that Wade had been responsible for signing Hannah away to some hospital. It distressed Anne that she couldn't help her sister; it all sounded so sinister. She might never see Hannah again. No one had the means to cross the ocean these days. She and Patrick didn't want for anything, but they certainly would never be able to afford a trip to America. Life had not worked out for Hannah the way it should have, and that made Anne so sad. Her sister deserved so much more. If only Andy had never gone off to war; it was he that she should have married, not that horrible man she wound up with. She and Hannah should be raising their children together, playing ragtime on the piano and dancing like fools.

Anne had gotten the most disturbing letters from Hannah over the years, mostly about Wade and his philandering. Why, the bastard had been a bootlegger. He'd cheated on her and tried to force her into an abortion. Anne shuddered. She couldn't bear that any man would disrespect her sister to that degree.

She'd been corresponding with Sister Vincetta ever since Hannah had learned that Andy was alive. The sister had written to say that Hannah came often to the church to thank God that Andy had survived. *It is clear how much she loved him*; she'd gone on to write. Their letters had continued, at least two a month. The correspondence between she and the nun had become especially important to her.

It made Anne happy that Hannah had a friend in the states for she was so far away from her family. Anne and Sister Vincetta decided not to tell Hannah that her papa had passed away. They didn't want to give her any more grief, not now, not while she was trying to survive being locked away in some loony bin. Before his death, her Papa had missed Hannah, missed her terribly, and in recent years he'd come to reminisce over and over again that Hannah did this, and Hannah did that in her youth. She was so free-spirited, he'd say, like her mother. It used to worry him, but then he'd smile, "my girl did okay though, didn't she?" And he would wink.

Anne never told John Reilly that Hannah was miserable in her marriage. Hannah wrote to him often, but she'd never mentioned it either. It wasn't anything to tell their father about. Hannah only wrote about how much joy her children gave her, and she'd send photographs. Before their papa died, he had those photographs of Hannah and her children all around him. Sometimes he'd laugh and say what a good nun she would have been, but perhaps her marriage was an act of fate. Life works out for the best, he'd say. How it would break his heart to know the truth, that for Hannah, life did not work out for the best at all.

But now, Anne wondered if she should have told him the truth, perhaps he could have done something? Patrick said they were helpless being so far away or they would demand that Hannah be released from the asylum she had been forced to enter. Anne had been so upset she couldn't sleep for days. She barely ate. She'd gotten that disturbing letter from the Sister, who always signed her name as Vinnie. Anne had come to call her that. She seemed to like it. Vinnie had written that Wade had signed his wife into a hospital for observation. Then Vinnie said that "hospital" was a polite word; it was really an asylum.

Vinnie's letters had become frantic recently, and she wrote more often. Hannah was to be released in three months, but they were refusing to release her. Anne felt helpless. She and Patrick wrote to the hospital demanding Hannah's release, but nothing was done about it and their letters were never answered. She asked Vinnie if the church had money for a lawyer, but of course they didn't, and Vinnie had none of her own.

Sean tugged at her sleeve. They had come to Dublin to shop for clothes and toys. It was coming on Christmas. The sky was bright, so rare in Dublin at this time of year. It seems Sean had stopped before a cocoa shop, a small café they often went to. Patrick laughed.

"Well, I could use some hot cocoa too," he said.

They settled themselves at a table and had placed their order for sandwiches and pudding for Sean. Anne just happened to turn her head and look toward the door. She barely recognized him; it had been so many years. But It was certainly Andy McGregor at the cash register paying his bill.

"Patrick, it's Andy McGregor," she said.

Patrick stood and called him over. Andy smiled; he was clearly glad to see them. He pulled over a chair and sat. Anne might not have recognized him so easily. His golden curls were completely gone, and his hair had thinned and was mostly grey. The mischievous expression he always wore had been replaced with a somber one. But aside from that he'd remained youthful, perhaps even a bit thinner than he'd been.

They spoke for at least ten minutes before he asked about Hannah. Anne knew he would. She exchanged a quick glance with Patrick. She wasn't going to lie to him.

"She isn't in the least bit good or happy," Anne said. She reached out and put her hand over his. "I'm sorry to tell you, Andy."

Andy's concern was immediate, and his gaze found hers with a great deal of intensity. Anne hated to tell him, but she knew the truth was best.

She started at the beginning of Hannah's marriage and ended with the cruelty of her forced entry into the institution. Andy did not speak for a long time. Anne ordered another cup of cocoa.

"And she can't get out of this institution?" he finally asked.

"Not without her husband's signature, and he doesn't respond to any requests from the hospital," Anne said with a sigh. "The hospital has absolutely no interest in the truth."

"She must give him the divorce then." Andy sat back in his chair. "Is that all it would take?"

"Yes, she's finally willing to do that now, but there is still no response from her husband."

"Why not?" Andy stared at one and then the other. "She's willing to give him what he wants; why doesn't he respond?"

"The letters have been returned unopened; he can't be found."

"He must be found." Andy looked at Patrick and nodded his head. "That should be easy enough."

Anne noticed how angry Andy became. She

noticed that his face was like fire.

"The Catholic Church in Jacksonville is trying to locate Wade, but even if they do find him, it seems that the hospital has refused to release Hannah under any circumstances," Patrick said. "They're less interested in finding Wade than keeping her locked up, unfortunately."

"I don't understand." Andy looked from Patrick to Anne and back again to Patrick while Sean began to lick his pudding plate.

Anne took the plate away from her son.

"They say she's dangerous," Patrick said.

"That's absurd," Andy realized he had shouted and glanced around the tiny café apologetically.

Anne squeezed his hand. She had not let go of it since they began to tell him about Hannah. "She has a friend in Jacksonville, a nun. We call her Vinnie." Anne smiled sadly. "We're all trying to do something."

It wasn't until they were outside standing in the cold bright sun that she asked about Catherine, his wife. She noticed how the corners of his mouth seemed tautly drawn.

"She's not well," he said.

"It's not serious, is it?" Anne asked.

"I'm afraid so," he said. "But we're managing."

He put his arms around them and took Sean's hand. "Give me a proper hug," he said to the boy.

Anne could see his eyes as he held Sean. They seemed to hold so much anguish.

"Keep in touch with me. I want to know about

Hannah." He waved and was off.

Anne watched him walk away. It was a disturbing day no matter how you looked at it. Sean began to pull her toward the stores that sold toys and tinsel and wreaths. She listened as the bells rang out, the haunting bells of Christmas, at least that year.

# Chapter Thirty

They screamed when she played the piano. Sometimes they sang loudly and off-key. There was one woman in particular whose scream was the most maniacal; it would often turn to laugher, and she'd fall out of her chair and hold her side screaming and laughing at once. There was an old upright in a room they called the Recreation Room. Hannah could not understand why they called it that for even though there were games and knitting and even an old radio, the women sat around and stared out like ghosts, ghosts who had found flesh to inhabit without being aware that they weren't dead.

They had ripped out the pages of the few books she might have enjoyed. It was only a matter of time before they ripped out the keys on her piano. She could find nothing to do that wasn't tainted by some impending act of destruction. Being so idle almost made her as mad as they thought she was.

She wasn't mad of course, but she was angry. She was furious at having to be there. She was subjected to people who pulled out their hair and defecated on the floor. She learned early on that she couldn't react. To react would mean the electric shocks. To react would mean she was too aware of her surroundings. No one liked awareness, they preferred their patients in a comatose state, one in which they would be less prone to violent outbursts or to complaints.

Hannah became more and more despondent as the weeks and months passed. In all the years of her marriage, she had never felt the kind of despondency she now felt. It was like a hopeless acceptance of a sudden death that one could do nothing about. Death would have freed her though. She couldn't get free without dying, that was the problem. Everyone she knew was writing letters to the governor on her behalf, and it was as if no one with any authority to do anything cared a damn.

Conversing was difficult. She only had a doctor to talk to, and he seemed to her to be a bit off himself. Always nodding his head, saying nothing. He doodled on a pad. He gazed into space. Sometimes he even bit his nails. She stopped telling him anything at all. What was the point? He wasn't hearing her.

She wanted to complain about Cassidy, the woman who always wanted to touch her. She touched her hair, her face. "Only trying to make friends. We can be friends. I won't kill you. I won't kill you." Hannah looked back into her detached expression and shuddered. She would never come into the Recreation Room if they didn't force her to make friends, to make friends with someone who was probably in there for stabbing her next-door neighbor to death.

Mostly, she would come to hate the odors. The halls wreaked of ammonia, the attendants of sweat, and the inmates carried around the stale traces of urine like old houses carry dampness. From the confines of a tiny room, she wrote to Sister Vincetta.

*The insane are haughty. They treat you as one of them. If they sense your intelligence, they play tricks with your trust. Some of them fool you into accepting them as equals, but they are not equals. They will slowly weave a web of illusions around you and when your vision begins to fail, when your world begins to resemble theirs, they will push you into darkness.*

She hated them. At first there was pity and compassion, but then the line between them began to dim and she had to strengthen it. She held herself apart from them and exercised her mind with memories. They tormented her. They screamed in her face for no reason. They spit in her food and tried to grab her hair and pull it down. She spent her days walking and reading. They would find her books and tear them to shreds. When she complained to the staff, she was called delusional and treated with suspicion.

"I demand to see my doctor," she told a large fleshy woman in white.

"No temper tantrums allowed here, Missy," the attendant said as she left the room and turned the small steel lock into place.

Hannah had been confined to the Florida State Mental Institution for one year. She had written to everyone she knew begging for help but had received no word on when she would be released. Sister Vincetta came to visit her once a week. They allowed them to speak in a small white metal room with little light.

Hannah had bitten her nails so badly that the cuticles were bloody. The sister noticed and looked away.

"Have you found him?" Hannah asked.

The sister shook her head. "We know he's in Saint Louis, but we can't locate him."

"Where the hell could he be? I'll divorce the bastard now. That's all he wants, isn't it?"

"Things have gotten complicated, Hannah."

"What do you mean?" Hannah sat upright in her chair.

"This damn hospital is saying you're not fit to leave yet. So, his signature on a release might not mean as much."

Hannah took her fists and hit her head with them. She did that several times before staring at Sister Vincetta. "What?"

"I don't understand these places. The administrators seem more insane than the patients. Look, we'll find Wade. He'll sign you out. We'll force him to do it. We'll play upon his conscience. The hospital will have to release you."

Hannah put her head back in her hands and began to cry. "He's probably already gotten his divorce. He's probably declared me insane. He doesn't give a damn if I rot in here."

"You would have received notice. Don't you think some sort of papers would have come to you with notification that Wade was able to divorce you?"

"They don't give me my mail. They don't let me read a newspaper. I am denied novels because they might excite me, but there are a few children's books I can get my hands on. The pages are all torn up, but it's something." Hannah had an odd expression of amusement on her face.

"We've got to try everything, Hannah."

"Did you hear Ty Lewis got married?"

Sister Vincetta shook her head slowly. "No."

"Seems he got tired of waiting for me." Hannah laughed. Sister Vincetta thought that she looked a bit deranged sitting there. Her hair had grown down her back, and she was as thin as a toothpick. It made her eyes huge.

"Not everyone has deserted you, Hannah."

"I know." Hannah reached across the table and held the sister's hand.

"Anne had another baby, a girl."

"Oh, how I wish I could see her."

Sister Vincetta slid the photographs across the table. "I know they confiscate your mail. But they can't confiscate me from bringing it to you."

"Oh, how pretty she is. Is that light hair on my niece?"

Sister Vincetta nodded. "I've been told. It's red as can be." It was good to see Hannah smile.

"Stay strong just a little while longer, Hannah. We'll think of something."

When she'd first arrived, she had seen Dr. Russell regularly, but after the first thirty days, she had been reassigned to group sessions. Twice a week she saw a new doctor who spent entire sessions coughing and picking his teeth. He had been the doctor who bit his nails and doodled.

"I am here for observation," she told him. "I was to be released in thirty days. Why are you keeping me?"

"You still have a problem relating to others," he told her as he rolled up tiny sheets of paper into small triangles and shoved them up near his gums.

"Yes, the insane are difficult to relate to. They don't have much to say." She stared in his eyes hatefully.

"And I'm still concerned that you get lost so much of the time," he mumbled.

She looked at him with disdain.

"Lost? Hard to get lost in this prison."

"Your husband told us you got lost in front of your house."

"Did he now?" She stared at him and then leaned in and found his insipid expression. "I'm from Ireland. The world looks different in Ireland. We don't have all those odd-looking trees that look like they're wearing dresses. They shoot up to the sky and throw shadows on the ground."

He leaned forward. "Are you afraid of shadows?" he asked her.

She threw back her head and laughed. "No, I'm afraid of fools," she answered.

He leaned back. She returned his stare. She hated these sessions that ended in his silent disapproval, as if she had failed to prove herself sane. She knew they were not going to let her out. Her frustration and her anger became greater than her hope. Soon it became greater than her faith. It filled her with a fire she could not contain. It was released like a bomb going off. She would bang her hands against the walls and weep uncontrollably. She would scream for help, and when she screamed, they put her in a straitjacket. When she threw whatever she could find against the floor, out of her intense despair, they sedated her for shock treatments.

Wade Jr. had come to see his mother for the first time during her third month of confinement, and that took all the strength he could muster. She had written several letters to her eldest son and asked him to get help. She told Wade Jr. to go to his congressman and tell him she was being held against her will and tortured for no reason. She begged Wade Jr. and Sister Vincetta to do everything they could to get her out, but their pleas and protests to the authorities continued to be ignored.

Wade Jr. put his head in his hands and wept when he saw her.

"Darling boy, stop your crying. Go to your father and tell him what they're doing to me. Appeal to his heart," she told him.

Wade's eyes hardened. "The bastard has no

heart."

"Then I want you to go to the head of this hospital and threaten him if you have to.

Tell him you're my oldest son and you want me out of here. Surely you have as much legal right as your father," she said as she brushed the hair from his forehead and took his hands.

Wade looked into his mother's eyes. They were so large and blue. He remembered the sparkle and the creases her laughter had caused, places he loved to touch as a boy. He stared at the pale white robe and felt as if his insides would burst open. He felt helpless. He reached out and took her hand in his.

"I love you, Mama," he said.

"My beautiful boy," she said softly. "Would you be terribly ashamed if I held you in my arms, child?"

He put his head against her shoulder and let her reach out and hold him. Soon he was weeping again. He felt her fingers lock around his hair. He heard her heartbeat against his ear.

"I'm lost here. I'm as lost as I've ever been," she whispered.

He was afraid. His mother had become thin and weary. He wanted to carry her off. If only he had brought a coat to throw around her. He could pick her up and carry her right through the open doors. He imagined himself picking her up and carrying her all the way back to Ireland. He saw himself carrying her through fields of flowers and into valleys of weeping willow trees, past black and white collie sheepdogs that leaped over fences and nipped at their heels. He would be so happy that he would dance with his mama in his arms as the old bagpipe music she loved played in the distance.

Suddenly, Hannah sat straight up and stared at her son.

"Are you all right, Mama?" he asked.

"I feel a foreboding," she said. "I feel I've lost hold of tomorrow."

Wade put his head back on her shoulder. He wanted to comfort her, but he couldn't find the words. He tried to get back the old images, but they eluded him. Her papa in Ireland had passed away. He didn't tell her about her papa, even though she continued to write to him. He would not have been able to leave her alone with her grief. His Aunt Anne kept writing and telling him to bring her home. But he couldn't get her released, and he certainly didn't have the money to cross the sea. They told him she could not take care of herself in the outside world. He wondered why they would say such a thing.

The sky had darkened, and someone went to close the doors against a sudden rain. He sat so still in his mama's arms that his hands went to sleep, and his neck became stiff. But he would not move. He lay quietly in her arms as the rain beat against the glass like slaps and the doors shook in response, as if they would unhinge and come smashing and crashing to the floor, shattering and breaking at his feet.

# Chapter Thirty-One

Hannah handed Sister Vincetta three letters that morning, they were all for Sheela.

"It's her birthday, you know," she said.

"Yes, I got her a new scarf and told her it was from you."

Hannah smiled. "And did it make her happy?"

"I think it did."

"Hide those letters deep in your pocket, those crazy bastards can smell my ink. They tear up everything of mine they can find."

"Well, they will have to turn me upside down and shake me good to get these letters from me."

"The thought of you hanging upside down between two loonies is quite an image."

The sister laughed. "I thought you'd find it amusing."

Hannah's expression changed quickly. "How much longer can I bear this, Sister?"

"Be strong, Hannah. We will get you out of here."

Hannah used to look at her with hope. Now she put her head down and nodded as if her head weighed a thousand pounds. She seemed so forlorn, as if she had reconciled to spending her life locked away like a lunatic.

The sister raised the shade in her tiny room and sat in her chair by the window.

"You sent for me, Sister?"

Sheela stood in the doorway, her hair in a red beret. Her plaid skirt fell below her knees, and her socks were folded just above her ankles.

"Yes, come in, Sheela, and close the door behind you."

Sheela entered and sat on the edge of the bed for there was nowhere else to sit.

"I've a treat for you, letters from your mother. There are three of them. I saw her this morning, and she is doing well."

The girl screeched and stood to her feet. "Can I see them, oh, can I see them, Sister?"

"Of course." The sister reached in her pocket and handed the letters to Sheela.

Sheela started to run down the hall, but then she circled back. "Would you like to hear them, Sister?"

"Why yes, if you'd like to read them to me."

Sheela positioned herself back on the bed and unfolded the first letter.

"*Darling Girl,*" she began, "*they have taken their meanness to the ivory keys of my piano and ripped them out like bad teeth. Still I sing as sweet as a yellow canary. My tongue is too much mine for them to harm. My books are gone too, torn like useless paper by these monsters, these loons that I cannot find within myself to love. So, now I write by my own hand, my words too much my own to lose."*

Sheela looked up and stared at Sister Vincetta. The nun felt her heart skip a beat. The girl looked so sad. "If you don't wish to continue…" she began.

"No, no, I do," Sheela said quickly and turned back to the letter. "*Sweet girl, I love you so much I ache from it. I may never see you again. There is talk of fiddling with my brain even more than they have. They're calling it some super-duper shock treatment. They say it will cure me, but it is they that need to be redeemed, not I. I am altogether whole, and my soul cannot be touched by their cruelty."*

Sheela looked away, and Sister Vincetta knew she was crying. "I don't think your mama meant to upset you."

"Is she okay?"

"She's fine."

Sheela wiped her eyes and picked up the next letter. "I don't always believe she's fine, Sister."

"She's trying to be fine. Look, if you don't want to read any more, we can save it for tomorrow."

"No," Sheela said. "I have to read them; she wants me to." Sheela picked up the next letter and began to read.

"*They have shaved my head and draw circles on my skull. But I will not let them take from me the memory of your dear face, nor the color of the mountains at dusk, or the taste of rain on my lips. No, I will not allow these thieves to rob me of my memories. To die in protest may be the most honorable thing that I can do. They threaten now to take my pen and throw my ink to the wash bucket. I must go quickly before they destroy my thoughts — all that ground me now. I am sorry to be so brief. Bless you, and your sister and brothers. Love, Mama"*

"I wish I could take you to her, Sheela, but they will not allow you in."

"I'm going to get her out. You'll see. I'm going to barge in there and get her out."

Sister Vincetta could see how angry Sheela had become. She wondered if she should have given her any letters at all. She knew the hospital was sending most of Hannah's letters to Wade, which meant they were probably never even opened and certainly he would never pass them on.

"I'll read the last," Sheila said and picked it up. "Darling Girl, *Jesus has been good to me this year. They repaired my piano, and they have locked it closed. So, though I cannot play it, I am at peace knowing that someone can. Sister Vincetta has written to me and tells me you are doing well. I pray for your independence. Let no one shatter your heart. My own heart is never still. I hold you there, and though I cannot see you, I feel your soul near mine. There is heaven, child, and in that place, there is no harm. Yes, meanness is a trait of the living. I do not understand it, meanness. But I do know that God will not accept it. The dying go to God free of hate, and only love survives His knowing. May your father, Wade Fournier, find his way. Be at peace and know that my heart will follow your path from this world and into the next, and it is my love for you that will allow me that journey.*

*Locking me up with the loons has taught me to find my own strength, and it will prevail, if not on this earth, then beyond it. Your loving mother, Hannah."*

The sister held out her hand. "Come here, child," she said.

Sheela walked into her arms and wept softly. "There are some people that I hate, Sister, and I don't care if it's a sin."

"Nor do I care," said Sister Vincetta. "Hate is good."

# Chapter Thirty-Two

The Great Depression of 1929 swallowed Wade in a myriad of pieces and swept across his dreams like cinders in a desert wind. Fear was a fist that he could feel against his heart; it threatened to cut off his breath and suspend him somewhere between light and darkness.

For Wade, even friendship was too precious to find during the years of the Great Depression. It was something he once had when his pockets were full, and his handshake was hearty. All around him the American dream was dying under the precarious winds of shattered hopes, and it lay across the future like a stick of dynamite. But God was present. Most certainly God was present, for no one seeks God more desperately than a man facing his own demise. Only a renewed faith in something greater than his own despair is going to keep a desperate man from firing a bullet through his brain. But sometimes faith is not enough, and those who don't have the courage to die, pray for God to take them, and lo and behold ... God does.

Aaron Lloyd lost the bank in 1929. Wade wound up with five hundred dollars in his pocket because Aaron insisted he withdraw it early. He secured himself a legal annulment from the Catholic Church on the grounds of mental incompetence and planned on marrying Lucy in the spring of 1930, but once the Depression hit, and Aaron's bank closed, Lucy spent every spare moment caring for Aaron and Lillian. Aaron had become despondent and was unable to consume even moderate amounts of food. Lillian was frail and frightened and depended on Lucy to help care for her father. Fortunately, Lucy's older brother had a law practice in St. Louis and kept the family from losing the house.

By this time, Wade could not get through his mornings without a drink. His temper flared easily, and he often passed out and had to be carried back to his apartment and put to bed. Once Prohibition ended, Wade was virtually unemployed. His contacts in Chicago had no use for him anymore. Eventually, he got a job tending bar at O'Rourke's Pub on Brearly Street. He thought that when he and Lucy married, he'd move into the big house with Lucy's family, get his real estate license, and make a killing selling land. He believed the Depression would pass swiftly, and he would be as prosperous as Old Man Lloyd had once been.

But Lucy didn't have time for him anymore. He heard she was helping at some church that was feeding the poor when she wasn't up in Clayton taking care of Old Man Lloyd. Wade didn't seem to notice that Lucy didn't look at him in quite the same way she used to. Her head was always tilted back away from him these days, and she'd hold her mouth open while her eyes looked up toward heaven. He'd gotten his legal annulment and still planned on marrying her, but she seemed not to care for him at all; the only thing he was feeling from Lucy these days was contempt.

The house in Jacksonville was gone. Those nuns over at St. Stanislaus came and took a trunk full of Hannah's linens and china, but no one was paying any rent on the house, so he just let them take it. Hell, he couldn't afford it now. The nuns kept writing him letters and asking him to sign a release for Hannah, but he had to keep her in that hospital until he married Lucy. Just until then. He'd sign the damn release after that. He figured that Lucy just needed time. Everyone was on edge. The Depression did that to people, put them on edge.

Hannah wrote to her children from the institution in care of the orphanage, but the institution feared that the letters would be upsetting for her children to read, so they intercepted them and sent them on to Wade. He never read any of Hannah's letters, but he did save them neatly tied in his top drawer with the intention of giving them to the children. But eventually, the letters stopped coming, and after a while, Wade stopped hearing from the hospital altogether.

Sister Vincetta wrote to Anne. She had to give

her the news that Wade had finally secured himself an annulment and had no more legal ties to Hannah, except where their children were concerned. Since Wade never saw his children, they remained at the orphanage under Sister Vincetta's care. Sister Vincetta tried everything under the sun to get Hannah released, but the hospital insisted that she wasn't ready to go, and because her husband had signed her in, he was still the one who had to sign her out.

"They're no longer married," she told them.

"Have him notify us of that. As far as we're concerned, he's still responsible for her."

"He does not respond back to us."

"That's not our concern."

Sister Vincetta slammed the phone down so hard it chipped the mouthpiece. She knew they were still giving Hannah shock treatments, shocking her into submission. Sister Vincetta also knew the danger of shock treatments. Shock treatments were likely to turn Hannah into a vegetable if something wasn't done quickly.

She had to think of a way to help. She sat down at her desk and started her letter to Anne. There was a way to put an end to all this suffering, if only they could pull it off. Hannah could break out of the institution, with Sister Vincetta's help, of course. But Sister Vincetta couldn't figure out how to keep the hospital from tracking Hannah down and bringing her back. As a divorced woman Hannah probably had less control over her destiny than she did under the contract of a marriage.

# Chapter Thirty-Three

Anne looked up from the newspaper. What she read surprised her. She got up and put her arms around Patrick.

"Catherine is dead," she said.

"Catherine?"

"Andy's wife. It was in the paper. She died of cholera."

"That's a sad thing."

"I should go see him. He may need help. He's got two sons. We should do something, Patrick."

"I agree. When do you think we should go?"

"She died on Saturday. He'll need us now. Poor man."

Andy was happy to see them. He put on a pot of tea, and they all sat around the wooden table in the kitchen.

"We're so sorry, Andrew." Anne reached out for him, and he held her hand in his.

"I'm sorry too," he said. "She was young. She's the mother of my two sons. She was a good mother, too. I'm glad the boys are nearly grown; it'll be easier on them."

"Never easy to lose a parent," Anne said.

"Her death has been easier than the illness; watching her waste away was the worst of it. It was so devastating for all of us."

Anne noticed how much better he looked than the last time she and Patrick had seen him.

"I'm glad to see you looking so well," she said. "Her death must have put a horrible strain on you."

"I'm feeling better than I have in years, God forgive me for saying it, but I'm feeling good."

Anne looked at her husband briefly. She saw the surprise on his face. She turned back to Andy when she heard him laugh.

"It wasn't a happy marriage," he said softly. "I have not been happy for some time, but despite our differences, Catherine didn't deserve to die. I mean that with all my heart. She didn't deserve to die, and I am grieving for her."

Both Anne and Hannah had known Catherine as girls. She'd been a bit high-strung, always demanding that things go her way as if one could will a friendship into being just by pushing oneself hard enough into it. She wondered if it had been like that for Andy. If she'd pushed him into loving her before he even had a chance to know his own mind.

"Well, she was a very determined woman, wasn't she, Patrick?"

Patrick seemed embarrassed. He coughed and blushed. Anne remembered how he used to call Catherine a *ganky*.

"You know, I never got over Hannah. I was so angry that she married someone else." Andy smiled sadly.

Anne nodded. "Yes, yes, you two should have been together. It seemed so fated. She loved you so much."

"Catherine just showed up in my life right after I visited you that day, the day I found out Hannah was married. There was to be no future for Hannah and me. It felt so final, so hopeless. Catherine started doing this for me and doing that for me. I thought it made sense for me to marry her. I did love her in my own way."

"Don't be hard on yourself, man," Patrick said.

Andrew shook his head. "I can't help feeling guilty, I thought about Hannah every day of my life. Maybe Catherine sensed it. She was like a shrew, always yelling at me .... I was weak, messy, stupid. She wasn't always like that. I'm sure I was the cause of her meanness toward me. She felt it in her soul, that I still loved Hannah."

Anne sighed. "I wish things could have been different for you, Andy."

"I think Catherine always sensed that I was carrying Hannah around in my mind and my heart. She probably hated me for it and that's how she took it out on me. She made my life miserable, forgive me for saying it, but she did. In the end, we weren't happy at all."

"Don' t blame yourself for her death, you had nothing to do with it."

"How is Hannah?" Andy asked.

"Things are not good for her. She's still at that

hospital. Wade got his annulment, and they still won't let her out. But Vinnie tells me to have hope, that she has a plan. I don't know what it is, but knowing her like I do I'm sure it is a good one."

Andrew looked up. "Yes, a plan is what we need, a plan is good. We can't let her waste away over there."

Andrew spent days thinking about Hannah. He began to feel happy. It was like waking from a long, bad dream. He saw them together again in his mind's eye. He imagined her smile, her laugh. He decided that life was short, too short for inaction. He paid Anne and Patrick a visit as soon as he was sure of what he wanted to do.

"Maybe I can get to America," he said, seating himself at their kitchen table. Anne put on a kettle of tea, and Patrick leaned back in his chair.

"What can you do there?" Patrick asked.

"Marry her," he said. "And bring her home."

"You might not find her the way you remember her, Andy. She's been through so much." Anne took the chair next to him and sat. "Besides, getting to America is expensive."

"You're right. I guess I'm being foolish." Andy closed his eyes for a moment.

Patrick and Anne stared at him. He drummed his fingers on the table and looked out the window onto a garden of purple flowers, so like the wildflowers that had surrounded him and Hannah that day in Boyne Valley.

"And then again, maybe I'm not being foolish,"

he said. "Can you tell me where I can find that nun?"

# Chapter Thirty-Four

She wasn't going to get anywhere with Father Timothy. He was refusing to give Hannah any shelter or support, save prayer. Well, the hell with prayer, she thought. Prayer is often the last resort, and she wasn't willing to accept any last resorts at all. It was more like using her brain and exerting her courage and changing a situation that needed changing. Praying for something to change wasn't always the answer. She must rise to the occasion and make change happen.

She was at the beach, sitting at the edge of the water. She had kept the male clothes she and Hannah had taken from Wade's wardrobe, and she managed to escape whenever she could, donning herself as a boy, with no responsibilities or heartache. With the water teasing her toes she was no longer Sister Vincetta. Sister Vincetta was imperceptible. It was Vinnie who sat with the sun on her face. It was Vinnie who could establish a plan to save her friend. Sister Vincetta was helpless to do that, bound as she was to subservience.

At the end of the church gardens there was a

rather large shed, big enough for garden tools, lawn mowers, and trunks, one of which was kept locked. They key to it now dangled behind the gold cross she wore around her neck. It was in the shed that she would change her clothes, and if anyone saw her leave the church grounds they would assume the gardener had called it a day. She and Hannah had laughed over it, wondering what poor Father Timothy would think if he ever caught her impersonating a boy.

She felt so close to Hannah being at the beach. It had been their place. Escaping to it was worth the risk. It was better than being in a church to be at the beach. God was more apparent, so much more alive on the ocean's wave than between the pages of a prayer book.

Andrew McGregor had written her. The poor man's wife had died. He said he wanted to come to America, to help Hannah get out of that god-forsaken place. Sister Vincetta appreciated his loyalty, but what could he do and how would he get here? For one brief moment Sister Vincetta thought of all the money the Catholic Church had in accounts and if she were only capable of withdrawing the funds, stealing Hannah from the institution and running off forever on some ocean liner.

But Hannah would never leave her children. Unfortunately, Sister Vincetta could not think of a plan grand enough to include whisking them all off. But she had to do something that would bring about legal protection, a legal decree once and for all that would prove her husband's motives and protect Hannah from that damn hospital's claim on her.

First things first, she thought, get Hannah out of that inhuman asylum and then work on legally securing her freedom. It was a daunting task, and she felt incredibly alone. If only Andrew really were there, if only someone were there to help.

The city frightened him; it was startling to see New York City for the first time, so grand and yet so loud and full of people. He wished he had more time to explore the mystery of it, beckoning him like some dangerous ogre with secrets too compelling to ignore. Maybe he would see it with Hannah. Maybe he would hold her hand and lead her up to the newly constructed Empire State Building and walk her through the curved pathways of Central Park.

He was probably taking the same trip Hannah had taken to Jacksonville. He couldn't see much of the city, and it was hard to sleep, but it was a fascination, and it had an electrifying energy, one he had never experienced before. God, how he would love to be there with Hannah. How he'd love to take her hand and lead her into Luchow's; he had heard so much about Luchow's. Hannah had loved brisling sardines. He knew brisling sardines were on the menu. He wondered if she still liked them. Boxty and coddle as well; did she still love boxty and coddle? What a gastronome you are, he used to tell her.

After leaving New York, which he did so

reluctantly, America looked to Andy like a city of shacks and fields. The American accent amused him, and he had to listen to people very carefully, the same way they seemed to listen to him. Sometimes he had to repeat himself twice, sometimes, even more.

Florida was a bit of a fascination. The heat was stifling, and he immediately took off his coat. He had no idea how long he'd have to make Florida home, so he bought a car and a map. He found a house to rent, a little house not far from the beach. It was a bit of heaven, that beach, but not the rest of it. Not the steamy heat or all those trees looking like sticks in grass skirts. After he settled himself and had a long nap, he looked up the convent of Saint Stanislaus and found that he wasn't far away from it at all.

She would never have expected him to look as he did. Hannah had described him differently, and only once. There were no golden curls that fell across his brow and the dimples in his cheeks had become lines. His hair was like the ocean now, grey and wavy. Sadness seemed to wane heavy in his gaze, and his youthful grin was lost behind the sadness in his eyes. But he was not unattractive, not with his tall, thin frame and his gentle expression. He was a good man; this she knew. Even before he reached out to shake her hand, even before he smiled and she could feel the strength of his grip, she knew it clear as day—this man was meant for Hannah.

"Andy McGregor," he said, meeting her gaze head on, waiting for her shock to pass, before releasing his hand from hers.

They walked together in the very same back gardens she had walked with Hannah for so many years.

"I could never forgive myself if I didn't do something," he said. "She was my girl back in Ireland; did you know that?"

"I know," Sister Vincetta said sadly.

"I loved her all my life; you know that too?"

The sister nodded. She felt that fate had dealt Hannah a harsh blow.

"How on earth did you get here?" she asked him.

He laughed. "Same way Hannah got here, on a ship, and a train. I guess Hannah never knew that I became rather well-off. Perhaps Anne hasn't even realized it. Anne takes no notice of things like that."

"I am happy for you, sorry that your wife died, of course, but happy that life worked out for you in other ways."

"Well, I enjoy what I do. I rent out properties, some of which I own."

"I will tell Hannah that; I'm sure she will be happy."

"I'd like to tell her myself."

"They won't let you see her. They only let the nuns in, or immediate family."

She watched as his expression darkened, and he looked to the ground. She pulled him beside her on a bench that was surrounded by hibiscus hedges and plumbago. The sky was nearly teal, as if someone were reflecting the Caribbean Sea onto it.

"I'm sick to death of the way she's being treated."

"Anne tells me you have a plan?" He watched her hopefully.

"Yes, but God knows if it will work and for how long."

His light blue eyes did not leave her face as she revealed what she was thinking. He seemed to hang on every word. When she finally stopped talking, a good half hour later, he looked up toward the sky. "I have a plan too. If yours works then mine most surely will."

# Chapter Thirty-Five

Sister Vincetta got off the bus. The trip was long. It took nearly three hours to get to the hospital, and then it was three hours back to the convent. All this to spend but twenty-five minutes with Hannah, but she'd been doing it for so long that by this time, she hardly felt the distance.

Hannah was seated at the table with her hands stretched out in front of her. Sister Vincetta had passed her a note the last time she was there. The note had been quickly passed back to the sister after Hannah read it. In the note had been explicit instructions as to what to do. The note was then torn to shreds and discarded back into the sister's pocket.

For the first time in two years Hannah looked hopeful, even happy.

"You've put on weight," the sister said.

"I knew I would need to." Hannah reached her hands out further to Sister Vincetta. "Do you have it?"

The sister looked around. They spoke in whispers, whispers that they hoped sounded like prayers. But no one ever paid attention to them. Who cared what a nun and a lunatic patient had to say?

"I have tied a belt around the package which you can adhere to your waist. It is flat as I could make it. It shouldn't show under that God awful robe of yours."

Sister Vincetta began the Lord's Prayer as she reached under her robes in order to drop the brown package that had been hidden by her habit and held close to her stomach. With her feet she gently kicked the package under the table to Hannah.

The sister nodded. "Hallowed be thy name," she said.

Hannah slipped her feet around the package and slid it over until it sat on the floor between her legs. The nun continued to pray.

"Do you think I'll be noticed?" she whispered.

The nun shook her head. "We are never noticed," she said.

Hannah reached down and slid the package up under her robe; a thin, white, starchy dress was beneath. They quickly looked past the door. No one seemed to care what they spoke of, or what they were doing.

"Thy kingdom come; thy will be done."

Hannah slipped her body up quickly and lifted the package to her waist.

"I've got it," she said.

"Tie it, I don't want it to fall," the nun said. "That will be the end of us."

Hannah reached her hands below her dress and

felt for the belt. She stood, and as if adjusting her underwear, tied the package around her. "I look pregnant," she said, slipping back in the chair.

"Hope they won't notice. If they do, tell them you've gained some stomach weight on account of the crap they feed you."

Hannah flattened the package against her stomach. "There, it's a wee better."

"The nuns come at seven thirty in the morning. Remember to be precise. I will meet you at the end of the street. There will be a car there, a black one."

Hannah looked nervous but determined. "On earth as it is in heaven," she said.

Sister Vincetta had not mentioned to Hannah that Andrew McGregor had come all the way from Ireland to help her get the hell out of there, that would be a surprise, but she didn't mention it because she didn't want Hannah to think of anything else but her escape. If she knew Andrew was waiting for her, she might have tried to fly out the doors. She had to be concentrated and precise.

"Soon, soon Hannah, you will be free."

"But for how long?" she asked.

"Pray, don't lose your nerve and be precise." The nun reached out and squeezed her hand.

Hannah awoke at dawn. Her room was dark for there was no window. She reached under the bed for the small package. She put on the robe she was made to wear each morning and tied the package once again around her waist. The attendants woke them at six and lined them up in the corridor. They were then marched in a row to the bathrooms. She tried not to look at the faces of the patients as she usually did; though their lunatic expressions depressed and frightened her.

"I need the toilet," she whispered to the attendant who stared suspiciously at her. She was midway between her room and the bathrooms before her.

"Can you wait?"

"No, I cannot. It is an emergency." Hannah jumped up and down on her feet and pretended great discomfort.

The attendant reached out for her arm and pushed her toward the toilets. "Be quick," she said. "I'll wait right here."

Hannah knew the next stop would be the showers where she would be stripped naked and marched into the stalls with three other women. She couldn't let that happen. Her heart was beating rapidly as she tore open the package and began to change into the habit. She could hear the attendants talking and an occasional loon was screaming. Hopefully, there would be enough distraction for her to quietly slip out into the corridor. She rolled her hospital dress up as tight as she could and hid it back behind the toilet. It would be a while before it was spotted, a long while she hoped.

"Are you all right in there?" The attendant knocked on the door.

"I've a bit of an upset stomach. Give me a moment please."

"Do you want to go to the infirmary?"

"No, just give me a moment and I'll be fine. It's

just a bout of diarrhea."

"Diarrhea? All right, I'll be back for you. They need me in the showers."

Hannah had prayed for that. Prayed that the attendant would not remain while she relieved herself. The mornings were busy, and it was unlikely that the attendant would find it necessary to escort Hannah back onto the line. Hannah had the same attendant every day for a month. She was younger and a bit kinder than the others. Hannah had to risk it, and it seemed to have worked in her favor. The only place to change her clothes would have been in the toilet.

As she stepped from the stall, she was immediately stopped by one of the nurses.

"Sister? How did you get here? These are the patients' bathrooms."

"Oh, I've lost my way," Hannah said. "I had such an emergency. Please show me how to get back to the main hall." She disguised her brogue as much as she could so no one would associate her to the Irish patient who caused so much trouble.

"Of course," the nurse said and led her out.

Hannah walked swiftly. A few nuns stared at her, but they did not show curiosity or alarm for it was not unusual to see a new novice among them.

It seemed like miles to the front entrance. Hannah continued to walk with her head slightly bowed. She was not far from the door when she felt a hand reach for her. She felt her heart race and nearly stop.

"You're new, aren't you?" the nun asked.

Hannah nodded and tried to smile. "Yes."

"And what convent are you with?" The nun seemed pleasant, not suspicious. Hannah tried to be nonchalant.

"St. Stanislaus," she said.

"Jacksonville, isn't it?"

Hannah nodded.

"Have you a moment? I could use some help in the cafeteria."

Hannah would not be rude under normal circumstances, but nothing about the moment was normal.

"I cannot," she said. "I am meeting someone outside and must hurry. Father Peter, he wishes me to help him with something, and I did promise."

"Oh," the nun said. "Of course."

Hannah saw the sunlight before her as she walked toward the front door. It was the light of day. She so rarely saw the light of day that she might have stopped to weep. She felt the stare of the nun behind her, the one who had asked for help. Perhaps she had not moved on. But Hannah would not turn around. She prayed she would not be called back. She put her hand on the front door and pushed. In an instant, she was free. Outside she looked around. The sun was blinding and hurt her eyes, but she would not stop walking. The day was hot and so blue. The clouds were white enough to compare to cotton balls and whipped cream. No one gave a damn about her now. She walked quickly forward down the block, trying to keep herself from running.

# Chapter Thirty-Six

Wade placed the phone back in its cradle. His sister wanted to take the girls. They were old enough now to help at the Sea Spray.

"What about Henry?" he had asked.

"I've no use for a baby, Wade, but the girls will be able to keep the rooms clean. I told you I wanted to take them. It will save me a lot of money not to have to hire anyone. No one has money these days, certainly not I."

Wade sighed loudly. He hated leaving his youngest son with the nuns, but he certainly couldn't take care of him. He had himself a new woman now, but she cared more for dogs and cats then she did for children. He certainly couldn't burden Sweet Sue with a little boy.

"All right, I'll call over there and tell that nun that you'll be coming for them."

"Yes, they might not release the girls to me if you don't."

"I'll make sure that nun friend of Hannah's knows. She'll see that my wishes are carried out."

"You okay?"

"I'm real fine, going to get married soon."

"I see." Rena paused a moment. "You think she'll ever get out?" she asked.

"Hannah?" Wade didn't know what to think. They wrote and told him she'd gotten worse but after a year or so of shock treatments she should be well enough to be released to his care in due time. It took a while for him to get the letters. For the longest time he had no address. He'd lost his apartment overlooking the old cathedral. For months he had slept on any woman's couch he could charm his way onto. Now, he had a home, Sweet Sue's home. Shit, what would he do with Hannah if they released her to him and what would he do about Sweet Sue; she certainly wouldn't want to see Hannah's face anywhere near hers? He guessed he could tell the hospital he was no longer responsible for her. In actual fact, he really wasn't.

"She'll never get out," he said. "Don't worry."

It was agreed that Rena would pick the girls up from St. Stanislaus and take them over to Clearwater. They'd be enrolled at the high school there and would have plenty of time to get the rooms in shape after school. The little one, Henry, would stay behind with the nuns. His older son was still hustling pool up and down the state of Florida and refused any contact with his father. Wade cursed him now. Got drunk and cursed them all. Even that Goddamned Lucy Lloyd had betrayed him. Eventually, she went and married some highbrow with hair so blond he looked like a fop. Wade had tripped over her baby carriage one day in front of the pharmacy on Carroll Street. It almost made him puke in the laps of those chubby little twin girls of hers to stumble so horribly.

"Excuse me, *Mrs. Anderson,*" he had sneered.

"Quite all right. Wade!" she had replied.

*If I ever get that fop husband of hers alone, I'll tell him a thing or two,* he thought to himself as he stumbled back to Sweet Sue's. He might be poor, but he wasn't dirt-poor like the men in the mines or out on the farms picking fruit. But he was poor all right. His suits were no longer crisp, and his face looked skeletal and pale in the light of the sun. The collars of his shirts had all frayed, and his two-toned shoes had become too dirty to clean. He had caught the white lace monogrammed hood of Lucy's baby carriage and the flicker of diamond and gold on her finger the day he had tripped over those damn kids of hers. "Fop bastard of a husband," he had mumbled to himself as he walked off, pretending he didn't give a good goddamn.

He had met Sweet Sue in 1931 and moved into her house only a week later. Sweet Sue took in any stray dog or cat in the neighborhood, and she'd feed anyone who showed up at her door. The animal hair was bothersome to Wade, but he put up with it. Sweet Sue's hair was orange, like one of her cats, and her eyes were such a watery blue that the color seemed to run. She held Wade up when he couldn't stand, and she wiped his mouth when he lost his food. She laughed at his tempestuous threats and rocked him to sleep when Hannah haunted his dreams.

Sweet Sue loved him like she loved her dogs and cats, and she cared for him as if he were a small, rescued puppy she had found at her door. He was happy not to be alone and welcomed her affection. He would frequently pat the top of her head and kiss the palms of her hands. He called her his "good girl," his "baby dear" when he was sober. When he wasn't, he called her a pain in the ass, a nag, and a bitch.

That didn't matter to Sweet Sue, though. She loved Wade, and she framed every one of his paintings and put them up all over her house, in every room. She proudly paraded every delivery boy, every postman, by them. Though his hands now shook when he painted, he couldn't stop doing it; it was a drug, he said, something he had to do. He used dark colors, for his subjects were always bleak. His landscapes were scenes of isolation, and his portraits were always of misplaced animals or forlorn children, but Sweet Sue told him it was the dark side of his genius and he was most certainly the reincarnation of Michelangelo.

"You ever think about having a baby?" he asked her as he mixed himself a drink. She was not the type of woman he ever saw himself with. She was not the delicate type. Her hands were as thick as his, and he probably could have worn her shoes.

"A baby poodle?" She laughed and put her legs on a table. Wade stared at the flesh around her knees. She didn't really keep herself up. He thought about a movie he'd seen with Louise Brooks. He wanted a woman that looked like Louise Brooks, some saucy, sexy siren to make his heat level rise.

"You gets what you get in life, don't you?" he said wearily.

"What?"

"You think you got what you deserve?"

"Yep."

"I have a son, Sweet Sue. He's sitting in an orphanage. Maybe I should think about raising him."

"He's got a mother, doesn't he?"

"She's nuts."

"'Cause you made her nuts."

He laughed and sat at her side. He ran his hands up her legs. "You look like Louise Brooks," he said.

She opened her legs wide to him and squirmed around. He closed his eyes while he reached for his belt buckle. "Louise, Louise, Louise," he said. "I got something for you, my beauty queen."

She squealed, and she screamed as she took him in deep. "Baby," she said. "You're my only baby."

# Chapter Thirty-Seven

Hannah opened the door to the black car that seemed to be waiting for her. It must have been a mirage. "Excuse me," she said quickly. "I thought you were someone else."

She was nervous and was thinking that perhaps she had been followed. She wondered where Sister Vincetta was. She looked around anxiously. The man had gotten out of the car and was walking toward her. She stared without expression.

"Hannah," he whispered.

Now she stared in disbelief.

"Oh, my God," she said. "Andy? Are you real?"

"Hello, Hannah."

"Andy?"

"Yes," he said.

"Surely I'm hallucinating? It isn't you, oh dear God, it isn't you?"

He looked into her face and then drew her into his arms. She began to cry as if storms inside her body raged, let lose suddenly, unexpectedly.

"I am not a mirage, I promise you."

"Oh, my God, Andrew?"

"Quickly," he said. "We must get out of here. I can't very well have a nun sobbing in my arms."

It was quite some time before her tears subsided. "Andrew," she said. "Is it really you or have I died and gone to heaven?"

"It's me," he said, and reached over to take her hand.

"How? Why? What are you doing here?"

"To see you," he said softly.

"You're a miracle. How long are you staying? You haven't moved to America, have you? Oh, Andrew, have you been living here all this time?"

"No, no, no." He laughed. "First time ever I have set foot in this fine land."

"Not particularly good circumstances. I don't know what to say....I can't believe you're here."

"I would never have forgiven myself if I didn't try to help you."

"Anne told me you married, have children."

He turned away. "My wife died."

"Oh, Andrew. I'm sorry."

"I'm sorry too, but still happy to be here getting you out of this mess."

"And just how do you propose to do that?"

"Well, I'm driving you away, aren't I?"

"That you are. Oh, Andrew. I can't believe this. Did Vinny know, did you plan it together? What about your children?"

"My sons are big boys; they can take care of themselves now."

"How did you have the means to get here?"

"I have the means," he said.

She reached out to stroke his hair. "Your golden locks are gone."

"But you have not changed a bit." He turned to look at her, his grin still infectious.

"Ha, I'm haggard and drawn, and perhaps a little defeated-looking."

"No, you are beautiful, a bit pale, a bit skinny, but we will fix that."

"And where are you taking me, Andrew McGregor?"

"I'm taking you with me," he said. "All the way back to Ireland." He turned to her and winked. "In due time."

He took her to the house he had rented near the ocean. It was a small white house surrounded by gardens, flowers in every color. He put her to bed in the second bedroom where she stayed for days. It was as if she could not get her feet to move.

"I want to sit outside so badly, Andrew, in the pretty garden, but I am so tired. All it seems I can do is sleep."

Andrew brought food up to her. He helped her eat. She told him what being in the hospital had been like. "Shock treatments," she said. "They take away your memory." She smiled. "But I remember you." She reached out and touched the side of his face.

He held her other hand more tightly. She wept as she spoke of the crying, the crying of the loons, as she called it. "I would sing, and they would cry.

They made horrible sounds. They would not stop. Eventually, I couldn't even sing anymore myself. I couldn't stand their crying."

He kissed her forehead and closed her eyes. "You'll be singing to me soon, Hannah, and you'll stop for nothing."

One evening he fixed her a grand meal of lamb and potatoes. He bought two bottles of wine that they almost finished, and before the night was done Hannah had the glow back in her face, and she laughed at something he said. It was music to his ears.

"I never forgot your laughter."

"I still have the music box," she said. "Well, I gave it to Sister Vincetta for safekeeping, to hold for my daughter, Sheela."

"We can put it on the mantle," he said. "Sheela can have it years from now, after we're gone."

She looked at him most incredulously. "And what are you saying, that you still love me after all this time?"

"Oh, I believe that is what I'm saying," he said.

"And I still love you, Andrew McGregor. I never stopped."

She looked at him for a long time. She watched as he came to her side. He put his arms around her slowly. "I know what you've been through. I know. I could never know firsthand, but I have a sense of it."

"I can bear anything in this life, but going back there, to that God-awful place."

"You're not going back."

She sighed deeply. "I can only pray for that."

He held her more tightly, and she took his face in her hands and kissed him.

"Take me to your bedroom," she whispered softly. "All my married life, I've missed you."

Sister Vincetta brought the children over every day, and they quietly observed Andy, as if he were a strange species. "You talk like Mama," Sheela said.

"I was born in the same town, and we grew up teasing each other for most of our lives." Andy lit his pipe and sat back.

"Do you tease her still?" Leda wanted to know.

"Why not?" he asked. "Do you tease your sister?"

Leda giggled and shot Sheela a glance. "She deserves my teasing, she's so full of herself."

"I'm not full of myself," Sheela insisted.

Andy amused them for hours with tales of their childhood, he and Hannah chasing each other around the farms of Boyne Valley. Kieran, her beautiful setter, that loved to chew his hats and hide them. How he brought their mama flowers.

"Why didn't you marry her?" Sheela asked.

Andy sighed and sat forward to look at them each in turn. "Now that's a long story, but one we'll get to in due time." And in his most gentlemanly fashion, he gave them his grin and told the girls that he would be asking their mother for her hand in marriage now, but not without their approval, of course. "Better late than never," he said.

"Marriage?" Leda cried out, "But what about Daddy?"

"Your daddy is out of the picture for now, but

you will see him again at some point, I'm sure."

The children went off in a huddle for an hour or so before they returned to give Andy their consent. Leda paused and sat before him.

"I don't understand how you can marry my mama when she's already married to Papa."

"Your papa got an annulment, young lady," he said.

"An annulment?" Sheela asked, "what's that?"

"It's like a divorce," he said.

Leda began to cry, and Andrew put his arms around her. "Believe me, your mama is better off than she's ever been. I will take good care of her, and of you."

"We are better off than we've ever been too," Sheela said. "Stop your crying, Leda."

Andrew knew how important it was that he and Hannah get married in Florida even though they would be returning to Ireland.

"I need to have the authority over you here in this state," he said. "If that damn hospital comes after you, they won't have any right to take you from me, your husband."

"But I want a big wedding," she said.

"And we will have one, in Ireland. That will be the real one. The one we'll have here will be the necessary one."

Hannah wondered, of course, if Wade would be notified of her escape from the hospital and try and interfere in some way, but she assumed he didn't have any legal right to insist that the hospital readmit her.

After only a month, Hannah was far enough away from her experience at the asylum to sleep through the night and to wake in the mornings not expecting to be surrounded by the stark white room she had hated. Nights were the most unsettling of all; she had to get used to the quiet.

She settled into a comfortable life with Andrew, as if there had never been a prior marriage, as if there had never been a bastard named Wade in her life. She felt God's blessing, like atonement for her grief. God was freeing her for the happiness she deserved, forgiving her for her betrayal of him, her lack of foresight.

She and Andrew were married at St. Stanislaus Catholic Church, and Sister Vincetta covered the couple in bouquets of flowers as they ran to their car for a four-day honeymoon in Miami Beach.

While Andrew and Hannah were away Sister Vincetta took the children back to the convent to care for them. She felt the darkness had lifted. That was why it was quite a shock for her to see Wade's sister, Rena, walking through the gardens toward the rectory. It would have been the last thing she'd expected. It was as if the Wicked Witch from every child's storybook had come to trample her beautiful flowers and turn the blue sky black.

"I've come for the children," she said. "Well, the girls. The boy will remain here."

"I will not relinquish the girls." Sister Vincetta stared into her face, held her gaze defiantly.

"Their father has asked me to come," Rena said.

"Their mother does not want you to have them."

"Their mother is in an asylum."

Sister Vincetta remained silent.

"Are the girls here?" Rena asked.

"Of course," Sister Vincetta said. "Would you like to see them?"

"That won't be necessary. If you won't let me take them, I'll be back for them. I'll have court documents if need be."

Sister Vincetta watched her ride off. She knew she would return; of course she would. She'd be ranting and screaming and waving court documents in her hand, and it would not matter a damn. The children would be with Hannah by then. She'd have no authority to take them from their natural mother.

Rena was red in the face when she called Wade. It had made her so angry that some nun, with absolutely no authority, had refused to relinquish the girls to her.

"We must get court documents," she told him.

Wade appeared stunned. It took a moment for him to get his bearings. "What are you talking about?" he demanded. "She has no right to my children. I'm their father, and I sent you to collect them."

"That nun would not let them go with me. We need court documents."

"I need no such thing. They are my children," Wade screamed. "Their mother is incompetent; she's institutionalized."

Rena took a deep breath. "Maybe she got out,"

she said. "You should check."

Wade called the hospital the moment he'd said good-by to Rena, promising to call her right back.

The hospital had only recently discovered that Hannah was missing, and when they did discover it, and no one from her family had notified them, they refrained from doing anything about it.

"You incompetent fools," Wade shouted.

"Sir, you did not inform us that she was missing, and we are overcrowded here."

"You did not inform *me* that she was missing."

Wade was fuming. The hospital was double-talking him. They didn't want the liability. But what they didn't know was that Wade was no longer responsible for Hannah. He had divorced her. Perhaps when they discovered that they would be less intimidated by his threats.

"I demand that you find her and bring her back."

"You will need to sign her in again. We cannot hold her here against her will unless she's a threat to society."

"She is a threat to society. She's crazy."

"We can no longer take your word for that, Mr. Fournier. You need court documents."

Wade was furious. It seemed he needed court documents for everything.

"I will get the necessary documents, and I want you to bring her back where she belongs. You didn't release her."

"Sir…"

"There is nothing more to say in the matter. I will sue the hospital over this. You didn't even know my wife was missing? You listen to me: you bring her back to that hospital or I'll have you closed down."

# Chapter Thirty-Eight

There were days in Florida when the air was a perfect caress of wind and the scent off the ocean was clean and fresh, made you want to breathe deep. The sun that day was friendly enough to warm the air without the oppression of too much heat, the sky so blue, like a deep reflection off the sea. Hannah could smell the crape jasmine tree behind the house as she opened the bedroom windows. She saw him there on the iron bench with his head in his hands. She watched as his shoulders made a sobbing rise and fall. She was perplexed. Would he cry from happiness, she wondered?

"Andrew," she called but he did not look up. She stood for a few minutes more and watched. He dried his eyes only to lower his head and sob some more. She felt an odd foreboding, brief and dark.

She was slow to take the stairs. She knew she was going to hear bad news. What would make her husband weep but bad news? But perhaps she was wrong, and he wept from happiness, that they'd finally be back in Ireland, a family, the way it should be.

She came to the garden quietly, as if to give him time to come to his old self, to rise to his feet and laugh, to tell her he'd been moved by something, as he often was. Sometimes he wept for nothing but the sun setting. But he remained in a trance of sorts, staring out.

"What has happened?" she asked as she came to sit at his side. "You are frightening me."

He took her hand and held it. His face was red, and his nose looked swollen. The tears still ran down his cheeks. He handed her the telegram that he had crumbled up in a ball.

She had to unravel it to read it. The words blared out at her and nearly stopped her heart.

"Michael is dead?"

He nodded and looked up to the sky. "No one is to blame. An accident."

"He fell?"

"Hit his head and died instantly." He nodded. "My oldest boy."

She took him in her arms as he stoically tried to regain his composure. "You must go home," she said. "Brendon will need you."

"He'll be lost without his older brother."

"I'm so sorry, Andrew."

"We will all go. It will take some time. You'll need passports for the children."

"We'll leave immediately." She held him more tightly and felt his grief like a closing in the back of her mouth, cutting off her breath.

She saw the tissues as she entered the bathroom.

They appeared hidden, buried under other debris like cotton balls and clean tissues, without the blood. She picked them up in her hand.

"Did you cut yourself, Andrew?" she asked.

He shook his head. "I don't know what it is, I'm coughing it up."

"Blood?"

"I wouldn't worry about it."

"I am."

"We'll take care of it, back home."

"Shouldn't you see a doctor here?"

"It's nothing to worry about. I've got bigger things than that to worry about."

Hannah put it out of her mind. She knew there was no talking sense to him until they got back to Dublin, then they would take care of it.

But in the midst of making travel arrangements, getting passports for the children and planning the move across the seas, Hannah received an order from the court. It was sent to the convent, and Sister Vincetta brought it over.

"Good God," she said as she sank into a chair. "Wade is suing me for custody of my children?"

Sister Vincetta rose from her knees and crossed herself. Andrew had left for Ireland to be with his youngest son, and Hannah was due in court to defend herself against the devil.

The sister knew that Hannah needed Andrew most of all, needed his strength, his good humor and his faith. But circumstances would keep Andrew in Ireland longer than expected; he was diagnosed with lung cancer. Hannah had not heard of lung cancer. She got word from Andrew's doctors that he was undergoing tests and could not travel, not for a while anyway.

Sister Vincetta felt an odd sort of fate, a dark one, one that was not going to permit Hannah the happiness she deserved.

So many people came forward to tell the court what a wonderful mother Hannah had always been, how she was never insane but forced into the hospital by her husband because he wanted to marry someone else.

Unfortunately, the hospital told the court of her deceitful escape, her many shock treatments, her erratic behavior, and her dangerous bad temper. The courts granted temporary custody of all three children to Wade. But what was worse, Hannah was ordered back to the hospital until the hospital declared her competent. If they released her, her children would be returned to her.

Sometimes there is just a sliver of light in the darkness. Hannah was not led off by attendants but expected to return to the institution of her own accord.

"Do they really think that I am going to lock myself away in that hell by my own accord?"

"We don't have much time." Sister Vincetta packed her a suitcase while Hannah packed two for the children. They had made quick and frantic plans for Hannah to leave Florida, to escape the fate that awaited her.

Hannah had gotten all the necessary passports before Andrew left and was ready to drive to New York, stopping along the way in North Carolina and then again in Virginia. Andrew had wired them the money for the trip and planned to meet them in Dublin when they stepped off the ship. She would be leaving the country as Andrew's wife, but the children did not carry his name. There had been no time for any legal adoptions. There was fear that they would be stopped, but no one knew of their plans except Sister Vincetta. By the time it was discovered, Hannah and the children would hopefully be safe back in Dublin.

"Do not be afraid," Sister Vincetta said as she kissed Hannah on the cheek and bid her farewell.

Leda sat in the back with the baby and Sheela upfront with her Mama. "Do you know where you're going, Mama?" she asked.

"Do you know how to read a map, my girl?"

"I'll learn soon enough," Sheela said.

"We're off on an adventure," she said, feeling a certain freedom behind the wheel, a certain optimism.

Hannah sang ragtime tunes all the way to North Carolina. The children joined in when they weren't sightseeing, staring at trees and cars along the way. Henry kept complaining he was hungry, so Leda fed him peanuts and bananas and pears.

# Chapter Thirty-Nine

Wade stayed drunk for about three days. He didn't remember that Rena was supposed to notify him when she had the girls with her. He came to at about two in the afternoon and wondered why he didn't smell bacon in the kitchen. Sweet Sue always woke him up on Sunday mornings to the smell of bacon and eggs. It took him another twenty minutes to realize it wasn't Sunday and he'd been drunk since Friday.

He staggered into the living room and found Sweet Sue playing with the latest stray, a sorry-looking hound with red eyes.

"He's very smart," she said.

"Don't doubt it." Wade found his chair and collapsed in it, the way someone might fall backwards into a swimming hole.

"No coffee in the kitchen. You going to make me some?"

Sweet Sue stared at him; he looked like hell, of course. His beard was coming in grey, but his hair was still dark. The rings under his eyes made him look like a prizefighter just been rubbed with eye black.

"Go shower, Wade. Coffee be ready when you get out."

Wade felt the cold water on his skin. He shivered but didn't warm the water. He needed the sudden blast; it was bringing him back alive after being in a comatose state. His head felt big as a basketball and just as beat up.

He realized, while he was soaping up his body, that he hadn't heard from his sister and she'd promised to call. It made him feel like he really got one up on Hannah; he'd gotten her kids from her, and she was going back into the institution. He didn't suspect they'd keep her long, just long enough to appease him. He'd call his sister soon as he had some of Sweet Sue's coffee, best cup of java in the whole damn state. Once the girls were with Rena, life would be back to normal. If Hannah got the children back, Rena would just have to deal with it.

As he dressed, he felt better. He shaved his face, didn't like facial hair. He spruced himself up good and decided it was the time to bring it up, about wanting to raise his son. Hell, Rena didn't want Henry, had no use for Henry but he was going to get Henry one way or the other whether she liked it or not. Hell, he'd failed with Wade Jr., but just maybe little Henry would bring him some joy and they'd have the father-son relationship he' d missed out on.

He didn't know how Sweet Sue was going to feel

about it, of course. She didn't care much for kids, but this was his son, had to be something special about that.

He found Sweet Sue in the kitchen with that new dog, the one she called Sammy. That old hound was following her around like she was Santa Claus. All the other dogs were sleeping; that's all they ever did was sleep. The cats, well, cats were strange creatures, just walked around and stretched all day. Got into one position, stayed there for hours and then got into a new position, after stretching. of course. Wade never saw them eat or take a drink of water, but they must have, a few of them were so fat they wobbled. He didn't much care for cats and kept telling Sweet Sue that their hair was going to kill him. He was breathing in hair, and animal hair was bad for his asthma, but Sweet Sue just laughed. "Cat hair never killed anyone," she'd say.

"I been thinking, Sweet Sue … "

She turned from the counter. She'd been pouring so much cream in her coffee that the liquid looked white, not coffee brown like coffee should look, just white.

"Now there's a lot of things you do better than thinking, Wade."

"Ha, ha." He laughed, never took her seriously, though she might have meant it. "I been thinking…"

"You said that, Wade."

"My son needs me."

"Your son is a man, Wade. He's old enough to take care of himself."

"I don't mean that son."

"You got another son?"

"Yes, Henry. I told you. Henry."

"Oh."

"He needs me."

"Why?"

"Well, cause he's my son, and he's only ten years old. It doesn't seem right to have him raised by nuns. I'm his father."

"Thought you said your sister was taking him."

"No, she's taking the girls."

Sweet Sue looked off. It was obvious to Wade that the conversation was over for her.

"I need to raise my son."

"How long has he been in that convent, Wade? It's just come to you? What, while you were in the shower it just came to you that you need to raise your son? He was your son ten years ago too."

"I've been thinking about this for days."

"You've been drunk for days."

"It's my duty."

"You don't give a damn about duty. You're just feeling guilty."

"Right, I'm feeling guilty. I need to bring him here."

Sweet Sue turned an odd shade of a listless color, maybe like some cherry soda that's been left out too long.

He stared at her as she picked up some things that were lying around and quietly left the room. A moment later, he heard the sweep of the broom and watched Sweet Sue through the glass as she swept the porch.

# Chapter Forty

Rena had the court documents in her hand when she walked into the St. Stanislaus Convent and asked that Sheela and Leda Fournier be released to her.

Of course, every one of the nuns at St. Stanislaus knew that Hannah's children were on their way to Ireland. They most certainly had reached North Carolina.

Sister Mary looked carefully at Rena Soldar. The nun thought she looked impatient and angry. The nun didn't like Rena's face; it was hard, and she appeared both haughty and insipid at once.

"Well?" Rena said. "Are you going to stare at me or are you going to collect my nieces and bring them to me?"

The nun wasn't sure what to do. Sister Vincetta had warned them all that Rena Soldar would come pounding on the door for Sheela and Leda. She felt afraid to tell the angry woman the truth, but she must. Or maybe there was a better way.

"Well?" Rena demanded.

"I'll get Sister Vincetta," the nun said and ran

off.

Sister Vincetta prayed that Hannah would make it onto the ship for Dublin before any of the authorities learned of her demise. She'd been praying for time and for miracles. She took a deep breath before she entered the room in which Rena huffed and puffed like a dragon staring at supper. Supper, of course, being Sister Vincetta. Her eyes were large as she fumed at the sister.

"Where are the girls? I have the necessary papers to take them."

Sister Vincetta knew she had to stall, to gain as much time as she could. There wasn't really much Rena could do, not with Hannah and the children so far away.

"They went to the cinema."

"What cinema?"

"Why, I'm not sure."

Rena paused a moment and walked around the room. Sister Vincetta cleared her throat.

"Why don't you come back tomorrow?"

"When did they leave for the cinema?"

"Only moments ago."

"Then I will wait the two hours for them to return."

"No need. I'll bring them to you myself. Friday there is no school. That should be a good day."

"I will be back later today for my nieces. They had better be here."

Sister Vincetta stood aside as Leda rushed past her.

It was nearly six when Sister Vincetta prepared to leave for the dining hall. Sister Mary was clearly upset when she burst into Sister Vincetta's room and nearly knocked her to her feet.

"What on earth?"

"There is a policeman downstairs with that horrid woman. They are speaking with Father Timothy. He told me to bring you down."

Sister Vincetta felt the shaking in her body, like some wild epilepsy, but she nodded. "It will be all right, I'm sure."

The policeman was taller than any man she'd ever seen. He was serious-looking too, not kindly at all.

"Sister," Father Timothy said. "I was just telling the officer that Hannah has left for Ireland. That's her home." He turned to the officer. "Ireland is."

Sister Vincetta said nothing. The policeman told her to have a seat. "You know she was ordered back to the Florida State Hospital by the court?"

The sister nodded but remained silent.

"I have the papers here in my hand. She should have been there yesterday."

Sister Vincetta made the sign of the cross. "A fate worse than death," she said.

"That's not for you to say, Sister." The policeman walked a few paces around his chair. "Where are her children?" he asked.

Sister Vincetta looked at Father Timothy who seemed confused. She wished she had told him the truth, but she feared telling anyone the truth.

"Sister, I asked if you know where her children are?" The policeman leaned forward. He was gruff when he'd asked her. She didn't like that.

Hannah looked at Rena, who sat like a snake curled on a rock.

"No, I do not know."

"They were ordered into the custody of their father," the policeman said. "And I think you do know where they are."

Father Timothy stood to his feet. "They are with their mother, where they belong."

"And how do you know that, Father?" The policeman walked to Father Timothy and put a hand on his shoulder. "How do you know that?"

Father Timothy still looked confused, perhaps more so than he had looked before. He stared around the room. "I saw them leave in a black car. Sister Vincetta, why don't I know what's going on? Why shouldn't they be leaving with their mother?"

"Because they have been ordered to be with their father, which is another fate worse than death." The Sister crossed herself.

Rena stood to her feet. "How dare you, nun or not, how dare you insult my brother?"

"Where did they go, Sister?" the policeman knelt before her and looked into her expression.

"I don't know."

"New York," Father Timothy said. "How else would they get to Ireland? Can't swim there from here." He laughed self-consciously.

"When did they leave?" the policeman asked Father Timothy who shrugged his shoulders.

"Why I don't remember," he said. "Do you,

Sister?"

"We are so busy here, it's hard to say."

The waiting was awful. Sister Vincetta didn't know what they would do if, in fact, they could do anything. Would Hannah have enough time to make it out of the country? The sister did not pray in the church for Hannah and her children. She prayed along the sand, by the rush of waves, and the welcoming sun.

# Chapter Forty-One

*Churches are such bunk*, thought Sheela.

The teenager was sitting in a wooden pew. Father Timothy's Latin mass was filling the silent room like music. The faces around her were bowed in prayer. Rosary beads were held and clasped like they were the hands of a precious God.

They had been there at the loading dock and taken back to Sister Vincetta. She didn't know where they'd taken her mama; no one would tell her. They put them on a plane. She was frightened. She didn't like planes.

"*The Lord is my Shepherd,*" she whispered. Jesus gazed at her from his cross. *He is so sad,* she thought to herself, *so sad. I am sad too.*

Little bells rang, and people knelt and beat their chests. Sheela sat still and silent and stared at Jesus. He looked so real. "They've made him look so real," she said softly.

Sister Vincetta sat beside her. She was crying. Her tears were soft and almost comforting.

Sheela's eyes returned to Jesus. It took her by surprise. The little figure on the cross was breathing. She followed his breath and the tear that fell down his cheek.

*He's alive!* she almost said aloud. *He's weeping. I can hear him weep.*

She looked around the crowded church to see if the others noticed, but they were too busy praying. Their hands covered their faces, and their rosaries fell around their fingers like precious strands of Jesus' hair. They did not notice his ribs move or his eyes lift over the mass of bodies that knelt before him. She heard his breath. She watched as the blood fell from his wrists and landed on the altar. She almost stood, but fear kept her seated.

"Jesus is alive," she said.

"What did you say, child?" whispered Sister Vincetta.

"Jesus is alive, Sister."

"Of course, he is," she answered and took the girl's hand.

Sheela looked back at the altar. Father Timothy was making the sign of the cross, and Holy Communion was about to begin. The congregation was standing and forming a line toward the pulpit so they could receive the flesh and blood of Christ. Sheela followed and knelt before the priest. She opened her mouth to receive the wine and the wafer, and as she did, she lifted her eyes once again to the cross. Jesus continued to bleed.

*He will leave a lot of blood,* she thought.

She couldn't wait to get back to the pew so she could continue to watch Jesus live, watch his tiny ribs move and follow his breath. His eyes were on her now while his chest swelled ever so peacefully.

He appeared to be smiling even as he wept. Then most curiously, he looked right at the girl and closed one eye.

"Jesus winked!" she whispered.

"What's that, Sheela?" questioned Sister Vincetta.

"He winked."

"Hush, child."

Sheela quickly returned her eyes to Jesus, but he had turned his head away. He had laid his head back against the wood and had shut his eyes as furtively as he had opened them. He had disappeared behind the language of Father's Timothy's Latin and hidden himself in the tiny beads of the rosaries that beheld the kiss of those who worshiped him.

"Sister Vincetta." Sheela turned to the Sister. "Jesus bled all over the altar. I swear I saw him do it. Come see."

"Don't swear, girl," Sister Vincetta said and took both her hands. The young nun's eyes were filled with tears. "When the mass ends, gather your sister and brother to me, child. I have something I must tell you."

The authorities had been waiting for Hannah in New York as she went to board the ship with her children. There were two men, one of them was kind to the children, who were terribly upset. They were put on a plane with the man who was kind. Once they landed, they were put in one car, their mother in another. Hannah was brought back to the hospital kicking and screaming, and the children were returned to the orphanage.

Sister Vincetta had rushed to Tallahassee to be at Hannah's side, but first, she had demanded to see the head of the hospital.

"You have no right to keep her," she said as calmly as she could. "She has remarried."

Dr. Mason Dunmore lifted his head. Sister Vincetta thought he looked surprised. "She is no longer married to Wade Fournier?" he asked.

"No, she is not."

He rubbed his chin. "Her husband is with you?"

"No, no, he isn't. He has returned to Ireland. It was an emergency."

"This is an emergency," Dr. Mason said.

"Yes, I agree. Look, her husband doesn't want her here," the Sister said. "Wade Fournier had ulterior motives. Andrew McGregor would never agree to this."

Dr. Mason was pensive. He had just been given the title, Chief of Medicine. Sister Vincetta had never met him before. He was new. Perhaps he could help Hannah.

"They held her here against her will." The sister added.

"Most patients are held here against their will, Sister."

"But she isn't crazy. She was never crazy."

"There are degrees of 'crazy,'" he said.

"Doctor, I need to get her out of here. She needs to repeal a court order that has released her children to an incompetent man."

"An incompetent man?"

"Her ex-husband."

"And that is your opinion of Wade Fournier?"

"Yes, yes, it is."

Dr. Mason Dunmore sat forward in his chair. "You will need a signed affidavit from...what is her present husband's name?"

"Andrew McGregor."

"A signed affidavit from Mr. McGregor, notarized of course."

"Thank you, Mr. Dunmore. Thank you."

"I will give you the necessary form for Mr. McGregor to sign. It will release Hannah to his care, and he will be responsible for her."

"She needs to get her children back. You have to tell the authorities that she is not insane."

"I cannot do that, Sister."

"Why not?"

"Her records indicate that she is."

The nun felt defeated. She knew that if Hannah lost custody of her children it would be like taking the life from her.

"Having a very hot Irish temper is not being insane," she said.

The doctor remained silent, but then he nearly smiled. "But you could get a second opinion, even a third," he added.

"Oh, my God. Yes, of course. Of course. We will do that."

"We are not the only hospital in Florida, Sister. And as you know, opinions differ." He smiled a real smile this time while she made the sign of the cross.

When Sister Vincetta was taken to the small room to visit with Hannah she noticed right away that Hannah's head had been shaved.

"What have they done to you?"

Hannah shook her head.

"There's hope now, Hannah. This new chief of medicine, he's not bad. He told me to get a second opinion, even a third, and we will take it to the appeal.

"Am I to get out of here?"

The nun nodded her head. "Oh, yes, with Andy's signature. I am going to write to him today and send him this." she held up the forms Dr. Mason Dunmore had given her. "He doesn't even have to be here."

Hannah barely acknowledged her. "I will wait for word," she said.

Two weeks passed, and Sister Vincetta had not heard from Andy. She quickly wrote to Anne and Patrick. The reply she received caused her entire body to collapse. Her hopes shattered, like shards of glass.

Anne wrote to tell her that Andy was being kept in the hospital. He had some disease of his lungs, but surely, he would get better, he'd been sick since his return.

"I must hold on," the nun whispered. "I must hold on."

Sister Vincetta continued to visit Hannah weekly, but she didn't tell her of Andy's turn for the worse. She complained about the mail, how long it took, how they must wait for the forms and be patient.

The letter she received from Anne a few weeks later was not welcomed or expected. Andy McGregor had died, quietly passing in his sleep. It seems the cancer had grown quickly. Sister Vincetta could not tell Hannah right away so she made up excuses as to why she couldn't get to the hospital, she wrote letters of apology. But Hannah had known her friend well and could read between all the lines that the good sister could not bring herself to reveal.

# Chapter Forty-Two

Father Timothy had not mentioned Hannah in the day's Mass, as he had promised. Perhaps he would not mention her at all. Hannah was a sinner and would not be laid to rest in Catholic ground. Sister Vincetta begged Father Timothy to reconsider, but he had refused.

"She was almost a nun, Father. She gave year after year to the church." Sister Vincetta had cried.

The father said nothing for quite some time. Then finally, she felt his hand on her arm. "She died in sin, girl. Pray for her soul."

"No," she wanted to say but didn't. "She died in distress, in despair."

She wondered why Sheela had imagined seeing blood. There had been much blood when Hannah was found, and the sister shuddered. Hate was an emotion she would never master, like anger, it ate at her soul.

Sister Vincetta watched as the children filed before her.

"Sit here in front of Jesus," she told them. "Hold each other's hands."

The nun shuddered as she looked into the eyes of Hannah's children.

"Your mother is with God," she said quietly.

She didn't tell them that Hannah had taken a knife from the dinner table and had hidden it in her gown. She did not tell the children that Hannah had opened the veins in her wrist and the veins in her legs and had bled to death in her bed. She told the children that their mother loved them and would always watch over them instead.

Leda and Hank wept loudly. Sheela was silent.

"Listen to me, children," she said as she prayed for the validity of her faith. "Sit very close and listen to me."

The children sat around her. And because she was a nun, and their mother's favorite nun, surely, she would provide them with a message from heaven.

"None of us really die. God gives those of us with faith, eternal life. You do know that, don't you, children?" she asked them.

They nodded, but their pain was not consoled any more than hers was.

"Perhaps she's an angel now."

The sister watched as they nodded, their tears streaking their faces, their noses red and running. She knew they did not really appreciate the spirit of their mother appearing to them in anything else but flesh and blood. She wanted desperately to comfort them.

"You will see her again," she told them. "In time, we all return to God."

# Chapter Forty-Three

Someone notified him in 1934 that Hannah was dead. He'd been between shifts at O'Rourke's when he read the telegram. "A suicide" was spelled out in bold black letters. There was a brief apology. An explanation. Something about her sneaking out a knife from the dining hall. Wade's eyes blinked involuntarily as he folded the telegram back up and put it away in his top drawer.

"How did this happen?" he asked his sister when he called.

"She was picked up trying to leave the country, Wade. That damn nun was protecting her, had her take the girls and run."

"How did anyone know where she was?"

"The police found out, notified the authorities in New York, and they picked her up when she tried to board the boat."

"Oh," he said.

"Did you know she was married?"

"What?"

"Married some Irish guy. That's where she was going, back to Ireland to be with him."

"With my girls?"

"I've been busy, but I'm driving over for the girls in a few weeks. You come see them soon, okay? You hear?"

Wade hung up the phone and sat for hours on the sofa thinking that life was not at all good.

Those damn animals Sweet Sue had all over the house were killing him. He could barely breathe. He'd been living with her for over two years now. Perhaps he had decided to ignore that he could not be around long-haired animals. Sweet Sue had six cats and three large dogs, and they were killing him for sure.

He tried not to think about Hannah. It didn't make sense, that she was dead. Would Rena kid him about a thing like that? He reached over for the telegram and re-read it. Dead? He took the telegram and placed it alongside the letters Hannah had written his children that he had never passed on. He had tied the letters all together and placed them behind his socks. He ran his fingers over the envelopes. He brought the letters to his lips. He could still feel her scent enfold him, and it made him feel unbearably alone. He felt himself overcome with despair, so much so, that he stood there crying with Hannah's letters to her children in his hands. He cried so much, he gagged on his own tears.

Finally, he made himself a whiskey and lay on Sweet Sue's couch. But he kept wailing like a baby and choking so much he could barely breathe. But then he drank enough whiskey to put him to sleep, and he quickly fell into a dream. He dreamed of Hannah and her beautiful auburn hair. In his dream he reached out to touch it, to feel it softly shine against his palm the way it used to. He bent down to kiss her hair, and as he did, he inhaled it, inhaled it so deeply down his throat that he could not catch his breath. Her hair flowed down his throat like water and lay across his lungs like a blanket from God.

Sweet Sue found him. His face all wet with tears. His eyes open. They say she shot all six of her cats after Wade died like that. They say she let the dogs go, but she didn't go with them. She left her house alone and never went back. All of Wade's belongings were shipped down to Clearwater to his sister, Rena, except for Hannah's letters. They were forwarded on to the St. Stanislaus Orphanage as they had originally been intended.

Sister Vincetta took Hannah's letters and placed them inside her old prayer book. She never read the letters. She planned to send them over to Clearwater to that horrible woman who was taking the girls. But she never did. Maybe it was just a part of Hannah she could keep close, her words, her thoughts. The nun tied the letters around the music box that played ragtime. And one day, in the far future, Sister Vincetta prayed with all her faith, that the music box would be opened, and the music would be heard again.

She knelt before the Blessed Mother and lit four candles. The scent of wood and incense filled the air as the tiny flames flickered below the statue's gaze. The stained-glass saints looked down from their window perches. She felt at peace. As she closed her eyes, she could almost hear Hannah at the piano. Her sigh filled the quiet church as she stood. She walked back to a wooden pew and knelt.

She put her head in her hands. Her rosary swayed in the gentle push of her breath. Suddenly, she felt a presence and lifted her head to the silent and so terribly forlorn Jesus. But there was nothing to see; no misty vapor fell before her eyes. Yet a lingering presence demanded something of her that she could not interpret. She lowered her head and prayed in full voice. But the presence would not be ignored and pushed itself beyond her prayers, challenging her with all the fire of life.

"It's unfair, isn't it? Go on and admit it, Sister Vincetta. It's unfair," the spirit whispered fiercely.

Sister Vincetta brought the rosary to her lips and kissed it. "For the love of God, be still, Hannah Reilly," she whispered back.

Sister Vincetta's family was proud of their only daughter, yet she often felt so little pride in herself. She had reluctantly accepted her father's wishes and had not made her own choices. Now she was hearing voices in her head like Saint Joan. How proud would they be to know she was quietly losing her mind, living in darkness the way she was.

"You'll serve God and not your own ego," her father had said.

Being a nun wasn't as sacred as being a priest. It didn't seem quite as important. But she was still treated as a messenger of God. She was treated sometimes as if she *were* God. So maybe she was entitled to hear voices inside her head. The upside of religion, talking to ghosts.

"Rest in peace, Hannah Reilly," she said and crossed herself.

But Hannah Reilly would have none of that. *Rest in peace? You want me to rest in peace while your Sisters of Mercy are torturing my son? Rest in peace while your Father Timothy practices his sermons before the mirror and dyes his hair as if he were Errol Flynn? You'd better not look for God behind priests' robes, Sister Vincetta, because God is more than a good sermon, and He sure as hell is not found in hypocrisy.*

The sister was furious and fell to her knees. "God forgive you, Hannah Reilly. God forgive you."

The spirit assured her: *He already has.*

Sister Vincetta prayed. *It is a good life to serve Jesus,* she thought.

Suddenly, someone entered the church, and Sister Vincetta turned to look behind her.

"Sheela?" she called out.

"Yes, Sister," answered the young woman.

"Has your aunt come for you and Leda?"

"Yes," the girl replied.

Sister Vincetta held out her arms.

"Come here, Sheela." She embraced the girl. "I've done my best for you, watched over you, haven't I?"

"Yes, Sister."

"You will always be in my prayers. Always."

"Thank you, Sister."

She searched Sheela's eyes, holding onto glimpses of Hannah's sparkle and the faint reflections of familiar expressions. The sister was about to tell her how much she resembled her mother, the impressive height, and the striking shape of her face, when they were suddenly startled by a loud crack. They went quickly to the statue of the Virgin Mary and saw that one of the little red glass cups had shattered from the heat of a candle.

"Come," said Sister Vincetta. "Let's light another one. They were for you and your brothers and sister.

Together they knelt before the Blessed Virgin and lit a new candle.

"Should we light them all?" asked Sheela.

"No, there are too many to light. These are special. They are in your mother's name and for you, Leda, Henry, and Wade Jr.," said the nun as the wick took the flame.

"Mama loved candles," the girl said sadly.

*Holy Mary, Mother of God, pray for us sinners now and in the hour of our death. Amen,* the nun prayed silently.

"Sister Vincetta?" Sheela turned and looked at her.

"Yes?"

"Why wouldn't Father Timothy bury my mama at St. Stanislaus?"

"Well, St. Stanislaus is Catholic. Don't worry, I had her buried elsewhere, child."

"Where?" asked the girl.

"Saint Mary's."

"Isn't Saint Mary's Catholic too?" Sheela stared at her earnestly.

"Oh, yes."

She'd had to change Hannah's name to get her

in, but damned if she didn't do it. Father Timothy said Hannah couldn't be laid in Catholic earth because she had killed herself and suicide was a sin against the church. Sister Vincetta had profusely agreed with the good Father Timothy, and she had enthusiastically nodded her head. She then proceeded to erase the *H's* from Hannah's name on the burial papers she had been told to fill out, and she had her laid to rest under a Catholic marker as *Anna Riley*. When Father Timothy inquired, Sister Vincetta told him that poor Hannah Reilly Fournier was lying on the far side of the cemetery over at St. Mary's in Protestant soil and wouldn't be meeting God with Catholic dirt on her soul.

"They said she sinned, Sister. Did she?" Sheela asked.

"We all sin, Sheela."

"Can sin kill me?" asked the young woman.

"Perhaps."

The glass broke again with a loud pop, and the haunting returned with a chill that made the nun rise and stare behind her. Even the girl seemed to feel it.

*And just what is sin?* The spirit taunted her. *Not eating fish on Friday? Taking the Lord's name in vain? Smacking a child across the hand till he bleeds? Fornicating on Sunday? Killing yourself to escape a loony bin when you're being held against your will and you're as sane as St. Joseph? Go on and define sin for the girl, Sister.*

"Sin is evil. Evil kills the soul."

"Oh," Sheela said.

The spirit seemed tamed by her response. It

seemed to linger in the silence of the altar. But then it smirked, *that must account for all the evil souls wearing the robes of Jesus.*

"Be still. For the love of God!" Sister Vincetta called out.

"Sister?" Sheela stood up. "Are you all right?"

"Yes, dear. I'm fine." And she took the girl's hand. "Do you believe in ghosts, Sheela?"

The girl laughed. "Do you, Sister?"

The nun did not answer. She knelt before the altar and crossed herself. The silence could almost be heard.

Sheela hated living at the orphanage, but she didn't want to leave. Sister Vincetta had been good to her. She and Leda always got the donated clothes before the others. There was always an extra cookie for them, and unlike the other children, they never felt the stick. Once, Sister Vincetta told Mother Superior that she would punish Leda for letting a cat into the dining hall, but she never did. Sheela felt sorry for her brother, though. He was staying behind, and Sister Irene was always beating him up. He was just a little boy, only ten years old, but he never complained. Sister Vincetta tried to intervene, but Henry's room was in the back of St. Stanislaus Orphanage, and Sister Vincetta's room was in the front with the girls. None of them knew what had happened to little Henry until they saw the cuts and bruises on him after the fact.

Sister Vincetta rose from her knees and stood up as tall as one so small in stature could. Sheela felt a pounding in her chest that made her want to cling to the nun's robes. She began to weep.

"I don't want to go." She reached out and held onto the nun's robes. "I'm afraid I won't be happy."

Sister Vincetta almost welcomed the emptiness she felt. For a moment, the spirit respected her sorrow. But then it whispered softly: *tell my daughter something she can use in the world, Sister. For goodness sake, don't bless her, and don't tell her to go with God. Be creative.*

"Shush. Do you hear that?"

"Only the whisper of the wind," Sheela said.

The nun held the girl close and put her lips to Sheela's ear.

"Beware the devil; he's everywhere you turn."

Sheela stopped crying. The nun stared back at the altar. The wind could still be heard moving through the chapel, causing the tiny flames to flicker in the darkness. Tall shadows leapt across the floor like demons and danced to the music of the flame.

The End

www.ingramcontent.com/pod-product-compliance
Lightning Source LLC
Chambersburg PA
CBHW050527110726
47899CB00005B/1625